EPIC IN THE
FORGOTTEN WAR

EPIC IN THE FORGOTTEN WAR

BY

KEN FILING

Order this book online at www.trafford.com
or email orders@trafford.com

Most Trafford titles are also available at major online book retailers.

Printed in the United States of America.

ISBN: 978-1-4269-6820-4 (sc)
ISBN: 978-1-4269-6821-1 (hc)
ISBN: 978-1-4269-6822-8 (e)

Library of Congress Control Number: 2011907044

Trafford rev. 05/09/2011

 www.trafford.com

North America & international
toll-free: 1 888 232 4444 (USA & Canada)
phone: 250 383 6864 ♦ fax: 812 355 4082

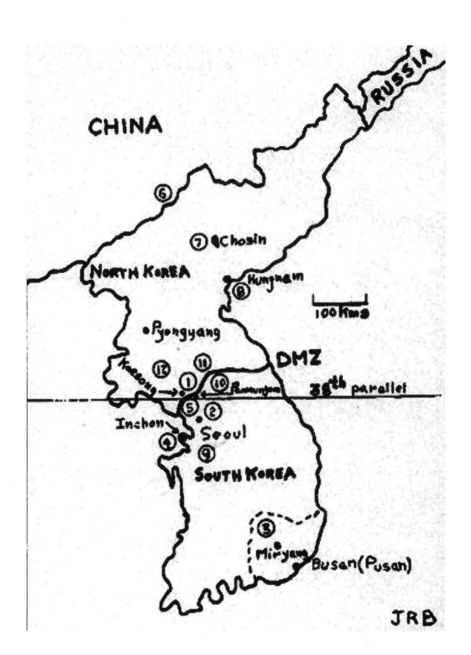

CHINA

RUSSIA

⑥

⑦ ●Chosin

NORTH KOREA

●Hungnam
⑧

100 Kms

●Pyongyang

DMZ

⑬ ⑪

① ⑩ Panmunjom 36th parallel

⑤ ②

Inchon

④ ●Seoul

⑨

SOUTH KOREA

③
●Miryang

Busan (Pusan)

JRB

To the men and women who unselfishly served in the *FORGOTTEN WAR* fought in Korea from 1950 to 1953. Especially remembered are the ill equipped Soldiers, Sailors and Marines who battled heroically when attacked by the North Korean Communists. They made a stand at the Pusan Perimeter until reinforcements arrived. Those brave men were the last hope for saving South Korea. If the Pusan Perimeter fell, the war would be lost. Lt. General Walton Walker issued the order to his troops to *STAND OR DIE.* These brave men stood and held until the Inchon Invasion changed the course of the war. Many of our brave troops were captured and suffered atrocities, especially in the early years of the war in 1950 and 1951. They were starved, beaten, tortured, subjected to experimental medical operations and coerced with Communist indoctrination. Yet when our troops returned home there were no parades, no waving of flags and no bands playing. Not a welcome or even acknowledgement that they were gone. Most found only their Mom and Dad waiting for them when they got off the train. The Korean War Veterans were completely ignored when the truce was signed. It truly had been *the wrong war, at the wrong place, at the wrong time.*

Finally, the Republic of Korea issued a special Korean War Service Medal commemorating the 50th anniversary of the war. Along with the medal came a beautifully worded letter signed by the President of the Republic of Korea, Kim Dae-Jung.

The author was proud to have received this medal.

PREFACE

Epic in the Forgotten War is a work of fiction. It loosely follows the travels of the author during his U. S. Navy enlistment and his shipboard life. He participated in the Inchon Invasion and the evacuation of Hungnam which are true historical events. However the personal exploits and the characters are purely fiction and are not intended to describe real people or real events. The author has tried to hold to the timeline of the action in Korea and the major events during this action to add realism to the story. Some of the timing may not be exact but needed to add flow to the story. These events and the timeline were researched through the use of the internet web sites entitled koreanwar.com, koreanwar/timeline.com, b-29s-over-korea.com and the map used from kvacanada.com/johnbishop.

CHAPTER ONE

"Well I don't know about you guys, but I'm tired of going to school. There's a whole big world out there to be seen and I want to see it" drawled Tony in his Midwest accent.

The other three teen age high school boys who were sitting with him in the detention room just chuckled and rolled their eyes.

Raymond looked up at him and said "Yeah sure Tony, just go down to your savings account and draw out those thousands of dollars that you've stashed away. Then you can buy a ticket on the next ship out of Cleveland."

The other two boys laughed and Tommy said "Yeah draw it out Tony and maybe you'll have enough to buy a bus ticket to Barberton."

This brought more laughter from the whole group including Tony who said "Yeah, that's part of the problem."

The group of pals were accustomed to that kind of kidding, all being much in the same predicament. They had been a very close knit group all through high school. They all played on any athletic team that was available to them when they weren't working part time jobs to help supplement their family's income. And they all excelled at one sport or another.

They had reached a crossroad in the game of life. High school commencement was in two weeks and decisions must be made. Which new road would each take at this intersection?

Times were tough there in 1949. World War II was over and many factories were changing from war work to consumer goods. Hundreds of thousands of veterans had hit the job market and were eager to start a new life. Many were enrolling in college to finish their education. This made for an overload in the schools of higher learning.

The conditions made it tough for a young man just out of high school. Coach said that he could work out an athletic scholarship for Tony and Jay but they'd be required to work some part time jobs at the school like serving tables and that kind of thing. Raymond had been contacted by a scout from a major league baseball team but nothing had been offered as yet and Tommy was thinking about joining the Navy and applying for electronics school to learn to be a technician.

"Ya know this Navy thing sounds like an idea, but I don't feel like going to another school" said Tony.

"I'm sure you could get sea duty and see the world that way, Tony, and I must admit the Navy sounds good to me. I checked into it and there are other opportunities available. Why don't we go into Akron and check it out further?" Tommy said.

Just then the outer door opened and Mr. Sauers, the Dean of Boys yelled into the room "Okay you hooligans. Time's up. You can all leave but you'll find yourselves back in here again if you decide to go swimming on school time again….even if it is close to graduation."

The four of them unfolded themselves from the hard back chairs and sauntered out.

One of them mumbled "At least we won't have to put up with old sour puss any more."

"I HEARD THAT! WHICH ONE SAID THAT?" yelled Mr. Sauers.

The boys just chuckled and kept on walking without looking back and when they reached the sidewalk, they took off running.

Mr. Sauers stood in the doorway with his hands on his hips and slowly grinned. His lips then parted slightly while a chuckle came from down deep.

He said to himself with a twinkle in his eye "I kind of hate to see them go. The four of them sure made life interesting." He sighed as he slowly turned and closed the door to the detention room.

The next two weeks flew by for the boys with all the preparation for graduation. But it soon was over and they were high school graduates.

They met at Jay's house so they could drive into Akron in his beat up old car to check out the Navy recruiting office. When Tony and Tommy arrived Jay gave them the latest news.

"Raymond won't be going with us. He called and said the New York Yankees want him to play baseball on their Lima, Ohio farm team. He thinks he has a good chance to make the team and who knows how far he'll go. He can really swat the ball and with proper coaching and some experience with his catching skills behind the plate, he just might do it. I told him to go for it."

And with that, the three buddies jumped into Jay's old '34 Ford Sedan and drove into Akron. They parked at the recruiting office parking lot and entered the building through the main entrance which led to a long hall with office doors on each side.

"Okay guys, we're here, now what do we do?" asked Tony.

"Well there's the door marked Navy Recruiting Office so I guess we go on in and ask questions" answered Tommy.

"Wait a minute" interjected Jay. "Right across the hall is the Marine Recruiting Office. They really have some neat uniforms. Let's go in there. Maybe it would be more fun to be a Marine."

"Oh right Jay. Haven't you heard about the training those guys have to go through?"

"Yeah but we've gone through some pretty intense stuff at football practice. Don't forget those scrimmages during those hot, humid August days."

"Not exactly the same" said Tommy.

"He's right Jay. Three months of Navy Boot Camp is all I want of that kind of stuff. Not a steady diet for three years" added Tony.

"I'm for the Navy" Tommy exclaimed.

"Me too" Tony agreed.

"Okay, okay you guys. I was only kidding. Let's go talk to the Navy recruiting guy."

They entered the Navy office and before they left, all three had committed themselves to a three year enlistment. They were to board a train to San Diego for Boot Camp on July 1.

When Tony broke the news to his mom and dad, they weren't overjoyed.

"I'd rather see you go to college Tony" said his dad.

"Gosh Dad, I know you can't afford to pay for my college education what with the orchard not doing well for the past few years and the football scholarships offered are not that secure. What if I don't make the team or get hurt?"

"But you could get hurt in the Navy too, Tony" exclaimed his mom.

"I know Mom, but think of it another way. They still have the G.I. Bill in effect and if I put in three years, I'll only be twenty years old. I can start to college then and the government will pay for it."

"Well, will you promise to go to school when you get out?" asked his dad.

"Sure I will Dad" answered Tony.

"Okay then" Mr. Marino said with a sigh "I guess I'll sign for you, since you're only seventeen. But I'm doing it with a heavy heart."

"Thanks Dad. I won't let you down. And Mom, don't worry, I'll be okay. The war is over so it will be a chance for me to see the world under peacetime conditions."

Those words would eventually come back to haunt Mr. and Mrs. Marino.

CHAPTER TWO

One year later, in June of 1950, found Tony home on a seven day leave. His ship, the USS Columbia, had docked in Norfolk, Virginia en route to New York City where it would set sail to Bremerhaven, Germany.

Tony left the ship in Norfolk and would return to it in New York at the end of his leave. He was fulfilling his dream and traveling to new and different places. He was assigned to the ship after Boot Camp and some additional "Special Forces Training" which involved intense indoctrination on small arms as well as automatic weapons and close combat drills. He had already been to Hawaii, Guam, Panama, San Juan and now would be going to Europe.

On the fifth day of his seven day leave, he received a telegram to report back to his ship in Norfolk at the end of his leave instead of meeting it in New York.

The telegram didn't give a reason but he was sure it had something to do with the outbreak of hostilities in the Orient in a country called Korea. The newspaper had some coverage on it and showed a map which placed the country across the Yellow Sea from Japan.

When he got back to the ship he asked his shipmates "Hey, what's going on? Are we going back to the Pacific?"

"We sure are" said Sully, the Coxswain "We're leaving tomorrow and not wasting any time about it. We're not stopping anywhere until we hit Hunters Point in San Francisco where they'll put all our guns back in commission. They've been in mothballs since the end of the war. So be ready to get underway right after reveille. We'll have chow after we're at sea."

"Wow. Must be serious" said Tony.

"Damn right it's serious kid. You're going to find out what the real Navy is all about. Get topside with the rest of the crew and make ready to make a move at 0600."

The trip south to Panama, through the Canal and north in the Pacific was not the leisurely, fun filled jaunt they experienced on the way to the Atlantic. The mood of the crew was different too. More business like and it was evident what to expect since the job of converting the cabins and holds to accommodate troops instead of civilian dependants was the prime duty for the deck crew.

The time spent at Hunters Point Naval Yard was short with no wasted time. The Yard crew worked 24 hour shifts to put the Columbia back to wartime readiness. Not only taking the guns out of moth balls but replacing the Motor Launches with LCVP's to be used for landing troops on a beach and other small boat runs.

When she was ready the ship embarked for the Port Chicago Ammunition Dump which was north through the bay, traversing San Pablo Bay and through the cut into Suisun Bay. It was there that the ship would pick up shells for its Five Inch, Forty Millimeter and Twenty Millimeter guns. Again work took place around the clock. No one now had any doubts about what the Columbia was being prepared for.

Fuel and supplies had already been addressed before she left Hunters Point so the next destination was the firing range off the coast of San Diego where all guns would be test fired and gun crews would be trained. The targets are drones, radio controlled by an operator aboard a training ship. It was two days of intense weapons firing.

Upon completion of the training exercise, the course was set for Seattle, Washington where the ship would take on troops from Fort Lewis Army Base and head for Japan.

The destination was Yokosuka, Japan where the troops would disembark for deployment. A U. S. Navy base was located there since Japan has been under occupation by the United States from the end of World War II. Tony had gotten word that after Jay had finished his tour with the Navy Drill Team on Treasure Island, he was transferred to this base. But he had no idea what Jay's duties would be. He mused to himself while taking a rickshaw to the base Main Gate "I bet he's got himself a racket of some kind. Jay was always good at getting the most out of the least."

He caught the base bus after showing his I.D. and Liberty Pass to the Marine guards and traveled to the Personnel Office where he asked a Yeoman if Jay Johnson was on the base and where he could be contacted.

The response was affirmative and Tony was directed to a small bungalow located behind the Officers Club.

"Strange" thought Tony "must be a small barracks or something."

When he passed the Officers Club, he glanced in and sure enough he saw Jay behind the bar placing bottles on the back shelf. He opened the door and yelled "Hey Jay. It's me Tony."

"Well I'll be damned" replied Jay. He came out of the Club and grabbed Tony in a bear hug.

"Come on into my shack and we'll have a beer and catch up on things."

Tony was speechless. He was certainly not used to this kind of military life. "What's going on Jay? Is this your job?"

"Sure thing , buddy. I'm in charge of the Officer's whiskey locker." Jay said with a twinkle in his eye.

"I knew you'd have some kind of cushy job, but old buddy you've really outdone yourself this time" said Tony in amazement.

"How long are you in for? Can you meet me at the base E. M. Club tonight?" asked Jay. "I don't have liberty" he said.

"Sure I can. How about 1900?" answered Tony.

"Sounds good. Hey have you heard anything about Tommy or Ray?" asked Jay.

"Last I heard, Tom finished Electronics School on T. I. and is stationed stateside somewhere in Texas. I think Ray is still playing ball for that Yankees farm team and working at his dad's bar off season."

"Hey look Tony, I've got to finish stocking the officer's bar. I'll see you tonight and we'll reminisce about the old days a little."

"Okay Jay. See you then."

That evening passed quickly for the two buddies. Tony told Jay that the ship was leaving in the morning to pickup a load of combat Marines in Osaka and probably head over to Pusan, Korea.

"The army guys are catching hell over there and need reinforcements. Our sister ship has already taken a boat load of soldiers over and they're now calling it the Pusan Perimeter. Those North Koreans are pretty well equipped and our guys were really caught short with all the cutbacks and punishing fiscal constraints after World War II. I guess a couple thousand of our guys already bought the farm. Now aren't you glad we talked you out of joining the Marines?" exclaimed Tony.

"Yeah, you're right. We'd probably be right in the middle of it. But Tony you might be seeing some action over there too. Better be careful bud. Don't volunteer for any of those crazy jobs. Be like me, a lover instead of a fighter" laughed Jay.

"You're a funny guy Johnson. Ha Ha. I've seen you in a few skirmishes and don't worry about me. I can take care of myself."

"Just be careful and keep in touch. I'll try to touch base with Tommy and Raymond. Wouldn't it be great to all get together again some day?"

Tony left soon after, since his liberty was up at midnight, and his would be an early start the next day. It would prove to be a long one.

CHAPTER THREE

The Columbia embarked for Osaka and picked up the First Provisional Marine Brigade. These combatants were ready for action. They were grim and armed to the teeth. They will be a welcome sight to the men defending Pusan. The 1st Battalion, 21st Regiment and the 3rd Battalion, 34th Regiment were getting slammed. Surely our military geniuses had a solution for this debacle.

Tony's ship anchored and the marines were picked up by L.C.M.'s and ferried into Pusan. It was now well into August and the heat and humidity was oppressive. The return trip to Japan was not easy. The passengers were Republic of Korea recruits going to Japan for training. Most were very young and newly drafted into the army. They were not happy for several reasons. First, they hated the Japanese since they were considered as slaves to their Japanese conquerors at one time. Also they didn't really want to become soldiers and lastly it seemed that almost all were prone to seasickness.

This made for intolerable conditions down below in the troop compartments. The stench was overwhelming and those who were sick refused to leave their bunks which made them even sicker. The ones that weren't sick refused to go down to the troop compartments and slept on the open deck.

Arrival in Sasebo, Japan was a welcome sight for all concerned including the ships company of the Columbia. After the ROK's disembarked, the skipper insisted that they send a crew back aboard to clean the holds. Even then it was days before they aired out.

But the crew was in a good mood because orders were to return to San Francisco and pick up another load of soldiers. One stop in Yokohama, discharge a few soldiers for some R. and R. and then out to sea en route to the States.

While they were anchored in Yokohama the Master at Arms approached Tony while he was coiling some lines on the main deck.

"Hey Marino, do you want to get in the anchor pool?"

"Explain what that is" answered Tony "I've never been in one but I've heard about it."

"Okay" said the M. A. "I've got 60 chances to sell at five bucks each. For your five bucks you get a number 0 through 59. When we get to the States, the quartermaster records in the log book the minute we arrive. Either when the anchor is dropped or when the first line hits the dock. If it's your number you win the pot. Three Hundred bucks. Do you want in or not?"

"Sure. Why not? I've got as good a chance as anyone. Here's my fiver."

"Okay your number is 13."

"Oh great. Thanks a lot for the lucky number." Tony quipped.

Just then the Bos'n whistle sounded and over the speaker and came the call "Away Number 2 LCVP. Away Number 2 LCVP."

Tony had boat duty. Since he was only a Seaman, his job on the three man crew was the Bow Hook which meant he was stationed at the bow of the boat and when they approached a dock he was to hook on to a cleat or bollard with a boat hook, jump off and secure the LCVP with a bow line. Then run back to the stern and grab a line from the Coxs'n and tie up the stern line. The reverse, of course, when they left.

Tony enjoyed duty on the LCVP and when the Coxs'n gave him the chance he'd grab the opportunity to learn how to run the boat. He even got to dock it and get underway a few times.

They got delayed at Yokohama a few days past the intended departure time and no one had an explanation why. It soon became evident.

It was now well into the first week of September and the ship left Yokohama but not en route to the states as originally scheduled, instead the next port of call was Osaka to pick up more troops. No more was said about where in Korea they would be going.

"Hey Sully" called Tony "where do you think we're going next?"

"How should I know, Marino" answered Sully, the Coxs'n "it's all hush, hush."

"I'll bet something's brewing. The old man was on the bridge last night when I had the mid watch on lookout. It's not like him to be up in the middle of the night just prowling around like he couldn't sleep or something."

"Don't get your shorts in an uproar Marino. We're probably just going to some port in Korea. Probably Pusan again" answered Sully.

"Yeah, we'll probably hear once we get to Osaka" said Tony.

They tied up at an Army Base deployment pier and loaded a full compliment of soldiers. As before the soldiers were combat ready.

As soon as they were loaded the signal was given to get underway and the anchor detail was called away.

"Hey Sully! Isn't that strange that we're going to anchor instead of heading out?" Tony asked.

"How many times have I told you, Marino. Yours is not to reason why, yours is but to do or die. Now you and your buddy, Peacock, stow those lines and secure them for sea duty. We won't be using them at anchor" yelled Sully as he walked away.

He passed the Chief Boatswains Mate as he strode away grumbling.

"What's the matter Sully? Those two young bucks getting on your nerves with their questions?"

"Yeah, Chief. But I'm only frustrated because I can't give them any answers" answered Sully.

"Well Sully, they're right about the strange things on this trip. I can tell you one thing from experience. It looks to me like a convoy is being assembled. Did you see the Diphda pull in right after we left the pier? They practically started loading her before she was tied up. There's about six more loaded attack transports anchored here and all fully loaded just like us."

"Any word on when we'll be getting underway?" Sully asked.

"Not a word" answered the chief "it's all hush, hush."

"Well I'm going down for some chow before those dog faces eat it all up."

"Hey you guys. Go down for some chow. We can get the rest done later" yelled Sully to his deck crew "we're going to be here for quite a spell I guess."

They all made a mad dash for the mess hall. When they were wolfing down their chow, the talk was all about where they were going. Of course there were at least a dozen theories and all of them were heard from very reliable sources. One sailor even said he heard the old man say they were going to Wonsan.

"You idiot" was the response "Wonsan is in North Korea. Do you think they have a dock reserved for us?"

"What makes you think I'm so stupid? Did you ever hear of an invasion? You're the idiot." said the sailor.

The chow table suddenly got quiet.'

"It kind of does look like we're gathering for a convoy doesn't it?"

"Hey Marino, finish up your chow. The Exec wants to see LCVP #2 boat crew. Pronto. So move it" ordered Sully.

"Okay, okay give me a minute" answered Tony.

"I said NOW Marino. Move it. I've still gotta find Peacock"

"Awright, awright. Don't get all touchy about it" said Tony as he wolfed down another bite and got up from the table "Peacock's back in his bunk. He had the mid watch."

The three of them made their way up to officer's country and knocked on the Exec's door. When he opened it he said "Okay let's go to the old man's quarters."

They all three gave questioning looks to each other as they followed the Commander. When they got to the skipper's quarters, the Commander knocked and a voice inside said "Come on in XO."

They all entered and the three enlisted men stood at attention.

The skipper said "Stand at ease men."

The Exec said "I haven't briefed them as yet sir."

"Okay then" said the captain and expelled a long breath.

He eyeballed each of them and said "This meeting is of the highest priority top secret. What is said here is not to leave this room. If that is something that any one of you feel that you can't fulfill say so now and you may leave the room. It will be as if you've never been here. Is that understood?" and he looked at each man individually.

Sully answered "Yes sir, I understand."

Tony looked at the skipper and said "Me too sir."

Peacock also answered "I'm good sir."

"This will involve a guerilla mission away from the ship and behind enemy lines. As always there is great element of danger and the possibility of injury, death or capture. It is strictly voluntary and again before I go further you may leave the room now if you don't care to participate with no danger of repercussion since it will be as if you've never been here."

"We're a team sir. We're in for the mission, whatever it may be" said Sully.

"Good. That's why you three were chosen. You've all been cleared for top secret data and had "Special Forces Training". He paused and looked directly at Sully. "Also, Sully, it's mainly because of a part of your personal history in between your Navy hitches from "1946 to '48."

Sully shuffled his feet, looked up at the overhead, lowered his gaze and sheepishly said "I thought I was cleared of all that and it would not be on my record if I reupped."

"Don't worry son. It is, and this time your experience is a benefit to your country" interjected the Exec.

"You'll understand once you hear the mission Sully, you're not in trouble" said the skipper.

The other two men looked confused.

"Okay. Here it is. The three of you will catch a flight to Pusan tonight. You'll be issued fatigues, side arms and two fully automatic weapons with sufficient ammo. When you reach Pusan you'll be met by a CIA operative acting as a Navy Lieutenant who is in command. He is an Old China hand, ex-CPO. When you meet him you'll understand why he was chosen to lead this mission. He's fluent in Korean and Russian. You'll pick up a sampan and that's why you're here Sully. You have the sampan experience and are familiar with the clandestine operation of one without being detected especially in the general area of this mission. Your two crew men were chosen because they are familiar with you as a Coxs'n. The Lieutenant will brief you on the rest of the team and where you are headed. Your duties are to run the boat where you are told and as armed seamen, return fire in defense, if attacked. Any questions?"

"No sir" the three answered in unison.

"Okay. Go down and put on you're dress blues as if you're going on liberty. If anyone asks tell them you're going over to the officers club to work security because of pilfering and may not be back for 3 or 4 days. The exec is riding over with you and will direct you to the deployment center to get outfitted. Good luck men. You all are doing a great service to your country."

"One more addition to this is the fact that this is a joint CIA-military operation. Any leaks of information would mean repercussions from the military and the CIA itself. I wouldn't want to be put into that position. So when you go to your compartment for your blues, not even your best buddy can have the slightest knowledge of this mission. Understood?" added the exec.

"We understand" said Sully.

They left the captains quarters and went below. There were the usual questions from their shipmates but they were satisfied with the explanation since several officers started some scuttlebutt about pilfering at the Officers Club under orders from the exec to do so. They were in the dark as to why but were experienced enough not to question the order.

The flight to Pusan was a short one and thankfully so since they were riding in a DC-3 cargo plane which seemed like it had seen better days. "Probably a left over from pre World War II" said Tony.

Peacock asked "Hey Sully, were you some kind of pirate or something?"

"Mind your own business Peacock" answered Sully.

"Hey, we're just curious Sully. What's the story?"

"All you've gotta know is that I can run a sampan and I know the area. Case closed."

"Okay. Don't get all bent out of shape."

"If we get out of this thing alive, maybe I'll clue you in on my two years of work on a sampan. But it's gotta stay between us."

"That's a deal Sully."

After they landed in Pusan and disembarked from the DC-3 they were met by a tough looking, weather beaten man in the same kind of fatigues. It was noticeable that none of the fatigues had insignias to designate rank.

"Follow me men" he directed.

They walked to a building where they entered a briefing room. In the room were three more men. One was an American and two were Korean.

They all sat facing a table where the man who met them, obviously in charge, stood behind the table.

He said "There are no ranks here and no names. I'm to be addressed as Bravo One. The army guy there will be Bravo Two. The two Korean military specialists will be Charlie One and Charlie Two. The head navy guy is Cox'n, the other two navy guys will be Xray One and Xray Two."

He hesitated and no one asked questions.

"Okay" he said "We leave at 0300 Hours. Cox'n, I have a chart for you to study but I'm told you're familiar with the area as well."

"Yes sir I know this general area but a specific destination was not given to me."

"Do you know Yonghung-do?"

Sully smiled "Yes sir. Pretty well in fact."

Bravo One also smiled "That's why you're here Cox'n."

"Let's get aboard the sampan. It's going to be home for a few days" he added "I'll brief everyone when we get aboard."

CHAPTER FOUR

The conditions aboard the sampan were anything but plush. All the men stowed their gear below in what was considered the crew's quarters. They couldn't help but notice just a few wooden bunks…. none with mattresses.

Bravo One announced "Okay here's the skinny…brief and to the point. MacArthur wants to cut off the N.K. from the Pusan perimeter. They've been knocking the hell out of us. We've been outmanned and unprepared for all these large military forces built by the Commies since the war. MacArthur wants to invade Inchon and the surrounding area. That's the closest way into Seoul and that's where they are the most heavily concentrated. Our job is to quickly….and I emphasize quickly…scout out the island of Yonghung-do, Wolmi-do and Palmi-do. We need to know the rise and fall of tides and the times of low and high at each locale. This is some of the highest in the world…some say 26 to 36 feet."

"Holy cow" exclaimed Tony.

"Yeah that's about right" said Bravo One "This creates huge mud flats. We've got to locate and chart them. Nothin' worse than some poor G.I.'s slogging knee deep through mud with Commies shooting at them at will. And where, there's not mud flats, there are steep, high seawalls for our guys to scale with assault ladders. In other words reconnoiter the whole invasion area. This is our mission in a nut shell. The Army guy and the Koreans have been briefed previously so they know their jobs. They'll do the scouting and make up the reports. You Navy guys will get us to the points of interest and hopefully back home. If necessary, help fight off any intruders. My job is to make sure the job is done and done right. I WILL come down hard on anyone that is not holding up his end of the mission. Questions?"

"Sir, I noticed what looked to be a covered gun mount on the bow. What is it?" Tony asked.

"Yes, you're right. It's a 50 caliber air cooled machine gun with some special armor piercing, heavy duty ammo in case we run into an armored vessel of some kind."

"None of us has fired that kind of weapon sir. Who do you want to man it?" Tony answered.

"That's going to be my job young man. And since you asked, you can be my ammo feeder. I'll show you how to keep the belts of shells feeding in and I will do the rest" said the boss-man.

Tony thought to himself *and I'll bet he does it very well too.*

"There won't be much time to sleep. Get what you can tonight. It may be the last except for some cat naps until we head back. Navy guys, be ready to get underway at 0300. Cox'n, stay here a minute and go over these charts with me. Army guy and Charlie guys can get a few extra hours shut eye. You'll have enough to do when we get there."

They all shuffled out to lay down on the hard wooden bunks and conk out for some much needed sleep. Sully and Bravo One stayed to study the charts.

It seemed like no time at all when they heard Bravo One yelling "OKAY SAILORS HIT THE DECK. DROP YOUR COCKS AND GRAB YOUR SOCKS. TIME TO GET UNDERWAY."

They were fully dressed so they wasted no time heading for the coffee urn and gulping down some of the worst coffee they had ever tasted. But it was all they had so it went down and hopefully would stay down. It was almost syrupy strong so it surely would wake them up. And there was no cream or sugar to cut the taste.

Sully kicked over the engine and surprisingly it started on the first try but it sounded like any typical sampan, sporadically running like it really wanted to quit at any time. Peacock listened with a trained ear. His job was to keep it running. He crossed his fingers as he listened.

They pulled away from the dock in the black of night with no running lights in evidence.

"Man I don't know how Sully can see where he's going" said Peacock.

"Don't worry about Sully. He's as good as they come." answered Tony "just keep a lookout. I'll take port and you take starboard."

They were soon out in the open water. The old sampan handled the chop very well as they plowed through the Yellow Sea around the southern tip of the Korean peninsula and then north to Inchon Harbor. It would be several days run.

The sailors ran the boat. Both Tony and Peacock relieved Sully on the tiller. There was no auto steering on this tub but it certainly was seaworthy and moved right along.

When they finally closed in on their destination it was in the dead of night. They stole into the channel and slowly drifted up to the island of Yonghung-do which was right in the mouth of the channel. They were a good ten miles away from the city of Inchon itself.

There was a small civilian population here and one of the Korean Charlie's had some contacts that could help in the reconnoiter.

Sully was also familiar with the island from his cloudy past and was able to bring the boat into a remote well hidden cove with a very small rickety dock. He had utilized this dock before. Tony and Peacock gave each other a knowing smile.

"Good job Coxs'n" said Bravo One "Okay Charlie One do you think you can locate your contact before light?"

"Yes, I'll head right out. He's expecting me" he answered as he climbed up to the high dock.

"Charlie Two and Bravo Two go ahead and get your preliminaries done while he's gone" said Bravo One.

"Coxs'n, you and one of your guys take a break and rest up. I want one of you on watch at all times. Set up a rotation."

"Yes sir" answered Sully. "Tony, take this first watch. Peacock will relieve you at 0700."

"That's good." said Bravo One "Go ahead and uncover the 50 caliber gun mount, Xray One. I'll check it out and at the same time show you how it's loaded. We want to be ready at all times."

Tony did so and the boss-man gave him his instructions. Being familiar with the 20mm's on board the ship, it came easy to him. Bravo One then went below to review his paperwork.

Tony kept a sharp ear and eye out but all was very quiet for several hours.

Suddenly he heard a slight rustling in the bush and strained to see something or someone. He heard it again and cocked his automatic weapon.

"Don't shoot!! It's Charlie One and a friendly" came a voice from the darkness.

"Walk slowly out on the dock where I can see you" answered Tony while he trained his weapon into the darkness.

Soon Charlie One and another Korean approached with their hands in the air.

"Whew" said Tony "Okay come aboard. I had to make sure."

"That's okay sailor. I'm glad you did. This man is Kim but I won't introduce you since he can't speak English anyway. He knows this island like the palm of his hand. I'm taking him below and pick his brain."

All the next day, a wealth of information was gathered from a whole group of islanders that just showed up. They were only too glad to help since the occupation by the N.K. had been brutal.

Yonghung-do was not heavily defended and would act as a staging area during the invasion. The assaults would be in three areas, Red Beach to the north off of Cemetery Hill by the 5th Marines using assault ladders, Blue Beach to the south on the salt plains where at low tide, a huge mud flat appeared, by the First Marines and at Green Beach which was Wolmi-do, a heavily fortified island.

Wolmi-do was the next spot to reconnoiter by our small group and would offer the most danger. They left under cover of darkness again and utilized Sully's past knowledge of a clandestine spot to anchor since no safe dock would be available. It was necessary to get in, get some data and then get out since the bombardment would commence by four cruisers, five destroyers and violent air attacks as soon as they got some critical intelligence.

They got what was needed and headed to Palmi-do where a non working old lighthouse was located. If it would be possible to restore it to working condition, the benefit to our invasion force would be priceless.

They were slowly drifting away from Wolmi-do to keep the engine noise to a minimum. And using binoculars, Peacock spied an assault boat bearing down on them.

He exclaimed "There's a fast boat coming right at us sir. I'm sure they've spotted us and it looks like they're coming at flank speed."

"Kick it in the ass, Coxs'n. Uncover the 50 cal sailor. Can you tell if they have any gun mounts Xray Two?"

"The only guns I see are the rifles that the soldiers are pointing at us sir. No mounts at all but it looks like they're almost in range with the rifles."

"They must have been trying to catch us before we got to the lighthouse and as we were leaving Wolmi-do. Looks like a full squad of about 15 soldiers. Probably thought they'd out man us" said the army guy.

Bravo One mused "I wonder how they discovered we were here. Might be a turncoat back on Yonghung-do."

"Okay Coxs'n, head right at them and we'll give them a taste of our battery. Load her up sailor. The rest of you keep your heads down. We should be in range with the 50 cal before they are."

Sully turned and bore down on the enemy assault boat. They were closing fast and Bravo One gave them a short burst with the machine gun. The shells fell short but not by much. He wanted to test the range.

He waited an agonizing long time before firing again. Puffs of smoke came from the enemy craft as the soldiers fired their weapons but none of the bullets hit home....yet.

Finally Bravo One cut loose with the 50. It was a long burst and the noise was deafening. The smell of cordite permeated the air as the armor piercing shells poured out of the barrel. Tracers showing the path of the shells provided Bravo One with the right trajectory to rake the deck with killing shots. What soldiers that weren't killed or wounded by the long burst ducked for cover behind the gun'l.

The enemy boat veered away from this hail of fire giving Bravo One a perfect broadside view. He cut loose again and with this burst he wiped out the boat operator and two more soldiers. One man tried to take the wheel and straighten out the now erratic course. The next burst got him and the next hit the gas tank. An orange flash blew out of the side of the boat and she listed badly. Bravo One fired relentlessly into the hull and it soon turned over on it's side and slowly slipped under water. The few remaining soldiers jumped into the water and either couldn't swim or the heavy gear they were wearing or carrying on their backs pulled them under.

After the boat completely disappeared there were only a few bodies floating near by and they were obviously dead.

Sully slowed to take a look and Bravo One commanded "Keep moving Coxs'n. We've still got work to do and then a rendezvous to make tomorrow evening, that is critical to this operation. Head for Palmi-do."

He gave a visible sigh of relief.

"Good job men. Cover the 50 cal, sailor, we may need it again at Palmi-do" he continued.

Sully kicked the engine back up to full power and headed northeast. It was a few hours run to Palmi-do.

They arrived at dusk and stole into the cove at idle speed. The old lighthouse was easy to spot in the receding light but to get to it meant disembarking and some overland travel.

"We'll split up after we tie up at that rickety old pier" said the boss-man "I'll take the two Charlie's and Kim since they know something about this old lighthouse. Bravo Two and the sailors stay aboard. If anything happens to me and the Charlie's, get out of here as fast as you can. Bravo Two, it's your responsibility to make sure all the data gets to the rendezvous point on time."

"How much time should we give you sir?" asked Bravo Two.

"Five hours max" he answered "We should be back quicker than that if we see it's a lost cause to get it lit."

The lighthouse detail left as soon as they tied up.

All four that were left aboard stayed topside and cautiously watched the surrounding area. They jumped at each strange noise but nothing was amiss….as yet.

Three hours passed and Bravo Two was nervously pacing the deck.

"I wish he'd stand still" whispered Sully.

"Well, you know Sully" said Tony "he's got a lot of responsibility."

"Yeah, yeah, I know but he's getting on my nerves."

Bravo Two finally sat on the fantail and stared at the lighthouse.

Another hour passed and Bravo Two leaped to his feet.

"I swear I saw a flash from the lighthouse" he said.

They all trained their eyes on the glass windows at the top.

"Yeah….hey look I think they have it lit" said Peacock.

"It is! It is" exclaimed Sully "they did it. They did it."

And they all gave each other slaps on the back and high fives, even the Army officer.

"Okay guys, get ready. As soon as they get back we're out of here" said Bravo Two.

It wasn't long and they heard the lighthouse detail hurrying down the makeshift road to the pier.

Sully kicked on the engine and the detail clamored aboard with big smiles on their faces. Mission accomplished.

"Okay sailors, get underway" said Bravo One.

They pulled away from the rickety pier and Sully asked "Where to next boss?"

"Head for Yonghung-do and we'll drop off Kim and then head out to sea to rendezvous with a Navy Frigate" said boss-man.

It was just at dawn when they reached Yonghung-do and the plan was just to pull up to the dock and drop off Kim.

But as they approached something seemed amiss. There were three or four villagers hanging around the dock and they seemed disoriented. As they got closer, it was evident that there was a problem. Two of them had bloody tunics and one was weeping.

Kim jumped off as they touched the dock and babbled in Korean to the one weeping. Suddenly he screamed and sobbed.

Bravo One asked one of the Charlie's. "What's going on? Can you understand them?"

"Yes. I think the North Korean's have punished the village for assisting us. It sounds like they've wiped them out. Maybe 50 people were killed. All of Kim's family was among them."

Kim returned to the boat and spoke in Korean to the two Charlie's. He sobbed and sobbed. "GO! GO quickly. The N.K. will be here soon. You must complete your mission."

"Pull away Coxs'n" said a composed Bravo One.

"But sir. What about....."

"I SAID PULL AWAY SAILOR. THAT'S AN ORDER"

"Yes sir" said Sully.

As Tony and Peacock pushed them away from the dock, Sully gave it full power and headed towards open water.

"Steer 270 when we are past the island. We should meet the fleet in four or five hours. They'll be watching for us and when they spot us a frigate will pick me up along with the army guy. The rest of you will head back to Pusan. I'll turn in my report and in four or five days the bombarding and air attack will start. You sailors will be flown back to your ship and make ready for the invasion. Don't forget this was a CIA mission and is still Top Secret. You'll be told when it is no longer hush-hush. Until then, if anyone asks, you were on a security watch at the Officers Club."

The sampan chugged along for a few hours and by noon a helicopter flew over and circled them for about ten minutes. When it left they could spot a navy vessel on the horizon bearing down on them. It turned out to be the frigate for the two Bravo's.

Before Bravo One started up the Jacob's ladder to board the Frigate he turned to the sailors and said "You'll all have a commendation in your records for this mission after it's all over. And don't worry, Sully, your past life is still off the record."

They gave each other a knowing grin and he scrambled up the ladder.

Sully pulled away and headed towards Pusan. The return trip was uneventful and as soon as they were tied up they were rushed to the same DC-3 for the return flight. They landed, took a well deserved shower and changed back to their dress blues. The mail boat was at the city pier so they clamored aboard for a ride back to the USS Columbia.

CHAPTER FIVE

On the trip through the harbor while on the mail boat, they noticed that it was jammed packed with anchored ships of all kinds. But mostly troop ships or assault ships with troops aboard.

They arrived at the gangway and rushed down to their living compartment as soon as they left the quarterdeck.

"Hey look whose back. The big time security guys" chided one of their shipmates.

Another one piped up "Did you guys break up the crime ring?"

"Yeah" said a different sailor in a falsetto voice "it was probably the Japanese Mafia."

This brought on some raucous laughter from the whole division.

"No" said Sully "we didn't catch anybody. After a few days of security, the pilfering just went away."

"Yeah, I knew that would happen" said the first sailor "you guys just had a big racket over there. Probably did nothing but drink beer and chase girls."

"That's for sure" said the other sailor "I heard about those good looking nurses that hang around the officers club and let alone the cute little Jap girls that work in the kitchen."

More laughter and then somebody yelled off color, descriptive remarks.

"Yeah, big deal" said another "while we're back doing all the hard work, you guys are having fun on the beach."

Peacock bristled and yelled "YEAH, YEAH. You guys just don't know all........."

"PEACOCK" yelled Sully "back off."

Tony jumped up and put an arm around Peacock's bunched up shoulders. "Hey buddy, I need a cup of coffee. How about you? Let's go to the mess hall and see if there's any in the urn."

"Good idea Tony" said Sully "I'm going to hit the sack."

The two buddies left the compartment and everyone quieted down. The untold message may have gotten across. No more was said.

The night passed lying at anchor and more ships gathered in the harbor.

Tony and his buddy Peacock were standing up forward on the fo'cs'le, looking out at the anchored ships early the next morning, wondering what was next.

"I count about 40 Tony. What do you see?" Peacock said.

"Yeah that's about what I see. Some more left late last night" answered Tony "there's also some tin cans cruising around outside of the harbor. See them out there?"

"Yeah, they just showed up this morning. I wonder if that means we're next."

It didn't take long to find out.

"MAKE ALL PREPARATIONS TO GET UNDERWAY" blared the loud speaker. "ANCHOR DETAIL PREPARE TO WEIGH ANCHOR"

All hands scrambled to their stations for getting underway and it looked like the other anchored ships were doing the same. The waiting was over and a sense of relief fell over the crew. Finally they could work off some of that adrenalin that had been collecting in their young bodies.

As the ships cleared the mouth of the harbor, they gathered together in the open water each falling into an assigned spot in a convoy. The escort destroyers met them after they formed their group and steamed along both sides and at the head. Off in the distance were several Cruisers and a Battleship cruising along at half speed or even less to keep pace with the slow moving transports and cargo ships.

As the day wore on, the weather took a turn for the worse. The seas were already rough and as the wind picked up the seas got rougher. The convoy speed got even slower.

The Columbia and the other ships were taking green water over the bow and the flat bottom LST's in the convoy were taking some tremendous roles almost capsizing.

Peacock came into the 3rd Division compartment shaking the sea water off of his foul weather gear.

"Holy cow, it's getting rough out there. I heard that a cargo ship had to turn into a port in Japan because some tanks broke loose and were beating the sides of a cargo hold" he said.

"What else did you hear? What do they say on the bridge about where we're going?" a shipmate asked.

"Don't know yet, but you can bet your ass it's somewhere in Korea and it's going to be with landing craft. Not tying up to a dock."

"Yeah, that's if we make it. This storm's getting bad."

"You'd think that they'd wait for better weather."

"Maybe that's all part of the plan dummy"

"Ah shut up and hit the sack."

"I heard the Officer of the Deck talking to the Exec when I was on watch and they were saying what a great General and strategist that MacArthur was. And this one would go down in history as being an outstanding coup."

"I just hope that this weather doesn't screw things up. There are a lot of sick soldiers on these boats. They'll probably be glad to get off even if someone is shooting at them."

Sully piped up "Okay you guys. Lights out was a half hour ago. Hit the sack!"

Dawn broke over the gray water. The seas had calmed down somewhat if you could call 15 foot waves as calming down.

The bos'n on watch piped reveille on his pipe over the P. A. system. Tony and his shipmates hit the deck and since it was still pretty rough they deferred the sweep down of the upper decks. The ships company was able to get the morning meal before the troops and they were happy to do so since the mess hall would literally be a mess after all those soldiers tried to eat chow being both sea sick and pretty nervous about what they had to do when they got to the target .

The latest scuttlebutt was that they were arriving at their destination early, early tomorrow morning. It was a Korean port called Inchon which was about 20 miles from Seoul, the Capital of South Korea. Seoul was now firmly under North Korean control.

Tony and Peacock smiled at each other when they heard the other sailors discussing this rumor.

It was now understandable. Invade at Inchon, an unlikely spot for several reasons. First and foremost Inchon had a 26 foot tide. Not a good spot for an amphibious landing since the beach from low to high tide would be enormously distant. The first wave of LST's will deploy at high tide which was early in the morning, land their troops and by low tide they would be completely high and dry on the beach, unable to back off.

Secondly, our forces would be 200 to 300 miles behind the front at Pusan. If the enemy has a force at Inchon it could be a disaster for our boys.

But by the same token if the North Korean's concentrated forces in Seoul and at the front, the U. N. forces could be in Seoul in a matter of days and cut off the enemy with a pincer movement.

The landing went well. Tony's LCVP carried 22 Marines from the 5th Marines who swarmed up over the seawalls on assault ladders at Red Beach. The resistance was there but minimal. The surprise of an invasion at an unlikely spot worked, proof of the capability of General MacArthur. The first wave of LST's went in with the mop up troops.

On into the night the Battleship Missouri and the Cruisers shelled the interior with their big guns.

The Missouri lobbed its 20 inch shells all the way into Seoul. The orange and yellow muzzle flash from the guns could be seen from the harbor and the shells whistled over the head's of the anchored ships before the sound of the blast could reach them.

This was a resounding victory for the U. N. forces and again it was proven that General Douglas MacArthur was indeed a military genius.

But it was not all easy. The North Korean army did not give up Seoul without a fight. There was savage infantry fighting and heavy marine casualties.

The Columbia stayed at anchor in Inchon Harbor. Several times General Quarters were called for an eminent air attack but they never came under fire. Our fighters must have knocked them down before they reached the ships in the harbor.

"Hey Tony" yelled Peacock "I heard that the North Korean's were flying fighter planes without props. They're supposed to be a Russian plane called MIG's and they use some kind of rocket propulsion."

"Those are jets Peacock. I also heard that the pilots were not very good and our Corsairs were shootin' them down."

"Why don't we have some of those kinds of planes?"

"Don't worry, we will. Our guys are just taking a deep breath after the so called *big war* that we just won."

"We're lickin' 'em any how" said Tony proudly. Threat of an enemy air attack after the first day or so was minimal so security relaxed a bit and the sailors had a ring side seat of some of the fighting on the beach.

The Navy Corsairs were dropping Napalm on the retreating North Korean troops. The planes dove and disappeared behind the mountain and dropped a few Napalm bombs. As they pulled up and appeared on the other side of the mountain a huge fire ball rose up into the sky.

Tony said "Man oh man, I'd hate to be on the other side of that mountain. Those poor devils....nothin' worse than Napalm. That jellied gasoline just explodes and sticks to anything or anyone in the area and incinerates whatever it sticks to.... makes me shiver."

They headed back down to the compartment just as Sully came bouncing in and said "Okay guys, get squared away. We get underway tomorrow morning for somewhere in Japan to pick up another load of troops. Make sure we're ready to go."

"Hey, I thought we were going back stateside. I was planning to see my honey doll. She's waiting for me in San Francisco" said a bellyaching Peacock.

"You know the saying 'Yours is not to question why'.....Sully said in a stern tone.

"I know...I know" answered Peacock "Mine is but to do or die but I still would like to see my honey doll. She misses me too."

CHAPTER SIX

They weighed anchor at 0800 the next morning and headed south to skirt the south end of the peninsula and turned toward Japan. The next port of call is Osaka on the south end of Honshu. Their ship, the Columbia, would arrive mid morning of the 3rd day at sea.

It was a relief for the ships company to be at sea with only a few hundred troops aboard, most of them with minor wounds or a few soldiers with some personal emergency to remove them from Inchon and en route stateside. The more severely wounded were sent to the Constellation which is a fully equipped hospital ship. Some were admitted to a MASH unit field hospital for treatment and then shipped back to Japan.

The ship anchored in Osaka harbor which was bustling with activity. The so called "Police Action" in Korea by the United Nations was really ramping up. The biggest problem seemed to be getting our troops properly equipped and the new troops trained. Delays were rampant and so the Columbia sat at anchor waiting to be loaded with badly needed replacement troops.

The latest scuttlebutt had them going to Wonsan in North Korea. That surely meant that we were pushing the North Korean troops back very quickly.

In the meantime life was good in Osaka. The crew had liberty two out of three days and the bars on shore were flourishing. The third day was duty on board with Tony, Peacock and Sully assigned to boat duty which meant many runs from the ship to several different piers on shore depending if it was a liberty run, a mail run or some special run such as picking up the officers softball team. All were pretty much run of the mill and Tony was getting good experience in acting as coxs'n. Sully was teaching him all that he knew since he was due to make 2nd Class Boatswains Mate soon and his duties of running the LCVP at that time would be over.

It was on a routine mail run with Tony at the wheel that a near tragedy occurred. The bay was choppy from a fresh breeze and the flat bottom boat was taking a roll from the wind and waves coming on the beam.

Tony was following close behind another LCVP from a sister ship anchored in the same area as the Columbia. It also was taking some pretty good rolls from the choppy water in the bay.

He noticed a crew member scrambling forward to retrieve a bow line that had slipped into the water and was dragging along side. The danger being that the errant line would be entangled in the prop of their boat and could cause a great deal of trouble such as a stalled engine, a bent or broken prop or prop shaft or just a slow ride. No good could come of it if not readily retrieved. That Bow Hook would get a chewing out for not securing that line when they got back to the ship.

Suddenly a rogue wave smacked the two boats from the starboard side and both took a huge roll, almost to the point of taking on water on the port side. Tony quickly adjusted to the wave and regained control of the boat but the other boat was not so lucky.

When they took the roll, the crew member up forward, retrieving the errant line, lost his balance and went tumbling over the side into the choppy bay.

As Tony was struggling to right his boat the boat ahead was trying to turn around.

Sully saw what had happened and alertly yelled "MAN OVERBOARD….MAN OVERBOARD. RIGHT RUDDER, TONY, RIGHT RUDDER."

Tony quickly turned the wheel as far right as possible and they came within a whisker of plowing right over the bobbing sailor. As their wake swallowed him up, his head disappeared under the choppy surf.

The other boat by then had reached them and the coxs'n yelled "HE WASN'T WEARING HIS LIFE JACKET."

Tony had cut the engine to idle and all three were scanning the water for a bobbing head.

"If he survives this he's going to get another ass chewing for not wearing his life jacket" mumbled Sully as he looked at his crew, both of which were sans life jackets.

"THERE HE IS" yelled Peacock as the sailor's head came up above the water, coughing and hacking.

"Tony, take us closer, I'll try to snag him with a boat hook. His foul weather gear keeps dragging him under" instructed Sully.

Tony eased his boat as close as he could.

"Damn it. I missed him. He's back under" said Sully as he stripped off his foul weather jacket and prepared to dive in the water.

He stood on the gunwale of the rolling boat, trying to get a glimpse of where to dive when he heard a yell from the other boat "I see him he's just ahead to the right."

Just as Sully spotted him and squatted to make his dive, he heard "I HOOKED HIM...I HOOKED HIM...BACK DOWN BACK DOWN. OKAY CUT IT. HELP ME PULL HIM ABOARD. HE'S WATER LOGGED AND HEAVY AS HELL."

Sully and his crew watched as they pulled the limp body from the drink and as they pulled him over the gunwale he coughed and gagged and water gushed from his mouth.

They saw the Coxs'n jump down into the well deck where he and the other crew member worked on the soaked sailor.

Sully waited a few minutes and then yelled "Ahoy there! Is he okay? Do you need any help with him?"

The Coxs'n stood and replied "He'll be okay now. Probably get sick from swallowing all the polluted bay water though. Hey, thanks to you and your crew for locating him. I'm not sure we would have found him by the time we got turned around. Your Coxs'n did a good job. We owe you guys a beer next time we see you on the beach."

"Glad we could help" said Sully as he turned and winked at Tony who was beaming with pride and had a wide smile on his face.

"Put her in neutral Tony. I got something to say" Sully said.

Tony throttled back and put the transmission in neutral.

"I know those kapok life jackets are cumbersome and a pain in the ass and I'm as guilty as anyone about not wearing them. But regulations say that we wear them while we're running this boat at all times, even when we're not in enemy waters but especially when we've got some choppy conditions. Now let's all put them on like good sailors. Some day we may thank God we had them on....Okay Coxs'n" said Sully proudly "head this baby back to the ship. I'm gettin' hungry."

"Yeah, me too, in fact I'm starvin'. Let's hit it" Peacock piped up.

Sully laughed and said "The way you pack it away, Peacock, you might just be the missing link between man and the great white shark."

Tony let out a loud guffaw, put it in forward and gunned the engine. It looked like Sully was going to let him take her all the way back and maybe handle the hoisting aboard. He felt very good.

Two days later they got underway for Wonsan in North Korea with a boat load of the 1st Marine Division. It was an uneventful trip and they off loaded without a hitch. It was now in the latter part of October. They now heard that Communist China had joined forces with the North Koreans, since the United Nation Forces had made such good headway in driving the N. K. back so. This was not good news since the Chinese had a tremendous advantage in man power. Their army was huge.

"Well the hell with them" said Sully "we'll just get more troops and drive them back across the Yalu River to Manchuria."

"Yea I guess we learned our lesson. After the war when we cut back on men and put all our weapons in moth balls, the Commies were building massive forces and building planes and tanks" Tony said.

MAKE PREPARATIONS TO GET UNDERWAY came the sudden announcement out of the squawk box.

"Okay guys! Turn to! Let's head to Yokohama for some good liberty" yelled Sully.

The voyage from Osaka to Yokohama was a breeze. Good weather and morale was high since the scuttlebutt now had them going to Guam with troops to be reassigned to light duty there and then they'd head back to the good old U.S.A.

Tony had the lookout watch on the bridge as the ship proceeded northeast along the coast of Honshu before they entered Tokyo Bay. He trained his binoculars towards land intently looking for a famous landmark.

"Train your sight line a little more north, son and you'll see it" said a deep mature voice.

Tony relaxed the binoculars away from his face and through his peripheral vision he saw the arm of an officer with four gold stripes on the cuff.

Tony snapped to attention and said "Good afternoon Captain" in a somewhat shaky voice.

The old gentleman chuckled and said "It's okay son. Everyone is anxious for his first sight of Mount Fuji. Take a look at the snow topped peak through your binoculars one time and then go back to your look out duties."

"Yes sir. Thank you sir."

Tony trained his sight to where he was told and sure enough he found it. What a majestic sight it was. It rose up out of the mist and it surely was snow covered. He could understand why many Japanese considered it holy ground.

When he pulled the binoculars back away and turned, he saw that the Captain had already left. Moments later his relief approached him to stand the next watch.

They would soon enter Tokyo Bay which was a huge body of water. After entering the bay, the ship steamed right on past Yokosuka en route to Yokohama. Tokyo was on further towards the closed end of the bay.

Tony's duty when entering port was on the fantail. He and the other seamen in the 3rd division were busy flaking out the hawsers that would be used in tying up to a dock.

Tug boats were approaching and would soon assist them in navigating through a very congested area to tie up. Also a Harbor Patrol boat was falling in behind them and riding in the smooth water in their wake.

The Coxs'n of the patrol boat had a bull horn and called "Is Marino close by?"

Sully said "Hey Tony that patrol boat is asking for you. What the hell did you do?"

"Beats me Sully" Tony said as he looked out over the rail.

"Oh my God. It's that crazy ass Jay Johnson. The last time I saw him he was tending bar for the Officer's Club. Now it looks like he's running a Harbor Patrol boat."

Tony waved his arms and yelled "HEY JAY"

"IF YOU GOT LIBERTY…MEET ME AT THE TIGER CLUB IN TOWN TONIGHT."

"OKAY I'LL BE THERE AT ABOUT SEVEN."

"Hey Sully. The bridge wants to know what that Harbor Patrol boat wants" said the fantail watch.

"Just tell them that they wanted to make sure we knew that tugs had to assist us. It's pulling away now" Sully said with a relieved tone.

The watch passed on the message through his microphone.

"Geez Tony. You sure got some weird friends" Sully added.

The whole 3rd Division was busting a gut in laughter and Tony was just shaking his head.

"Only Jay could pull off a stunt like that. This liberty tonight should be a real doozey. Who wants to go with me?"

"I'll go" Peacock quickly said.

"And I'm going too" Sully said "but only to keep you guys out of trouble. I'm very familiar with what can happen at the Tiger Club."

That night, as the three of them sauntered into the loud, blaring music filling the Tiger Club. Sully lamented "Oh my God, it's even worse than I remember it."

"Hey Tony, over here" came a shout from the dimly lit interior, hardly audible over the music.

It was Jay and he sat among three young ladies clad in western attire, all enjoying tall cool drinks of unknown liquid refreshment.

"Come on over here. The first round is on me and I'll introduce you to my good friends" laughingly said Jay.

The three sailors made their way over to the table with Jay and his female friends seated around it.

Jay stood up and shook hands with Tony and then with Sully and Peacock as Tony introduced them.

He then turned to the three girls and said "Boys, I want you to meet Makiko, Michiko and Shizuka."

The one called Michiko grabbed Tony's arm and said "Hey cute saila' boy, what your name?"

"Ah, ah, I'm called Tony."

"Okay Tony-san, you come sit by me. You know how Jitta' bug?"

"Yeah, I can jitterbug a little bit. But I'd kind of like a beer first."

"Okay saila' boy. I go get beer for you. How 'bout you guys?"

"Sure" said Sully and Peacock in unison.

After Michiko returned it was a continuous round of beers and dancing for the next few hours. Everyone seemed to be enjoying a good time when suddenly an irate Shizuka stood and shoved Jay against the wall.

She said in an angered voice "I told you before Jay. I not pom pom girl. You want pom pom girl, you go find rickshaw driver and he take you to one."

"Okay, okay Shizuka don't get all bent out of shape. I'm going to leave anyway. I got early duty in the morning."

He turned to Tony and said "You want to go with me? Maybe we'll find us a rickshaw driver first."

"No thanks Jay. I'd rather be safe than sorry. We've been told that these big city girls are a little suspect for giving you a bug, doing some of that kind of action."

"Okay, okay. Maybe I'll see you tomorrow. Got liberty?"

"Nope I've got the duty tomorrow and we're leaving the next day or so. Maybe we'll be back in a month or so. I'll look you up."

"Okay pal. Sayonara." Jay said as he staggered off.

"That was a wise move, Tony, very wise." Sully said.

"Hey let's do Jitta' bug" said Michiko as she pulled Tony to the dance floor.

Tony was enjoying letting off a little steam and felt relaxed for the first time in months.

When he got back to the table, Sully said "I hate to throw a damper on things but, the group of rough looking foreign soldiers over there keep looking at us. I think they're Turks."

"Oh, oh the big tough one is coming over here. Let me handle this." Sully said as he stood up.

The very big and dark complexioned Turkish soldier dressed in fatigues stopped at the sailors table.

He spoke in very broken English and said "Hey sailors, what name of your ship?"

Sully answered as he drew himself up to full height. "The USS Columbia. Why? What seems to be the problem?

The Turk soldier stepped back. "No, no. I have no problem. My men and me, we just came back from Korea. We come on your ship. One of my men thought he recognize this sailor."

He pointed at Tony.

Tony said "Oh yeah. We had some Turks aboard. One was on a work party to help clean up the troop compartments but he couldn't understand a word I said so he got off pretty easy when I got tired of using sign language."

"Yes, yes. My man say you treat him good. We want to buy drink for you. All of you. Even girls. Okay?"

"Yeah sure. Why not?" Sully said and sat down.

"Okay. Send girl up for drinks. Tell bartender Big Turk buy them and bring special Turkish drink for Big Turk. I drink with my friends."

Peacock piped up "How about your buddies? Do they want to come over and join us?"

"Sure. Why not?" said the Turk as he called to his friends in a tongue that none of them could understand.

The three soldiers all stood and cheered as they dragged their chairs over to their new found friends, carrying a bottle of a dark looking liquid and three glasses

Soon it was a raucous party where the differences of language did not impede the drinking and new found friendship. The bond of a common cause outweighed all disadvantages. Even the Japanese girls were caught up in this happy group of warriors.

The Big Turk hugged Tony as they were about to call it a night and made him promise to look him up if he ever got to Ankara.

"Sure I will, but what do I do? Just go into this city of two million people and ask where does the Big Turk live? They'd probably throw me in jail."

"You very funny guy, Tony. I like you. Call me Hakan. Here, I write a note in Turkish with my name and address. Note will say you my friend and will help you find me."

"That's great Hakan. Are you headed back home now?"

"No, no. We go back to Korea in about two weeks. That's enough rest. This time I hope they let us use bayonets on those little guys that come at you all yelling and screaming and blowing bugles. We gonna get 'em."

"Well good luck to you and your men. Maybe we'll cross paths again some day."

They all hugged as they parted company. The girls got their share of hugs from both sailors and soldiers and giggled with each one.

Big Turk herded his staggering group out the door laughing and whooping as they went. It was a happy group of drunken soldiers.

Sully said "Okay guys. Liberty's up at Midnight and we can make it easily if we leave now so let's hit it."

As they stood, Michiko grabbed a hold of Tony in a bear hug and said "No, no. I no let Tony-san go. You stay, saila' boy. Stay with Michiko."

"Hey, I've got to get back to my ship baby-san. I like you too but duty calls."

"Just one more jitta' bug saila' boy. Please."

Tony looked at Sully and Sully gave him the old evil eye not saying a word but getting his message across.

"I can't do it Michiko. I gotta go" as he extricated himself from her death grip.

"Okay saila' boy. But you come back. Okay?"

"Some day….maybe….but not tomorrow." Tony said as he and the other two made their way to the exit with Michiko trailing behind.

Peacock was almost doubled over with loud guffaws. He said "Wow Tony, you turned out to be a real heartbreaker. I think that girl wants to keep you forever." And he ducked when Tony tried to swat him.

Sully just walked ahead and shook his head at the antics of his two best friends.

CHAPTER SEVEN

Days later found them at sea en route to Guam. The crew was festive because when they dropped off troops at Guam and picked up others there, they were going to return to their home port, San Francisco.

This was the relaxing part of going to sea. The weather was good. Temperatures were moderate and the island of Guam was a United States possession so no danger was involved. There were no big towns on the island and conditions were extremely rustic but the locals were very friendly.

Typically the skipper would give permission for the enlisted men and the officers to have a softball game and he would furnish a keg of beer for each game.

When they arrived in port a week or so later, the chief organized the enlisted men's softball game. Since there were plenty of volunteers the chief made up two teams. The Swab Jockeys and the Snipes were the chosen names of the two teams, which meant the deck force sailors versus the below decks enginemen. Of course extra men volunteered to help out since they too would be eligible for beer. No one that wanted to go was turned down. This was to be a day of fun and it was. The skipper wanted them to relax because he knew that the next bit of news, that changed their destination, was not going to be well received. He would wait until they were underway before releasing the information. At this time only he and the Exec knew that the trip to San Francisco would be delayed.

It was hot and humid. The beer flowed from the tap in an almost steady stream. By the fifth inning many of the young sailors were staggering.

The Swab Jockeys were up to bat and Peacock was at the plate. The score was tied at six runs apiece and those had all been scored before the fourth inning. Most of the batters were now missing the ball by a foot or more.

The pitcher lobbed a high arcing pitch to the plate and Peacock reared back to take a mighty swing. He was going to send this one out of the park. As the ball crossed the plate he swung with all his might, missed the ball by a mile and on his follow through, the bat slipped out of his sweaty grip. Since his swing was so mighty the bat went flying, spinning like a helicopter propeller, all the way to the bench of the now screaming Snipes. The bat landed in the midst of them, conking two of them on the noggin, one of which was a particularly hefty looking Snipe.

He took great offense at the antics of the now laughing Peacock who was prone on the ground and rolling in the dust. As Peacock rose to his knees the charging Snipe knocked him head over heels and then landed on top of him. He grabbed him in a bear hug and being almost twice Peacock's size, the wind came rushing out of the sailor with a loud whooshing sound.

The Swab Jockeys rushed to their shipmate's aid and all charged the huge Snipe at about the same time the Snipe team steam rolled in from their bench.

It was one huge collision of tipsy sailors. There was a lot of pushing and shoving and some wrestling and a few swings that ended up as misses. By the time the chiefs were able to intercede and break it up all concerned were more than happy to do so.

It was then decided that the game would end as a tie and all participants would finish off the keg and the return to the ship.

The trip back had them all singing dirty songs and laughing their heads off. They all staggered aboard and took well needed showers.

The next day was a duty day for Tony and the boat crew. Sully was to be Boatswain Mate of the watch, so Tony was assigned to ferry the officer's softball team to and from the athletic dock. This was Tony's first official duty as Coxs'n and both he and Peacock were hung over from the previous day's antics.

The trip in was uneventful except for some reluctance in his approach to the small cove where the athletic dock was located. But he took his time and made it without any mishap even if some of the officers were agitated at the slow ride in just before docking. Tony let the snide remarks slide off his back. After all they were officers and he really couldn't get smart with them and besides they were just as anxious to open that keg as the enlisted men were the day before. So Tony unloaded them and headed back to the ship. He knew he had a mail run later at the main dock and he wanted to get some much needed coffee and rest.

Time seemed to drag on and the hang over didn't subside the whole day long.

The officer's softball team had apparently decided to make a full day of it so Tony and crew were still on standby at 1700 which was chow time.

Peacock was sacked out on the deck sleeping on a pile of foul weather gear, snoring up a storm, his mouth agape and slobbering. Tony couldn't stand it any longer. He aimed a swift kick at the sailor's posterior and yelled. "Hit the deck you slob. Let's go get some chow before we get called away to pick up the gold braid at the athletic dock."

"Okay, okay" came the reply "you don't have to get physical. Why can't you wake me up gently?"

"Because the way you sleep, it's the next thing to being unconscious" Tony barked back.

He was not in a good mood.

On the way to the Mess Hall they picked up the third crew member who was a young apprentice and very anxious to crew with these two popular members of the 3rd division.

The chow line was long and slow. Just as they reached the trays, to start loading the evening meal, a loud message blared from the P. A. system.

"AWAY #2 LCVP—AWAY #2 LCVP"

"Wouldn't you know it" complained Tony "come on you two, we've got to go get the Brass. We'll have to eat when we come back."

"Aw geez, Tony. The mess hall might be closed when we get back" moaned Peacock "and I'm starving now."

"Make a move sailor. You're on boat duty and that means NOW" commanded the stern cox'n.

"Boy, give a guy a little power and it goes right to his head" mumbled the complaining sailor as he grudgingly set his empty tray down.

"I don't like it any more than you do pal" answered Tony "let's get a move on. Maybe we can make it in record time."

The crew hurried to their boat which was tied up along side and headed in to the athletic dock.

Now that he was more familiar with the channel, Tony made better time than before and when he tied up the officers slowly boarded the boat. They were tipsy and the below decks officers were complaining since they lost 13 to 2 to the Line officers.

"We only lost because we were short handed and had to use some of the chiefs who had never even seen a soft ball before, let alone played the game" complained the Chief Engineer.

"Go on. We're just better all around athletes" came the good natured reply.

While all this was going on, Peacock and Tony were standing on the dock snickering at the exchange.

"At least they didn't have a riot like we did yesterday" said Peacock.

"Yeah, let's get them loaded so we can get underway. I think we can still make chow time if we hurry." Tony added.

"Hey Tony, why don't we cut inside that aircraft mooring buoy that you've been using as a channel marker? I'll bet it's not really there to mark the channel. It sure would cut off some time if we didn't go around it."

"It really would get us back sooner but I don't know. It's there for some reason and I forgot to ask Sully."

"Well I looked it up on the charts and it designates it as an aircraft mooring buoy and not a channel marker buoy" asserted Peacock.

"I know, I know and I cut it pretty close this morning. There sure seemed to be plenty of water around it."

"Okay Cox'n, we're all loaded. How about getting underway?" said the officer in charge.

"Yes sir" answered Tony.

"Okay Peacock, cast off. Let's get some chow."

"Aye aye, sir" came a chuckling reply from Peacock.

Tony swung the boat away from the dock and headed out of the channel. As he got past lands end where the channel markers took him on a southeasterly course to open water, he reached the point where the only buoy was the one in question and it continued him southeasterly. Following the course used in the past he would go past the buoy and then make a hard turn to port and go northeasterly to the ship. If he made his turn now, before reaching the buoy, he could pick up a good 15 or 20 minutes.

He decided to chance it. It looked like good open water to him and there seemed to be plenty of water this morning just six or seven hours ago.

He was going full bore towards the ship and was feeling pretty good about himself when suddenly the LCVP hit something and the bow seemed to rise up and then slammed down with a loud teeth rattling, body jarring sudden stop. It threw Tony against the wheel and knocked the breath out of him. Peacock went flying down into the well deck where all the officers were being flung forward to slam up against the ramp with the ones in the stern landing on top of them.

The officers were yelling "What the hell's going on here" and they came struggling out of the well deck screaming uncomplimentary cuss words.

The boat was hard aground.

Tony tried to collect himself as the officer in charge asked "Cox'n what the hell's going on? Are we aground?"

"Yes sir. I don't know what happened. I thought we had plenty of water."

"Well it's obvious that we don't. Can you back her down and get us off?"

"I'll try sir but we're pretty far aground. We're a flat bottom and it seemed to skip when we hit."

Tony put it in reverse and slowly increased the revs to full power without any movement at all.

"I'm afraid we're going to need a tow sir."

"Oh great! How the hell are we going to get a tow. There's no radio aboard."

"I'm hoping the gangway watch is expecting us and when we don't show they may try to spot us with the binocs. Sully is Boatswains Mate of the Watch and he's usually the Cox'n with this crew. I hope he's watching."

Tony was right. Sully, knowing it was Tony's first day as Cox'n had his eye trained on them.

He had alerted the Officer of the Deck when he saw what happened.

"Why in the hell did that young man go out of the channel?" said the O.D.

"I don't know sir. It's not really a channel buoy although it's being used as one. I've seen other boats do it but it was always at high tide. It's dead low tide right now. Just Tony's luck and on his first day."

"I'll call another V.P. away to unload the passengers and lighten it up and then pull them off if needed. I hope it didn't tear out the bottom. It should be okay. Those flat bottom boats are built to run up on a beach. If only it's sand or mud and not rocks or coral, that's what will make a difference."

In the meantime Tony was eyeballing the ship with his binoculars when he saw #1 L.C.V.P. being lowered into the water and leave the gangway.

He said to the officer in charge "Okay sir, there's a boat on its way. I just saw them leave the gangway. Should be here in 15 or 20 minutes."

When #1 arrived, the Cox'n who was an old hand pulled up behind #2 and sarcastically asked "Hey do you guys need a lift?"

"Ha Ha" Tony said "Just slowly back your stern up against mine so I can unload the passengers. Should be enough water because I can run my engine and the prop just kicks up some sand and mud but it turns."

"Okay. Here I come."

When the two boats were married together, the officers gladly clamored aboard the rescue boat. After they were all off and Tony's boat was much lighter it was no problem getting off the shoal with just a little help from #1.

Both boats then made their way back to the mother ship. When Tony's boat arrived he was instructed to pull under the boat davits to be hoisted aboard so the bottom could be inspected.

After a thorough inspection and it was determined that new paint on the bottom was all that was required, Tony was told to report to the Exec.

His Division Officer, Lieutenant jg Nelson, accompanied him and they reported to the exec in his quarters.

The Exec, who was the same mustang that sent them on the secret mission, was silent for what seemed to be a long time.

Tony squirmed.

Finally the old gentleman spoke. He said "Were you in a hurry son?"

"Kind of sir. We missed chow."

"I hope you have a better excuse than that, Marino" said the XO sternly.

"Well sir, the buoy was not really a marker buoy and earlier it looked like deep water there. And yes sir, I guess I was in a hurry when I should have used better judgment. I also should have checked tide conditions. There was a 4 foot difference in tide from this morning to this afternoon. It was low tide. It's my fault sir."

"Yes it is son. This will be a lesson well learned and since there was no great damage to the boat I'm not going to put you on report. But I am going to require you and your crew to scrape and paint the whole boat and you'll do it on your next off duty day. No liberty. Understand?"

"Yes sir. I understand and I've learned my lesson on respecting the navigation aids and tide conditions."

"Okay son. You're dismissed."

"Thank you, sir."

As they left the Exec's quarters Lieutenant Nelson said "You're pretty lucky Marino. Getting restricted aboard with no liberty is sure no big deal when you're anchored in Guam. Where the hell would you go?"

"Yes sir, I know. Good thing the old mustang was an enlisted man once" said a smiling Marino.

"Okay. Just do a good job painting that boat and count your blessings" said Nelson, also with a grin on his face.

CHAPTER EIGHT

The stay at Guam was a short one. They got underway the following day which was several days before they were scheduled to embark for San Francisco..

After they were at sea and the 3rd Division sailors were stowing all the hawsers and rat guards that were intended to be used to tie up at a loading dock for passengers, Peacock asked "Hey Chief, I thought we were going to take a bunch of soldiers and marines back stateside with us. What's going on?"

"Don't ask me sailor. All I know is what I was told and that was to weigh anchor and get underway."

"Somethin's goin' on" Sully said.

They continued their work to make the ship seaworthy when the bos'n piped *All Hands* on his pipe over the P.A. system.

"All hands stand by for a message from the Captain" came the announcement.

A slight delay and then next…."This is the Captain speaking……Men….we've had a change in orders…..Our next destination will not be our home port of San Francisco…..We have been ordered to return to Japan in all possible haste to a port called Moji. It is located on the southern coast of Honshu in the Strait between the main island of Honshu and the small southern island of Kyushu…..This is a very small port….mostly a fishing village, but an arsenal is close by. We will rearm and await further orders on our next assignment…..I don't anticipate a long stay….Moji is one of the closest Japanese ports to Pusan, Korea…….I know many of you were anticipating a reunion with your loved ones in the States. I'm sorry to inform you that it will be delayed and to advise that all approved leaves, upon reaching San Francisco, have been put on hold......I did not divulge this information before we left Guam since it is top secret and I knew that some of you would be writing to the folks back home.....Bear with me.....I'll pass on to you as much information as I am allowed..... That is all, please return to your duties."

The crew stood quietly looking at each other with blank looks on their faces.

Peacock piped up "Hey, I wonder if we'll get liberty at Moji?"

"You jerk, Peacock" said Sully. "Okay sailors let's turn to. Get back to work."

The sailors went about their assigned duties griping all the way about how they could run this Navy much better. But then gripes were no different than before. There was always something to gripe about and there was always someone who felt he had a better way of running "this canoe club". And so it went, soon everything reverted to everyday shipboard life....lookout watches, chip and paint, sweep downs. And all the things that sailors do at sea.

One quiet night when Tony was on lookout watch from Midnight to 0400 and Sully was Bos'n Mate of the Watch, Sully came out to the wing of the bridge and said to Tony "I just overheard an interesting conversation between the Marine Captain of the group of marines we're hauling back to Japan and the Officer of the Deck. He just came up for a cup of coffee because he couldn't sleep. Anyway he's had more than his share of battle in Korea and he's had quite a bit of experience with the Turkish Brigade over there."

"You mean like those guys that we met in Yokohama?"

"One and the same. According to him they are some of the fiercest fighters in the war. I guess they weren't kidding when they said they hoped to use their bayonets. That seems to be standard procedure with them. He told some pretty harrowing stories about some of their battles. I don't know all the details but the Captain said at the Sunchon Pass where our 2nd Division came up against a stone wall, the bayonet of the Turkish Infantry once again asserted its rule and helped open up the pass which had been under enemy control for two days. With this attack, in which our infantry and tanks were able to advance, the battle came to a successful conclusion."

"Wow" said Tony "I'm sure glad they liked us. They were a pretty good group. I still carry Big Turk's note. He said he's called Hakan. I never did find out his last name. He told me but I couldn't understand him and I sure can't read what he wrote. I wonder if we'll ever see them again."

"I doubt it" said Sully "unless you decide to take a trip to Turkey after the war and then it would be a long shot."

"Who knows? Stranger things have happened" mumbled Tony.

The next day the weather took a turn for the worse and a severe chop developed but the ship drove on into the pounding sea. By that night she was taking green water over the bow and the Captain had to reduce turns because the stern was coming out of the water and vibration of the screw when it cleared the surface was severe.

It continued throughout the night and looked like it might subside a bit by morning. Unexpectedly there was a change in course and the chief came hurriedly bursting into the 3rd Division sleeping quarters where the sailors had just gotten back from a breakfast of beans and cornbread and yelled "Okay sailors we've got some preparation to do. We've been ordered to take a derelict tanker in tow. She's lost all power and is drifting without control. We should be there in about 2 hours. There's a long 2 inch wire cable in the stern locker. Break it out and flake it out along the deck where it won't get hung up as we pay it out. It's really heavy and hard to handle so be careful. Use the thick gloves because wire rope has a lot of sharp pieces of wire sticking out and it will rip your hand wide open. Sully, you're in charge."

The men scrambled up topside and started working on the coiled up wire rope. It was hard work and they were sweating.

Peacock said "How the hell are we going to get this heavy bastard over the side and hooked on to that tanker?"

"Think about it Peacock" said Sully.

"I guess we'll throw a heaving line and then a painter hooked on to the cable. Huh?"

"Close but not quite. We won't be able to get close enough to throw a heaving line. Gunner has a special shot gun in the armory. This shot gun doesn't shoot a regular shell. It has a metal rod in the barrel that's hooked to a spool of very strong line that's mounted on the stock of the gun. A special loaded shell is behind the rod. When we get in range, Gunner will shoot the rod over to the tanker, high enough not to hit anyone but placed so the crew can grab the line. They'll pull the line which will be bent to another line about the size of a heaving line which in turn is bent onto another bigger line, probably a painter and if we're close enough we'll tie that to the eye of the wire rope. That's the tough part. Since the tanker has no power they will pull it aboard manually. The captain will take the ship as close as he can in this rough weather. If there is too much wire out it will be too heavy for them to muscle aboard. That's the program….and it's up to us to see that the right amount of wire rope is paid out."

Shortly after they had the wire cable flaked out properly, they felt the ship slow down. Off to the east they could make out a small tanker bobbing in the waves. As they got closer they could see a rag tag crew along the rail waving frantically. The ship was an unkempt pile of rust. It would probably break in half with seas any higher than they were. Old tankers didn't have much support amidships and were notorious for sinking in extreme conditions. They needed a tow badly.

The captain pulled along side as close as practical heading in the same direction that the tanker was pointing. Gunner fired the shot gun and the metal rod flew in a high arc, landing on the forward deck behind the mast. A good shot.

The tanker crew scrambled for the line and pulled out all the slack. The second line was bent on and they pulled it across the open water. Next came the painter which was a much heavier line and a little more difficult to pull. It sagged into the water and the Chief yelled over the bull horn for them to pull harder. They did and the line rose free of the drink.

The painter was already bent on to the wire cable and Sully's crew fed the eye out through a chock. They waited until the slack in the painter was as little as possible and then started feeding out the cable. When the cable was about half way to the tanker it was in the water.

"PULL…..PULL" yelled the chief.

He knew it was inevitable that the wire would disappear in the drink, as heavy as it was, but he wanted it as taut as he could get it.

Again he yelled "PULL….PULL"

The end of the wire and a good 20 feet was still under water and the tanker had every available man pulling. Soon, the tip of the eye showed itself above the trough of a wave, and then disappeared again as the wave broke over it.

"PULL…..PULL. You've almost got it"

It seemed to give them a burst of strength. Maybe some adrenalin kicked in. They pulled harder and then the whole eye was visible. Sully's crew cheered and the tanker crew cheered back as they pulled with all their strength.

After a great burst the eye was aboard and they struggled getting it through a chock and secured on a bollard.

They all collapsed on the deck in great relief.

"Okay..Okay" yelled Sully "let's get it secured on our end after we've let out some slack. When we start towing we only want to see our end and their end. The middle section must be in the water. If it gets too taut it will snap like a rubber band and you don't want to be any where near it if that happens. The bitter end could slice you in half as slick as if you were butter."

The captain then eased ahead of the tanker and slowly took her in tow. It would slow them down considerably but according to maritime law you must render all assistance to a vessel in distress and a sea going tug was several days away.

A watch was set up to observe the tow cable along with the regular fantail watch who had a radio link to the bridge. Any change in the cable would be instantly reported to the bridge.

Unfortunately the weather deteriorated, the seas got higher and the cable rose and fell with the pitching ships. As long as the center of the cable was under the surface, the tow was secure. Throughout the night it was difficult to see the cable even with two spot lights trained on it but finally a gray day came upon them and they still had a successful tow.

Suddenly just as the new watch was taking over, a huge wave broke under the Columbia. First the bow rose up and the O.D. slowed the turns but then the stern rose up and the cable came completely out of the water it was so taut it was singing a shrill song. Some of the minute wires on the outside popped and sprung out like barbs but it held as the stern sunk into a trough and the center of the cable again sunk beneath the surface.

The wave continued. It was huge. The little tanker rose up like it was a bobber. The tow cable again rose completely out of the water just as the second wave lifted the Columbia and the cable snapped like a piece of string.

The four sailors on the fantail scrambled as the cable writhed like a snake. The parted cable rose into the air 50 feet from the stern of the ship, the strands unraveling as it whipped about like a whirling dervish. If the break would have been closer or on the deck of the ship it would have sliced the sailors up like so much meat. Luckily the break was a good 50 feet away.

"Fantail to Bridge. Fantail to Bridge. The cable has parted. Repeat. The cable has parted" called the fantail watch on the intercom.

The O.D. stopped all engines. The danger now was getting a cable wrapped around a screw. Then there would be two ships in distress.

Sully felt the sudden difference in the action of the ship and raced topside with his crew.

"Okay men, let's get that cable in. Be careful. Those broken strands are sharp as razors."

The fantail watch said. "Hold it Sully. The O.D. wants to talk to you. Here take the ear phones and mike."

"Sully here sir. Go ahead."

"How much cable is left Sully?"

"I'd estimate 50 feet or so sir but the last 10 feet or there about is useless."

"Okay. The old man says to throw it off the bollard and deep six it. We can't use it for anything now."

"Aye aye sir."

"Okay guys. We got an easy one. Deep six it."

Up on the bridge, the captain had already asked the radioman to call for instructions. He knew that they could not leave a vessel in distress and he only hoped that help was already en route.

After several hours he got the word that a sea going tug had left an island group the day before and its E.T.A. would be about mid afternoon the following day. The Columbia was to circle the tanker until its arrival and stand by to take on survivors if the tanker broke up. They could then proceed to Moji, after the tug gets hooked up to tow.

CHAPTER NINE

The sea going tug arrived at 1400 and the derelict tanker was taken in a successful tow. The tow line used was a harness with two points of connection for easier steering and the tug secured the cable to a capstan that would release tension in case of a surge similar to the one encountered during the tow by the Columbia. The tug was equipped to do this exact type of a job.

When all hook up was completed, the Columbia turned north to resume its course to Moji. The rest of the cruise was uneventful except for the fact that they ran close to flank speed to try to make up for lost time which made for a bumpy ride.

Ordinary shipboard work again took place when the Bos'n Mate of the Watch piped *All Hands* over the P. A. system.

"All hands stand by for a message from the Captain"

"Men this is the captain speaking. I want to share with you a message that we received by radio today. It reads:"

From: Commander Service Force, Pacific Fleet
To: U.S.S. Columbia; U.S.S. Reclaimer

Comserpac recognizes the fine seamanship required to pick up and tow S.S. Gulfhaven under ensuing conditions and commends Columbia and Reclaimer for their respective parts on a job well done.

After a pause.

"I also want to add my praise and approval of all of your fine efforts in the past few days. I'm proud of you. You're a good crew."

Sully spoke in admiration "And he's a fine captain too. We're lucky to have him."

The next few days passed quickly and they soon were entering the harbor at Moji. It was a small harbor and had very little ship traffic. The only other naval vessel at anchor was an Australian Destroyer. A merchant man was tied up at the only dock suitable enough for a large ship and it looked like it was loaded with cargo and preparing to get underway.

They dropped anchor about mid morning, shortly after 1000 and the deck force was making things ship shape. Tony and Peacock were assigned to chipping and painting a few spots on the stern bulkhead.

"Hey Tony, we've got liberty today starting at noon. Wanna go over and see what's in this town?"

"Oh I don't know. I'm kind of broke but I guess it would beat what we're doin' here." Tony answered.

"I've got a few bucks stashed away. These street guys like to trade Yen for green backs so maybe we can get a good exchange rate here." Peacock added.

"Yeah, 360 Yen for a dollar is usually what you can get. Okay I've got a few bucks too. Sully said this is one of his old stompin' grounds and he knows a couple of good bars. Let's see if he wants to go."

"Hey Marino" came a deep, gravely voice from behind them.

They turned to look and Peacock whispered "Oh, oh it's the Master at Arms. What kind of trouble are you in now Tony?"

"Hell I don't know. Nothin' that I know of." answered Tony as he eyeballed the big, hairy Boatswains Mate 1st Class walking towards them. Typically the Master at Arms was an old salt who kept the peace among the crew. He was also in charge of the brig and rumors had it that you never wanted to be in his brig on bread and water 'cause that's all you got. No favors from this old taskmaster with five red hash marks on his sleeve. He also felt that anyone with less than ten years service was still a rookie so these two tadpoles were prime meat for him.

Tony spoke up in as confident a voice as he could muster up "Yeah Boats. What do ya need?"

"I don't need nothin' wise guy. Just come down to the shack and get your money."

"Money? Hell I didn't leave any money down there, Boats."

"Well you lucky little shit head, you won the anchor pool. You might know a rookie would win it. Just come down and get it." And he turned and walked away.

Whatta ya' mean? I thought that was for when we went stateside?" Tony exclaimed.

"Well we decided to do it at the next anchor drop since we're not going stateside for awhile." He growled as he continued on.

"Wow! How much did I win?"

"Three hundred bucks dummy. Don't you remember nothin'?"

Peacock grabbed Tony in a huge bear hug and they danced in a circle. He said "Well I guess we got liberty money now. Let's go find Sully."

Sully had just finished showering when our dynamic duo charged in the compartment after Tony had picked up his money.

"Hey Sully did you hear?"

"Yea Peacock it's all over the ship. Tony's the big winner."

Tony piped up "Hey Sully, let's all go on liberty on me. Maybe you could show us one of those bars you know about."

"Oh I don't know. This place has a few memories from in between my hitches. Maybe I should stay aboard."

"Ya' mean when you were a pirate?" said Peacock.

"Hey I never said I was a pirate. Where'd you get that idea?"

"Well you never said what you were. But it had to be somethin' like that."

"Tell ya' what. How many guys are going?"

"Hell let's take the whole liberty party from the 3rd Division. Me, you, Peacock and 5 or 6 other guys."

"Sounds like I'd better go just to keep everyone out of trouble."

"Maybe we can find a place and pay enough to make it an exclusive party. Whatta yah think?"

"Just get your showers and get ready to go at noon. I hope you left some of that money in the M.A. shack safe." Sully added.

"Yeah, I only took a hundred. That should be plenty for this burg. Don't you think?"

"More than enough. Plenty good for Moji."

All the 3rd Division liberty party departed on the first liberty boat at the same time. When they got to the pier, the rickshaw boys were awaiting them. They rode two in a rickshaw, Sully gave directions to the lead one and told the others to follow.

They took the main road for a short distance then cut off on a side road and then cut off on an even smaller road.

They finally got to a small bar and restaurant that looked kind of unique. Not the run of the mill wild type sailor joints that they sometimes frequented.

"Hey Sully. Are you sure this is a place that we can have a good time?" asked Tony.

"Don't worry sailor. It's a place where we won't be bothered with Shore Patrol or some wild ass soldiers. There will be plenty of action and no trouble."

The other rickshaws arrived and Tony paid them with the Yen he had exchanged at the dock.

They entered the bar and a little old Japanese lady yelled "Hey what we got here? You guys lost? This nice place. No wild stuff here."

Sully piped up "Don't worry Mamma-san. These guys are with me."

"I don't believe it" she screamed "it's Sully. Maybe come back from the dead. Sully-san where you been?"

She reached up and grabbed Sully's head and gave him a big kiss.

"I don't believe it" she said again "Keiko, Keiko come quick. Sully come back. He's here."

A young Japanese girl came running from the back room and launched herself into Sully's arms, laughing and babbling "Sully-san, Sully-san. You come back."

The sailors all stood with mouths agape.

"Well I guess these really were his old stomping grounds" interjected Tony.

"Okay, okay ladies just relax. I'll fill you in later but first of all my shipmates and I want to have a celebration. Can we have one here? We can pay for the whole day if you can lock the doors and keep the place just for us."

"Sure. We can do. Anything for Sully and his friends."

Sully pointed to a table and said "Let's you and I and Tony sit down and make a plan. First of all, I see that you have a couple of customers back there. What's the deal with them? Are they here for awhile or just stopping by."

"Oh they two good Aussies. They come before. Make no trouble. Keiko likes one of them very much. Maybe can stay?"

"I'll go talk to them" said Sully.

He walked over to there table and introduced himself.

"G-dye mate" said one of them "looks like you boys are ready to celebrate. Just get in on the transport?"

"Yeah we did and we've all got a thirst. Are you guys planning to spend the day here?"

"Yes we were but since you outnumber us I guess we'd be foolish to object to your plans."

"Well now don't get upset. Mamma-san speaks well of you and I understand that one of you is sweet on Keiko so maybe you can join the party if you don't mind a bunch of American sailors" answered Sully.

"No worries mate. We get along quite well with you Yanks. We'd love to stay."

"Good. I'll pass the word."

As he made his way back to his table he passed Keiko and said "don't worry Keiko-san, they can stay."

"Oh thank you Sully-san. You the best." And she scurried off to the Aussie table.

In the meantime Tony had talked to Mamma-san and agreed that she would furnish good booze like Canadian whisky and mostly American beer. But maybe some Japanese beer too. She would have to leave after she set up the bar and go buy enough food for the group and maybe some more whiskey. She would also bring some more girls to serve and dance with the sailors.

The charge would be 20,000 Yen up front for food and drinks and free juke box. Anything else would be extra in case a sailor would really like one of the girls.

So the party began with the sailors ordering drinks from one of the girls and then the dancing started. Everyone was having a very good time and Mamma-san soon returned with two rickshaws full of groceries.

She motioned to Sully to come into the back room.

She gave him a cautious look and quietly said "I must tell you something Sully. But I'm not sure if you want to know."

"What's the problem? You know we don't have any secrets."

"Okay. About a year ago Sun-Hi came in and asked if I knew what happen to you. I tell her I don't know. You never come back after I hear about the trap set for you and your guys in Korea."

"Yeah. Well I had to make a deal with the Navy and Sun-Hi and the guys got carted off by the Korean government. I figured they were all in prison."

"Sun-Hi is very clever girl. She somehow make her way here and I think she work for Nippon Export/Import now."

"Mamma-san I think you know more than what you're saying."

"I say enough for now. Let's go party."

CHAPTER TEN

The party was in full swing and the sailors were having a ball. The Aussies fit right in with the Yanks. The type of food was not familiar to them, but surprisingly very tasty, and was being served in abundance. After some initial apprehension it turned into a feast.

As promised by Mamma-san, the whiskey was Canadian and most of the beer was American with some Japanese beer available for those who didn't mind a headache the next day.

A knock came at the front door and Mamma-san rushed to open it and she talked to the visitor, a tall, shapely woman. Mamma-san looked around the room and saw that everyone was engrossed in the party. So she opened the door and the visitor entered. The woman then took off her coat and walked to the sliding door entrance of the party room.

She stood leaning on one foot in the doorway with one hand on her hip. She took a long drag on a cigarette and let the smoke drift out of her mouth rising up past her face while she surveyed the room.

The party noise in the room subsided and all heads turned her way. Her dark hair draped over her right shoulder hiding part of her cheek. The hair on the other side fell behind her revealing a bare perfect shoulder. The white blouse was loosely fitted but still framed an elegant body. Her black silk skirt ended at mid calf but the slit along the side revealed a long, graceful leg. She was stunning.

Her eyes were wide set and round which gave thought that somewhere in her ancestry was some Caucasian blood. Her lips were full and had just a hint of lipstick. They parted and in perfect English, with a throaty whisper, she said "Hi there Sully. Where the hell have you been?"

All heads turned to Sully's table.

He was dumbstruck. He slowly unraveled himself from the arm chair....stood....and a wide grin spread across his face.

"Well I'll be damned" he said.

He took a step forward and then stopped as she dropped the cigarette and slowly glided, rather than walked, to where he stood.

The room was deathly quiet. There was only an occasional whisper. A respectful "Wow" came from a back table.

She stopped, looked at him with misty eyes and said "I missed you Sully."

"I missed you too Sun" he rasped.

She melted into his arms and they embraced with a tender kiss.

Cheers erupted from the gallery of sailors and after some boisterous laughter and kidding remarks about *lover boy Sully,* the party resumed.

Tony and Peacock both stood and sheepishly said "Aren't you going to introduce us?"

Sully said "Oh sure, this is Sun-Hi a friend from the old days."

"Looks like more than just a friend to me" Peacock quipped.

Both Sully and Sun laughed and Sully said "Will you guys excuse us? Sun and I have some catching up to do."

The two turned, Sully took her arm, and they walked to a table in the rear, out of the hustle and bustle of things.

On the way he called "Hey Mamma-san bring us a drink and some Kim-chi to munch on. Sun and I are going to be awhile."

It was much quieter back here. As they sat facing across the table, they joined hands and stared into each others eyes. It was one of those tender unplanned moments that neither one could have foreseen. It was only through a sudden separation of two years that both realized how much they meant to each other.

"I thought I had lost you forever Sun" Sully whispered.

"I never lost hope that I would meet you again some day Sully. But I wasn't sure that you would feel the same."

Sully answered "When those CIA guys turned you and the crew over to the Korean Feds, I wanted to go with you. But they decided differently and one of them must have given me a good clout on the noggin. When I woke up I was laying in the bottom of a fast moving boat cuffed to a stanchion. When I started yelling, one of them came down and said to shut up or I'd get another one only harder. I asked him what happened to my crew and he said not to worry, the South Korean government was taking care of them especially that North Korean girl. I knew then it was probably lights out for you and the guys."

Sun-Hi squeezed Sully's hand and with deep emotion said "Oh darling, when I saw you struggling and that big burly American hit you with that rifle butt, my heart rose to my throat. I screamed and tried to get to you but they pinned my arms back and roughly pushed me on to shore. They herded me, Jin-Sang, Chin-Ho and Chung-Hee to a troop of awaiting soldiers. Poor Chung-Hee thought he saw a chance to escape and started running. He didn't get very far before they cut him down with rifles. They threw us into the back of a truck and took us to Inchon where they locked us in a jail cell. It was a filthy place. They kept me in a separate cell next to the men. We stayed there over night and I had to literally fight off one of the guards. Jin-Sang tried to come to my aid through the bars and got a broken nose for his efforts but it gave me a chance to defend myself with some of the martial arts training you showed me. We made enough of a ruckus that some other guards came and told him to leave me alone or they would turn him in. Thank God it worked."

"Sweetheart, if only I could have helped you. I thought you were dead or at least in prison. Just one more run and we would have hung it up and gone to the States like we planned. I should have known better and not even tried to keep gun running."

"Well then, darling, we probably wouldn't have met" she said.

"Yeah that's true. But how did you get out of that filthy prison?"

"They decided to send us to Seoul for a trial by the feds. When we got there, the jail was a little cleaner and more modern. I was in a women's wing when the guards came and said I was going to the Captain's office to be interviewed. This guy was a real sleaze bag and he gave me an oily grin and said that I could make things easy for myself if I cooperated a little bit. I didn't think he meant giving him any evidence or stuff like that and I was right."

"Oh my God. What did he do?'

"He didn't really get the chance. I played along and said that I was interested in his offer and he explained the scenario, meaning I would become his mistress. He said he had an apartment where he had another girl that was becoming bothersome. I found out later that she was pregnant. He said he would take me out of the prison on the ruse that I was going to show him some evidence and he'd put me up in a hotel until he made an arrangement with his mistress. I thought that this was my only chance of escape and I agreed. They let me keep my rucksack with some personal items in it. During the search they did not find the cash that you made me sew into a pocket, at the bottom of the sack. I thought that once in the hotel I could some how escape."

"Well that was a break" Sully said.

"Yeah right, except he handcuffed me to the radiator and said when he returned we would make pleasant music. It was three or four hours later when I heard a key in the door and I prepared myself for a battle."

"That dirty bastard" interjected Sully.

"Well he was a bastard, but I never found out first hand because it was the mistress that showed up. She had the key to the hand cuffs and said she would set me free if I would leave town and never return. She had told the Captain that she would get an abortion if he would let her stay even if he wanted to keep me along with her and have two girls. The pervert agreed to that, saying he would bring me over tonight and all three of us would spend the night together. She convinced him to have a drink and she put something in it to make him fall asleep. She stole his keys and came to the hotel. She said she had it too good to share it with another girl and if I didn't agree she had a brother that would take care of me. I wouldn't be good for any man after he was done with me. That girl was one mean cookie."

"Sun this sounds like a real ordeal. Let me get a few more drinks. I've got to hear more."

He signaled one of the girls to bring some drinks.

"Well needless to say, I agreed to leave town as soon as she freed me."

Sully asked "What about the Captain? Wouldn't he be pretty pissed off when he found out what she did?"

"She had that figured out. We'd close the cuff on my right hand only part way to make it easier to slip out of it. There was a sink within reach with some soap on it. We put the wet soap on the cuff to make look like I used it to make my wrist slippery. The other cuff was hooked to the radiator pipe. She hurried back and put the cuff key and hotel key back in his pants pocket so when he woke up and got dressed he wouldn't realize she had left. When he got to the hotel, all he'd find was a pair of empty cuffs and figure it was his own fault."

"Did he buy it? I hope that poor girl didn't suffer."

"I don't know about her but I knew he'd be very upset and would have to answer to higher ups so I moved fast. Before I left the hotel I changed into some better clothes which were in my rucksack. I was within walking distance to the train station so that's where I headed. I bought a ticket on the next train to leave, which was to Pusan. I saw two local young girls sitting in the waiting area so I sat next to them and started a conversation. I found they were also going to Pusan so I kind of joined up with them like we were traveling together. As I boarded I saw two policemen questioning passengers and was relieved when the train pulled out. But I knew they suspected that I was on the train. I thought I saw two plain clothes policemen board at Wonju so I hid as well as I could and when the train stopped at Chech'on I got off and melted into the crowd. I changed clothes again, putting on a blouse and pants like a peasant girl and washed off all makeup. I walked to the market bazaar area and looked for a likely farmer who I might talk to. I saw an older couple who looked needy and not very sophisticated. I approached them and started a conversation telling them that I was a refugee from the Communist north and was trying to get to some family members farther south. But I was in need of food and a place to stay for awhile. I would work in the rice paddies for food and a place to sleep if they knew where I could go. They said they didn't have much but I could stay with them during harvest. I agreed. It was very rustic but I knew the police would not look for me there and after a month or so the hunt would cool down."

"You are a real clever girl Sun. But how did you get here?"

"I got lucky. After six or seven weeks, when I felt things were quieted down, I asked to go into town with the farmer and his wife. I hid my rucksack in the wagon and when we got to town I slipped away from those good people who helped me. I took the train to Pusan and checked into a cheap hotel on the waterfront when I got there. In the same block was a company called Nippon Imports/Exports. I overheard a conversation between two girls, while in a store, that one was leaving and they would need a replacement. I applied and got the job. It turned out to be a pretty good job and after six months I was well liked. I learned that headquarters was in Moji so I bought a passport from a local forger and asked for a transfer, if and when one ever came up. Lucky me. Or maybe it was because the boss' wife wanted me gone, he kind of liked me. Anyway, I got the transfer.

"You are a shrewd one Sun. I'll give you that. What next?"

"After I got to Moji, and got settled in, I went to see Mamma-san to see if she knew anything about you. She told me that she had heard that you were captured by the CIA and disappeared. One of our old contacts told her that you were sent back to the States and were probably in jail. I kind of gave up looking after that. I then planned on going back to my home in Korea if the United Nations was successful in driving the communists out of North Korea. But then a miracle happened and today Mamma-san came to Nippon and told me that you were here. I told them that I was sick and had to leave work. I'm so happy to be with you. How long can you stay?"

"My ship leaves tomorrow afternoon or maybe the next day in the morning. But I'll be back. I don't want to lose you again Sun."

"Oh darling, I want to be with you forever. But tell me what happened after the CIA got you on their boat?"

"Well as I said I woke up handcuffed to a stanchion and no one would answer any questions. I did overhear them talking and one laughingly said."

"Did you see that crazy gook try to escape and get cut down by the soldiers? He should have known they were just waiting for someone to try that. He didn't have a chance."

"When I heard that, I knew we were set up and it wasn't good for all you guys. We finally got to Pusan and they took me to a Navy transport and threw me in the brig. I had no idea what was in store for me but I got better treatment from the Navy guys than from the CIA guys. When we got to Yokosuka they transferred me to the lock up there and I waited for days before they came for me and took me to a room where I sat at a table with two Navy officers and two civilians. They told me that they were familiar with my service record during the war and were also familiar with my smuggling of foreign made guns and ammo and supplying them to a Middle East contact. It seems that after the war, the Soviet Union got a piece of different countries and wanted to spread communism even further. One place they were going to make an attempt was Afghanistan. The U. S. didn't want this to happen but couldn't politically do anything about it. They knew that my guns, which I was buying from an agent in North Korea and were made in Russia, were going to a Middle East agent. The CIA wanted to help keep the Soviets out and try to stem the flow of communism world wide. They wanted to use me to set up my contacts with them so they could increase the arms flow through a clandestine operation. I was hesitant since I knew the personal dangers involved when you give up that kind of information to government agencies. They assured me that the sting that just came down would disappear from any records and my involvement would never be revealed. They also said that they would reinstate my Navy career and my record would show that I never left the service. I agreed. It was a complicated procedure but I was able to satisfy their needs and I eventually ended up on the Columbia with these guys. All anyone, except my commanding officers and my boat crew, know is that I've been in the Navy since 1942. That's about it. Since I'm going to be promoted to Boatswains Mate 2nd Class soon, I'm considering making it a career. I'm almost half way to retirement at 20 years."

Sully took a swig of his beer and saw Sun's eyes rise and look at someone behind him.

He turned and looked up at the grinning faces of Tony and Peacock.

Tony said "Okay Mister mystery man, the three of us have been through an awful lot together and we think it's high time we were given a little more information on who you really are."

"Pull up a couple of chairs and I'll give you enough to satisfy your curiosity. What you really want to know is who this beautiful woman is and why she knows me."

"You got it pal" piped up Peacock.

CHAPTER ELEVEN

The two sailors each grabbed a beer and settled in at Sully's table with anxiety on their faces. At last they were going to find out about this man of mystery that both admired so greatly and best of all maybe some juicy tidbits about the beautiful Korean girl that seemed to be quite infatuated with him.

"After the war was over in '45 I stayed in to finish out my enlistment which ran until '46. During that post war year things were very loose. I got some shore duty here in Japan to help set up some bases and got acquainted with some local people that were to help move some goods and set up operations. Graft and corruption was rampant, both Japanese and American. I made a deal with some Korean nationals to take my discharge here and then return to Korea with them. By then the Soviets were already making moves to control the world and these Koreans had some contacts to buy and sell arms. Everyone wanted to make some money after the war in a world of shortages and dishonest people. They had the contacts, the money and a boat but limited knowledge of how to sail it or how to navigate it and move the goods. I was the last piece of the puzzle."

"We were doing well. Plenty of guns were available and we had a buyer with cash. The heroin made from poppies provided a lucrative supply of money to pay premium prices for guns and ammo."

"We typically picked up guns in the communist part of Korea which already was becoming an unpopular place to live. Many civilians wanted to move to the more popular south where Americans were in charge."

"Jin-Sang, one of my partners, said he had a cousin that wanted to escape from the north. This cousin and his wife along with several friends were willing to pay for passage on a boat that asked no questions. We agreed to transport them."

"Everything went without a hitch. One of the passengers was a beautiful young Korean girl with dual citizenship and had lived in America before the war. She had gone back to Korea just before the attack on Pearl Harbor. She was stuck there until now and wanted out. Her name was Sun-Hi. I became interested in her when I found out that she was unattached and little did I know that she also was interested in the 'American sailor'."

"We unloaded the passengers at P'ohang dong and I made note of the family they would be staying with."

"As time went on I made it a point to get to know Sun and she was always available when we made port there. She ran into some difficulties with the family she was staying with. The usual thing. A husband made a pass at her. She was distraught. I gathered up my courage and asked if she would stay with me on the boat. Much to my surprise, she accepted. After that we were a couple and made plans to somehow get out of the smuggling business with enough money to both get back to the states and settle down in a normal married life."

"We would have made it but Jin-Sang and Chin-Ho had made a deal with the Middle East Agent to make a heroin run. I had refused to do this on a previous occasion knowing that this could bring other factors into the picture and besides I didn't like running drugs."

"Unknown to me word got to the authorities, in South Korea, about a boat running drugs. They got in touch with the CIA who already had feelers out about the gun running boat and found out we were one and the same."

"That's when they set up the trap. We got caught with a boat load of guns and drugs."

"It was a joint operation with the CIA and the Korean Federal Police. Since I was American, the CIA took me back to Japan. We cut a deal which allowed me to be back in the Navy. I had to divulge all of my contacts on both ends. Because they were Korean, Sun-Hi was arrested with my three crew men, one of which was killed by the soldiers. Through a series of events Sun escaped and made her way here over a period of about a year. Is that enough to satisfy your curiosity for now?"

"Yeah that will do it Sully. Thanks for taking us into your confidence. Can I dance with Sun?" said Peacock.

"You're a good shipmate Sully." said Tony. "And now I'm going to get my little Japanese gal and get a jitterbug promise before the next dance starts. We'll have to get out of here pretty soon."

The party continued on into the night. The drinks flowed, the food kept coming and the music blared on. It was approaching midnight and the last liberty boat would leave the dock at that time.

Sully came over to Tony's table and said "Hey sailor, I'm going to Sun's place. You make sure all the guys make it to the liberty boat."

"Wait a minute Sully. Are you going to make it?"

"Just don't worry about me sailor. I can take care of myself."

And with that he left. Sun was waiting for him by the door with her coat on and they left together.

Tony thought to himself "Oh boy, this can't be good. I don't have a good feeling about Sully."

Quite a few of the sailors were tipsy, including Peacock, so Tony started rounding them up. He told Mamma-san to send someone to get five or six rickshaws for transportation to the dock.

When they got there he started loading them up and sent them on their way. Everyone was gone except him and Peacock.

Tony said "Let's go buddy. We don't want to miss that boat."

"Hey Tony" slurred Peacock "Michi wants me to stay. I told her you wouldn't let me so can I take her back to the ship. Maybe we could sneak her aboard."

"Are you out of your mind?" yelled Tony. "Get out here and into this rickshaw."

"Aw she's so sweet. Bye Bye, Michi. I'll be back and see you on the next trip."

"Okay Virgil. I see you again next time. You stay longer. Okay?"

Tony eyeballed Peacock. "Did she call you Virgil?"

"So what, Tony. That's my name and she likes it."

"Okay, okay don't get bent out of shape."

He turned to the old lady standing in the doorway. "You're a good Mamma-san. We'll be back some day."

The rickshaw bumped down the rutted street and they were on their way.

When they arrived at the dock, all of his shipmates were on the liberty boat except for Sully.

The cox'n asked "Is that it Tony? I'm ready to shove off."

"Hey can you wait just a little longer? Sully might just show up" begged Tony.

"I'll give it another ten minutes and then we're gone" he answered.

Tony clamored up on the dock and peered down the main drag for an approaching rickshaw. But none showed up.

A shout came from the boat "We're shoving off with you or without you Tony."

"I'm comin'. I'm comin'. I just wanted to make sure he wasn't on his way" said Tony as he jumped aboard.

The boat pulled away from the dock and Tony stared back at the shore and just shook his head.

Sun lived close by with a Korean family that was friendly with the company owner. They were a respectable family with no children and had room for a renter in a small attached apartment.

Sun said "We must be very quiet. I don't want to wake them. They are very good to me. I will explain my relationship with you but I'd rather do it tomorrow."

"I don't want to get you in trouble Sun. Maybe I should leave."

"Sully, I am a grown woman. I love you very much and I want to be with you. Please stay."

"I love you too Sun. I can't leave you....I want to stay."

They entered her apartment as two star-crossed lovers. He took her carefully into his arms like something fragile.

Her tense body softened and he could feel her shaping it against him from her knees to her bosom. He looked into her eyes as he kissed her. Her lips parted, moist and sweet. He closed his eyes and the earth seemed to tilt. He gently swayed.

She said "Wait darling. Let's go into the bedroom."

When Sun awoke the next day, Sully was standing and gazing out of the window. The view was of the harbor and he could see the anchored ships in the distance.

"Yes, my darling, I know that you must go." Sun said.

Sully turned and faced her.

He said "Things sure look different in the light of day."

"We were foolish to think that we would have anything more than one beautiful night together" she said. "I would give anything to have you stay with me forever, but I know it is impossible. My love for you is great enough to know that I must let you go and only hope that you will return to me some day."

"My beautiful Sun. You mean the world to me. If I don't go back to my ship right now I'll be a hunted man and we may never be able to live a normal life together. Some day, some how, when this so called war is over we will be together again and never be parted."

"Go now, my lover. Go before I lose my courage and beg you to stay" she sobbed.

He kissed her and said "I'll write to you at the Nippon Company and let you know when we're coming back."

"The company has ways of keeping tract of shipping. I sometimes can even identify military vessels. At least I'll try. Hurry back to me my darling. Now go, please go." Sun said.

That morning at 0800 muster, the Chief reported one man, BM3 Sullivan, as being A.O.L. and a report would be made to the Shore Patrol to assist in returning him to duty.

The Chief also informed the division to make ready to get underway at 1200 and to go about their normal duties until then. He wasn't very happy.

As Tony and the rest of the 3rd Division were making their way to the stern, they heard a commotion from up forward on the fo'c'sle.

"I wonder what all the yelling is for" asked Tony.

"Ah, those 1st Division guys are always making some kind of ruckus" answered Peacock.

"Hey. I think there's a little civilian row boat coming towards the gangway. You know, one of those weird wooden boats that the rower propels it with one single oar on the stern. Never could figure out how that works."

"Well it does and he's sure enough coming along side."

"Hey there's some one standing up in the bow. It looks like a sailor."

"My God…...It's Sully."

Tony and Peacock went running towards the quarter deck among the cheers of the whole deck force, standing along the rail. The tiny boat pulled up to the gangway and the lone passenger climbed out of it, stepped on the gangway and boarded the ship.

The two buddies stopped short of the area where the Officer of the Deck was standing and waiting for the A.O.L. sailor to come aboard. Yes, it was Sully.

Sully stood at attention, saluted the colors, turned and saluted the Officer or the Deck and asked "Permission to come aboard sir?"

The officer returned the salute and said "Permission granted."

Sully then waited for what was expected next.

"Sullivan, consider yourself on report. Go below, get out of those blues and report to your Division Officer immediately."

"Aye aye sir" said Sully and he left the quarterdeck and went below to the crew's compartment.

His two boat crew members were waiting for him and before they could say a word, Sully eyeballed them and said "Just leave me alone for awhile guys. We'll talk about it later. I have to go and see Ensign Jackson."

With that he changed to his dungarees and went to officer's country. He knocked on Ensign Jackson's door. When he came out he said "Okay Sully, let's go see the Exec and get this over with. The old man is so pissed off he said for the Exec to handle it. He doesn't want to talk to you right now."

They walked to the Exec's cabin and knocked. The Exec yelled "Come on in."

They entered. Both saluted and the Exec returned the salutes.

The Exec just looked at Sully. Not saying a word for what seemed like an eternity.

He then said in a low menacing voice "You damn dummy."

It was quiet again.

He then continued "You've been around long enough to know the seriousness of what you pulled for a few hours of enjoyment and the near tragedy of what could have happened if you would have missed the ship all together. You've got the potential of going far in this man's navy but things like this can have lasting effects on your record."

"I know that sir and that's why I came back. At first I had other thoughts in mind."

"I don't even want to hear about it, Sullivan. Fortunately for you, the old man just got a report from a source pretty high up on the outstanding job that you and your crew did at Inchon. Also the results for BM2 are in and yes you made it. Now since you haven't officially been awarded the new rank I won't have to bust you. I'm just going to not give it to you. That way it won't show on your record. You will remain BM3 and a promotion will just have to wait. You'll continue as Coxs'n."

"Thank you, sir. I understand."

"Well there's a further reason that you will remain a Coxs'n. Our next stop will be Hungnam in North Korea. Experienced boat crews are going to be in great demand. This next assignment will not be an easy one. In fact in the kind of weather and what we are going to be required to do could be a disaster waiting to happen."

He hesitated and then said with a sigh "You're dismissed. Let's make preparations to get under way. Ensign Jackson, stay here. I have some further instruction for you."

"Aye aye sir."

When Sully had left the Exec turned to Jackson and said "Things have taken a turn for the worse Ensign. Ever since the Chinese really got into this thing in November we've taken some beatings. We were confident that after we crossed the Yalu River that we could end this thing by Christmas and reunify Korea. Now we're retreating and I understand that President Truman has threatened the use of Atomic power but I guess he's been shot down on that by politics. Anyway, since you are the officer in charge of the boat crews, I want you to make sure all boats are mechanically perfect. We probably are going to take part in a huge evacuation at Hungnam. Make sure all crews are equipped to make runs in foul weather gear. It's going to be brutally cold. Prepare them for the worst. We'll also be taking wounded and battle weary soldiers aboard. Warn the crew to do what ever is necessary to aid them. That's about it. We'll have a meeting with all the other divisions to pass the word. You're dismissed."

"Yes sir" he said as he slowly turned and left the cabin.

CHAPTER TWELVE

The Columbia weighed anchor at noon and got underway en route to Hungnam in North Korea.

Since it was well into December by now and very cold and windy, the work topside was relegated to only necessary duties. The 3rd Division crew was working below in the troop compartments which were all empty. They were checking and repairing the four high bunks, all of which would be needed eventually.

"Isn't it strange to be traveling empty?" Peacock said.

"Yeah, I understand things aren't going very well in the last few weeks now that the Chinese are sending troops in. When I was on lookout watch I heard the Captain tell the O.D. that four Chinese Armies attacked the 1st Marines and the 7th Infantry at the Chosan Reservoir last week. That's pretty heavy stuff." Tony said.

"Looks like we might be going to Hungnam to pick up some guys there. Maybe some of the wounded are being replaced with back up troops from somewhere in the south" said Peacock.

"Well I know one thing, the LCVP's are being checked over from stem to stern. We're going to be making some boat runs."

The USS Columbia steamed into Hungnam harbor two weeks before Christmas and dropped anchor. It was snowing and very cold. There were several other ships in the harbor, one of them was the hospital ship USS Consolation. The small boat traffic seemed to be predominately going from shore to the Consolation with wounded and returning to shore empty.

It was late in the day when they dropped anchor. The evening meal was one of the better ones served aboard the Columbia. It was only ship's crew. No troops. They had recently provisioned and the cooks seemed to want to do something special. Everyone sensed that the upcoming period of time was going to be one that everyone would carry in their memory banks for a long time.

It would definitely be the case especially for our LCVP #2 boat crew.

The next morning all boat crews gathered in the mess hall. They were all issued foul weather gear, new life jackets and side arms.

Ensign Jackson announced "Men, all boat crews are subject to be on call 24 hours a day. There will be no off days. When your boat is called away, the Coxs'n will immediately report to the O.D. for your assignment. The two crew members will report to your boat whether it is tied up to the ship or in the davit ready for launching. While waiting for the Coxs'n you will make all possible preparations for getting underway. Your assignments will mostly consist of trips to a given spot on shore, possibly a dock, possibly a beach or cove and pick up Army or Marine personnel. You may be assigned to make a run to the USS Consolation on occasion. Each Coxs'n will be given a rough chart of the harbor. Use caution. Depths may or may not be correct."

Peacock glanced over at Tony. Tony rolled his eyes and turned red.

Ensign Jackson continued "Remember men. Its winter time here and the water temperature is 40 degrees or lower. If you go in the drink, you won't last long. Those new life jackets will keep you afloat for a while but hypothermia will set in before you drown anyway. Good luck and be careful. Any questions?"

It was quiet.

"Okay. You're dismissed."

The boat crews filed out of the mess hall and made their way back to their respective compartments. The demeanor was not upbeat. As the #2 LCVP crew went aft to their compartment, Sully said "It's going to be a little different than it was at Inchon."

"Yeah, you get a different feeling being on the defensive rather than on the offensive" Tony said.

It was only about an hour later when the P.A. system blared "Away number 1, 2 and 3 LCVP's."

"Okay guys here we go" Sully said. "I'll see you at the boat."

Tony and Peacock rushed down to the starboard side cargo hatch and boarded the boat which was tied along side. They kicked on the engine and waited for Sully who boarded soon thereafter.

As he climbed aboard, Sully said "All three boats are going to a spot where there's an old rickety dock. There's a whole company of soldiers that are pretty well shot up. Some of them may need to go to the Consolation. We'll make a decision when we get there."

All three boats cast off and headed towards shore. It was a bright sunny day but the temperature was just above freezing and with the wind at 10 knots it felt well below. The boats fought choppy water all the way in with LCVP #2 leading the way.

As they approached shore they spied a group of soldiers coming down the hillside finding their way to the makeshift dock. They were a sorry looking bunch with a variety of winter uniforms. One man even had a pea coat on. Sully pulled up to the dock and made fast to the one standing bollard.

He shouted "I'll take as many as we can hold and then the other two boats will get the rest."

"Okay sailor. We got some wounded guys I'd like to load first."

"Load them up. Do you have a medic that can go with them? We don't have any medical supplies on board."

"Our medic is one of the wounded. He got hit trying to attend to one of the guys. Dirty bastards shot him on purpose. He's got a round lodged in his spine and can't move his legs. We've got him in a stretcher but he's in bad pain even loaded with morphine."

"We'll do what we can for him Sarge. Do you think we should take him to the Consolation?"

"He says he wants to stay with the outfit, but I don't know what to do. Do you guys have any doctors aboard?"

"Yeah, they assigned a couple before we left Japan. Guess they anticipated something. We just had a Chief Pharmacist Mate before that but he's really good too." Sully said.

"Hey what's the name of your ship?"

"We're on the USS Columbia APA 59" came the reply.

"Oh yeah, I remember you guys from Inchon."

"We were there" answered Sully "hey that's a long way from here."

"Yeah. Seems like I've been all over this God forsaken country. Lost lottsa good men too. Okay if you've got as many as you can carry, send in the next boat. I'll stay until the last one."

"See ya later, Sarge."

Sully eased away from the rickety dock and waved #1 in to replace his boat.

The trip back was rough and cold. The wounded medic moaned loudly with each lurch when an unexpected wave hit them. His fellow soldiers tried to comfort him and finally they reached the ship.

Sully pulled along side by an open cargo hatch. The soldiers gently lifted the wounded man up and through the hatch. Then they struggled through themselves. All had some wounds as well as feet and hands that were numb with the cold.

Before Sully could pull away, a messenger stuck his head out and yelled "The O.D. said to go back to the same dock and pick up another load. Some more soldiers showed up."

"Okay. Will do but did I see an LCM pulling away as we were coming in?"

"That's right and it was the second one today with more on the way. We're going to have one hell of a load of soldiers, most of them are in bad shape. You better shove off. It's getting bad."

"Okay. We're on the way. Save us some chow."

The three LCVP's from USS Columbia, as well as boats from the other ships in the harbor, made trip after trip to pick up fighting men from the many countries that made up the United Nations. These were the forces that were battling the communist aggression from the north, which now included a massive Chinese army.

On one particularly nasty day with the harbor so choppy that all small boats were stored hanging from the davits, out of the water, LCVP #2 was called away.

The two crew men reported to the boat and boarded it while it was hanging, ready to be launched while Sully, the Coxs'n, reported to the quarter deck for the assignment.

It was close to dusk and a mountain of dark grey clouds hung low in the sky.

Tony said "If we don't hurry we're going to get caught in a blizzard."

"What are you, a cloud expert now?" Peacock quipped.

"Listen buddy, living in northern Ohio all my life had the side benefit of experiencing unexpected weather conditions. There's a saying back there 'If you don't like the weather now, just wait an hour and it will change' and believe me it happens."

"Yeah, those clouds do look kind of nasty and the wind is blowing a gale. I hope we're not going far."

Sully hustled to the boat deck and told the lowering crew to make ready to lower away. He hopped aboard and said "Get ready to kick on the engines Peacock. We'll need to pull away as soon as we unhook in this weather."

"I'll kick them on as soon as they start lowering" Peacock answered.

"Where are we going Sully?" yelled Tony.

"Not far. Over to the Consolation. They have a cargo net full of plasma and oxygen that they'll lower into the well deck. We've got wounded aboard that are badly in need of it."

"Man oh man, the way we'll be bouncing around they better lower fast."

Sully yelled above the howling wind "We'll go in on the lee side. The wind and waves will be a little quieter."

Tony whispered to himself "I sure hope so."

"Get ready! Shove us away as soon as we touch."

The VP hit the water with a jolt on a rising wave. As the wave receded the boat dropped like a stone and the wire slings snapped taut causing the pulley blocks to spring back to vertical with a sound like a shot gun firing. If either of our two crew men had been standing next to the blocks they would have been knocked over the side. Thank God they weren't.

Sully gunned the engine as Tony and Peacock pulled the release lanyard on the hooks and then pushed the VP away from the side of the ship.

They were under way in very rough water but it was a short run to the Hospital ship and Sully was at his best under these kinds of adverse conditions.

When they reached the Consolation, the cargo net of medical supplies was already hanging free of the deck, ready to be dropped into this little landing craft.

Sully saw the location of the cargo net and positioned the boat along side the ship as well as he could. There was no reason to try to tie up. Tony and Peacock used their boat hooks to hold them in close while the net dropped. As soon as it hit the deck, Tony dropped his boat hook and released the cargo hook from the eye of the net. Perfect. As the hook rose clear, Sully gunned the engine and pulled away. Everything went just as planned.....so far.

They made the trip back, taking water over the bow all the way since now they were going right into that north wind and Tony's weather prediction came true. It became blizzard conditions. The snow was heavy but the lights from the Columbia became visible and Sully zeroed in on them.

Tony yelled "Pour the coals to it Sully, it's getting real nasty."

"I'm peddling as fast as I can" Sully yelled back.

The plan was to come in on the lee side again so there was already a boom swung out and the hook over the side ready to drop into the boat. As soon as they swung in under the hook the crane operator dropped it down and Tony snagged it through the lifting eye of the cargo net. In an instant, the operator took up the slack and the medical supplies were free of the small boat rising up to the main deck of the Columbia....... and not a minute too soon.

Just as the cargo net was clear of the boat a huge wave lifted the VP and the force threw both crew men off of their feet and they went sprawling in the well deck.

When the wave cleared, the boat fell into a deep trough and rolled into the side of the massive ship almost capsizing. Water came pouring into the well deck drenching the two crew members. Sully came close to being thrown over board from the cockpit but managed to grab on. The boat was out of control and was being buffeted by the raging storm.

"Hold on! Here comes another one" he yelled.

They had risen on another wave and were now back in a trough slamming into the side of the ship but this time the boat had swung bow in and the landing ramp hooked onto a scupper on the side of the ship. As the next wave propelled them back up the snagged ramp ripped open. Suddenly the whole bow was gone and exposed to the high wave action. They were going under......and very fast.

"Abandon Ship" yelled Sully "swim for the side cargo hatch."

All three hit the drink. It was so cold it took their breath away. They tried to swim but it was almost impossible. It seemed like an eternity before they were at the side hatch but in reality it was only a few yards away. They almost reached the open hatch when another massive wave engulfed them and threw them away from the ship. All three came bobbing up gagging and hacking up sea water but their life jackets were keeping them afloat. Instinct alone caused them to swim for their lives but their heavy foul weather gear seemed like it weighed a ton. Again they were close to the open hatch. All three knew that they must get out of the freezing water soon or hypothermia would do them in.

A cargo net was hanging over the side from the hatch. If they could reach it they could grab onto it and climb up. Their shipmates had thrown life rings into the water, tied to lines, so they could help them get closer. The, now tired and freezing, boat crew each grabbed a life ring. The sailors on board pulled them close enough for them to grab the webbing on the cargo net.

The three tried to climb the 10 feet to the hatch but they were exhausted and struggled. Finally Tony and Sully made it with help from two sailors that climbed halfway down so they could boost them up.

Where was Peacock? He was really struggling. He couldn't seem to get clear of the water. Each time he got a good purchase, he would slip back. Finally he was so tired he seemed to give up. His shipmates cheered him on "Come on Peacock. You can do it."

He looked up and got a determined look on his drenched face. He gave a final gigantic heave and was clear of the water but he had no strength left. He just hung there with fists locked on to the webbing. One of the sailors, half way down, went even lower, almost to the water. He grabbed Peacock's lifejacket and pulled. This extra help seemed to give strength to the struggling survivor. They slowly climbed together and finally made it to the top where many hands grabbed both men and pulled them onto the deck.

As the heroic sailor caught his breath Peacock said "I owe you one buddy" and gave him an exhausted grin in great appreciation.

The three drenched survivors lay on the steel deck shivering violently.

A Pharmacist Mate took charge and bellowed orders to the rescuers "Okay you guys, grab them and get them up to sick bay....NOW...... hypothermia can happen fast.

"I...I...c-c-can't g.g.get up.p-p" moaned Tony.

"Help him sailors. Let's move it....fast"

All three were scooped up by strong arms and half dragged and half carried to sick bay which was equipped to handle freezing bodies what with all the evacuees now on board.

The rescued men were stripped of the wet gear and under clothing and dried off vigorously with toweling by medics. They were laid in bunks with pre warmed blankets covering their bodies but they still shivered so badly that it was difficult to talk so they didn't.

The warm blankets were interchanged and soon the violent shivering abated. A grizzly old chief entered with a bottle and said "I don't know if this really helps or not but it's going to make you relax and feel a little better."

He opened the bottle of brandy and gave each one a good slug and laughingly said "This is premium stuff so don't get used to it 'cause this is all you're going to get."

"Thanks chief. It sure went down easy" Sully said. The other two just smiled and closed their eyes. Soon all three were asleep. They were exhausted from the ordeal and from the lack of rest for the last several days.

CHAPTER THIRTEEN

Hours later Tony opened his eyes and lay there trying to remember where he was and how he got there. He turned his head and saw his two shipmates in adjoining bunks. Then it all came back to him.

As he lay there he suddenly realized how close to death he had come. Emotions suddenly took over and his eyes filled with tears. He whispered "Thank you God. I know you were watching over us."

A Pharmacist mate appeared and said "I thought I heard some rustling around. How ya feeling Tony?"

"I think I'm okay."

"Can you sit up? I've got some coffee if you can handle it."

"Man that would be great. I sure could use a cup of hot coffee."

"Me too, doc" piped up another voice.

"Might as well make it three" said the third one.

"Okay. Three cups of Joe and it sounds to me like I'm going to lose three patients."

When the medic came back with the coffee, the three survivors were comparing notes on their swimming prowess.

"Hey doc, I was wondering how that soldier medic that we brought in the first day was doing. Did they send him over to the Consolation? I hadn't heard anything."

"Oh yeah. He was one of the first wounded we got. Poor kid. Couldn't have been more than 18 or 19. Naw, he didn't make it Tony. The docs worked on him and did everything they could but he went into shock and never came back. Damn shame."

The three got very silent.

"Dammit" said Peacock.

"Yeah, we've had several that didn't make it. Had to turn one of the coolers into a morgue. At least we'll get to take them back. I guess some poor devils are still on shore, both dead and alive."

Sully jumped out of his bunk. "Come on guys. Let's see if they can get us another boat. Maybe we can bring some of those other guys back."

The three went back to the compartment to dress in clean dungarees.

Sully said "I'm going to talk to Ensign Jackson and see what's in store for us now."

Tony and Peacock were the center of attention with the rest of the 3rd Division crew. A general bull session was going on when Sully returned.

He called his crew aside and said "Ensign Jackson got us a boat. They're bringing it over from the Diphda. They won't need it any more. They're loaded and leaving this afternoon. We have orders to stay another day to pick up any stragglers. We leave tomorrow, Christmas Eve. Nice Christmas present huh?"

"It must be bad. There's a lot of shooting going on now."

"That's not the worst news. General Walker was killed. They think General Ridgeway will take his command."

"Let's go check out the new boat in case we have to make a run."

The other two boats were making runs into the beach but Ensign Jackson held Sully's crew back. He told them to rest up from their ordeal but the LCVP #2 crew members were ready to go.

They were in the mess hall drinking coffee and shooting the bull with some soldiers. Tony asked "Did the old Sarge from the first load make it aboard?"

"Yeah he's a tough old bird but he sure felt bad when we lost our medic. Hit him pretty hard. I think he knew him from before."

Just then Seaman Angel sauntered by and said "He sure is a tough old bird and take it from me, he's no one to mess with."

Tony laughed "Sounds like you had an encounter with the old boy, Angel."

"I sure did. He had just come aboard with a load of his rag tag soldiers and they had been through some bad stuff. There were about five or six of them standing in a group trying to thaw out."

"I had been saving a bottle of booze...Seagram's V.O....good stuff...I figured I could sell it and make some liberty money in the right situation and this looked as good as any. So I walked up to the old Sarge and asked if they'd be interested in buying some booze. He said, sure they would and how much did I want. I said, a hundred bucks and that old bastard pulled out his forty five, put the barrel up to my forehead, cocked back the hammer and said, "HOW MUCH?"

"I handed the bottle to him and said "It's on the house."

"He holstered his forty five and took the bottle, popped the lid with the palm of his hand and unscrewed it. All the while he's looking me straight in the eye. He took one long, long pull on the bottle, wiped his mouth with the back of his hand and handed the bottle to a soldier."

"The soldier took his share and passed it on until it got back to the Sarge. Sarge then handed me the bottle and said "Have a drink on us sailor."

"I took a big, big drink…..and handed it back. Sarge then proceeded to drain the bottle."

"He slapped me on the back and said "Come back and drink with us any time, son" and then they all turned and walked away. I'll tell you what Tony. My knees were shaking so bad, I had to wait a minute before I could walk away".

They all had a big laugh at Angel's encounter. It was one of those light hearted, unexpected moments needed by all.

Everyone had a restless night. Nobody got much sleep what with the noise of battle within earshot. It was one of the few times that the boat crew was up before reveille. They all met in the mess hall and drank coffee until reveille sounded. It wasn't long after that the call came for #1 and #2 LCVP's to be manned.

The crews reported to their boats and awaited the arrival of their Coxs'ns to hear their assignments. It was not a trip that any of them were looking forward to.

Finally Sully arrived and jumped into the cockpit and kicked on the engine. The two crew men anxiously looked at him, waiting to hear some word on where they were going.

"Okay guys this should be a quick one. We're going to the same old dock that we went to on our first trip, if it's still standing. Seems to be about the only place left, that's not overrun with Commies. We've got to pick up any stragglers from X Corps. These are the last guys to leave. We'll let #1 go in first, load up and then get out fast so we can get in, load up and get back to the ship. They've already got the engines ready and the Columbia is pulling out this morning…..with or without us. All those explosions that we were hearing over night was the X Corps blowing things up that we don't want to leave for the enemy. They should be ready to go when we get there, I hope."

Both boats pulled away and headed in to the pick up area. The city pier was a shambles and thick smoke was rising from the destroyed buildings in the background. Gun fire and mortar explosions could be heard all along the coast line. As they got closer to the pick up point they could hear small arms fire and the rattle of an automatic weapon.

LCVP #1 pulled into the dock and the crew jumped out and pulled on the lines to hold the boat in close.….no tying up today.…get in and get out. It didn't take long. The X Corps guys were as anxious to leave as the sailors were. LCVP #1 pulled away and waited while #2 pulled in.

Sully yelled "Hang there for a minute. It shouldn't take us long and we'll go back together."

The Coxs'n on #1 waved a 'thumbs up' and idled his engine.

Tony and Peacock jumped out onto the dock and held the lines so the boat was snug against the dock.

Sully yelled "Okay soldiers load up and let's get out of here"

About ten men were waiting and jumped aboard.

"How many more have you got?" Sully asked.

A young Lieutenant said "This is about half of us. The rest are coming down the hill now."

"I hope they hurry. I can hear mortar fire that sounds close."

"Yeah. They're a little ticked that we blew up everything last night."

Suddenly a mortar round exploded in the midst of the soldiers on the hillside. When the smoke cleared, bodies were strewn all about.

"Oh my God" yelled the army officer "come on. We've got to help them."

He and three other soldiers leaped out and ran up the hill just as another round exploded close to them and they were thrown to the ground. Only two got back up.

"Dammit" screamed Sully "Peacock, take a turn on that cleat, get aboard with the bitter end of the line and hold us in. Tony, drop your line and let's go up and see what we can do."

The two sailors scrambled up the hillside. The Lieutenant was wounded but still alive. Two of the soldiers were dead. About half of the original group was dead and the rest wounded.

"Come on Lieutenant, let's get what we can back to the boat. We'll have to leave the dead guys."

The bedraggled bunch started down the hill and were close to the boat when heavy machine gun fire erupted. A few more soldiers went down and the rest took cover in a ditch.

Peacock yelled "Hurry. Hurry I can see them coming at the top of the hill."

Suddenly mortar rounds came one after the other. Tony yelled back to Peacock "We're comin'. We're comin'. Just wait a minute."

As he said this a round hit the boat. A huge flame erupted as the fuel tank exploded. Tony could feel the heat on his face. Bodies flew out of the boat, some on the dock but more into the bay.

Tony rose up and bellowed "PEEEACOOOCK" and started to run to the boat when his whole world went topsy-turvy and he was flying through the air. But there was no noise....only a hard impact.... and then everything went black.

When he woke up he couldn't move..... he couldn't hear. Yes he could see....little was left of the dock and a burned out hulk of a boat....his boat. But....why couldn't he get up?

He felt a movement on the back of his body and suddenly the pressure was relieved. When he realized it he saw that someone had been lying on top of him and when he looked he saw Sully standing above and looking down at him.

Sully's mouth was moving but no sound was coming out of it.

"What?" said Tony. "Why does my voice sound so strange? Oh my God. I can't hear."

Sully pulled him to his feet and they stumbled through the dead soldiers to a grove of trees where they hunkered down.

Sully put his finger to his lips giving the sign for quiet.

They both lay still and watched as some Chinese soldiers carefully approached the bodies lying on the hill, checking each one for life. Every so often a pistol shot would ring out.

Tony could hear the shots in a muffled way so his hearing was slowly returning.

The Chinese soldiers then went to the dock to set up a machine gun but the boat off shore pulled away. They surveyed the damage then left, satisfied that there was no one left alive.

Tony and Sully stayed where they were until dusk. By that time Tony's hearing had returned.

It was still light enough to view the harbor and when they rose up to look they could see that it was empty of any ships.

They were stranded. The Columbia was gone.

CHAPTER FOURTEEN

LCVP #1 had lay off and was waiting for #2 to finish getting loaded and leave the dock. They could then join them for a run, in tandem, back to the USS Columbia. Suddenly all hell broke loose on shore.

As Jonesy, the Coxs'n of LCVP #1, watched through his binoculars, an explosion wiped out a group of soldiers that were approaching the dock on the hillside.

"Oh my God their under attack by a horde of Chinese soldiers" said the sergeant in charge of the squad on the boat.

Jonesy trained his binoculars on the hill "Wow, the mortars are still coming in on them. There goes Sully and Tony with two soldiers running up to help them."

"We gotta go in and give them a hand." said the sergeant.

"Okay I'll ease her in but I think most of those guys are history."

Jonesy slowly headed towards shore when a tremendous explosion rocked the boat and a gigantic fireball erupted from the docked LCVP. He could feel the heat on his face from the blast.

"THEY HIT #2!! THEY HIT #2" he screamed as he quickly backed down the engine and brought his craft to a halt.

"Good God look at it burn. Must have been a direct hit on the fuel tank. Can't be anyone left alive on that one."

"What about the guys on shore. Can you see anyone?"

"All I can see is a bunch of Chinese soldiers coming over the hill" said the Sarge "and we're taking some fire from those riflemen."

"Okay we're getting out of here."

"Jonesy...Jonesy I see a body floating. Looks like a sailor. He has a life jacket on."

"Can you grab him with the boat hook?"

"Yeah...Just get a little closer. Okay.....okay...I got him. Hey you guys, help me pull him aboard."

The two men struggled and pulled the unconscious sailor into the boat.

"Can you tell who it is?" called Jonesy.

"His face is burned and most of his hair is gone but I think It's Peacock."

"Better get moving Coxs'n, they're setting up a machine gun on the dock."

Jonesy jammed it in Forward and open it up with full RPM's. His orders were to return to the ship with as many evacuees as possible and he had a pretty good load. If only he knew what happened to his ship mates. Whatever...it was not good. There was a lot of shooting on that hill and it was all coming from Chinese guns.

When he was within sight of the Columbia he could see that they were already weighing anchor.

"How do we unload?" yelled the bow hook sailor.

Sully ordered "We'll pull along side approaching from the stern. She'll be moving forward at a slow speed. They'll throw us a painter line from forward. Bend it on to a cleat and they'll pay it out until we're under the hook from the 5 Ton boom. With this load, they'll need it to lift us. Hook on and hold on tight. They should be able to lift us aboard to the main deck."

Everything went as he said and when they got to the main deck the soldiers disembarked.

Jonesy yelled to the sergeant "Take your men to the fantail. There's a mustering station for you soldiers. They'll direct you to whatever you do next."

"Thanks Jonesy. You saved our bacon."

"No problem Sarge. I wish we could have gotten the rest."

Two corpsmen ran up with a stretcher and one said "Your bow hook said you have a wounded sailor aboard. Maybe a burn case?"

"Right. Better get him to sickbay quick. He may not make it."

The empty boat was then lifted and stored in its cradle ready to be lashed down for sea travel.

A messenger from the bridge ran up to Jonesy." The Captain and the Exec are on the bridge and they want you to report there and give them a rundown."

"Okay. I'll be right up as soon as I batten down the boat."

He instructed his crew and left for the bridge.

The Captain was in his chair and the Exec was standing along side.

Jonesy saluted and said "Jones, Boatswains Mate 3rd reporting as ordered sir."

Both Captain and Exec returned the salute and the Captain said "Stand at ease son."

"Thank you sir."

"From what we could see from here it looked pretty bad in there sailor. Can you brief us on what went on?"

"Yes sir. Sully and I took our boats in as ordered. Sully had told me to go in first, load up and get out. Which I did….without incident. We got about 20 soldiers and then I lay off while he went in. He loaded a squad and was waiting for the rest of the group to come aboard. They were about halfway down the hill when the shooting got intense. Mortar shells were dropping around the group when one exploded right in the middle of them. They all lay strewn about when Sully, Tony and two soldiers ran up to help them."

"I'm not sure what happened to them next because all of a sudden the other VP exploded. A round must have hit right on the fuel tank because it was one big fireball. We could feel the concussion clear out where we were."

"I wanted to go in and help but the Chinese were streaming down the hill and started firing at our boat. I couldn't see any life on the hill and the enemy was setting up an automatic on the dock which would have wiped us out. I opted to head out. I really wanted to go in and see if we could get our guys but sir I think I would have really jeopardized our whole boat load. We were able to rescue one survivor off of #2. It was Peacock. His life jacket saved him but he's got some bad burns."

"You did the right thing son" said the Exec.

"Thank you sir. I'll never forget the sight of that boat exploding. I'll carry that with me for the rest of my life."

"We've all got some bad memories of this encounter Jonesy. Have you got any kind of a feel of what may have happened to the other two men from the boat crew?"

"It doesn't look good sir. One of the soldiers said he could see a Chinese officer going to each body and putting a round in their head if there was any movement at all."

"Those bastards. But maybe they're just as well off from what I hear they do to prisoners."

"If I had to guess sir, I'd say Sully and Tony either got killed or wounded and certainly captured if they survived."

"I agree son. We'll report them as Missing in Action for now. We may get a report from the enemy but it usually is not accurate any how."

"Okay Jonesy. You're dismissed and it was a job well done sailor. You're in for a commendation as well as your crew. Give their names and rank to Ensign Jackson. He'll take care of it. You'll be getting a medal son."

Jonesy left the bridge. He went to the sleeping compartment, sat on his bunk, covered his face with his hands and sobbed. His shipmates went topside and gave him some time to himself.

The USS Columbia steamed out to sea en route to Pusan to unload some of the soldiers, others would go to Moji and still others to Yokosuka. It was a trip that would be etched in the memories of all aboard.

The Columbia was equipped to transport 2,000 troops. On board were in excess of 4,500 soldiers and marines. All of which came directly from the battlefield, some within hours of doing battle in extremely adverse conditions. Not only adverse from the plight of being grossly outnumbered and grossly ill equipped, but also the worst weather conditions imaginable.

The trip, because of the terrible weather, took two and one half days instead of the usual two days. This meant two nights at sea with 2,000 bunks to sleep 4,500 men and their equipment. Tempers were short and nerves were frayed.

To add to this quandary was the physical condition of many of the young warriors. Frost bitten hands and feet were prevalent. When warm conditions on board allowed thawing to happen, the pain was sometimes excruciating. Toes would turn black from lack of circulation and would certainly require amputation when a proper hospital was reached. The stench in the troop compartments from blood and rotting flesh was unbearable.

And of course there were those with wounds from bullets and shrapnel which required immediate treatment under very limited resources in the sick bay of the Columbia.

But maybe the worst of all were those who suffered from battle fatigue and post traumatic stress. No help was forthcoming for those poor souls. As a result, when morning dawned, there were men missing who were on board the night before. Several theories were rumored as to the reason for the missing men. Suicide was the most common theory but there also was a rumor of possible retribution for some unfortunate situation that may have happened on the battlefield.

One case in particular involved a particularly very regulation officer that lost most of his men, a battle that some thought was poorly handled. No one will ever know what really happened but he was no longer on board after the first night at sea.

When the ship docked at Pusan you could almost hear a sigh of relief. Most of the army men still able to return to duty were offloaded at Pusan as well as some of the wounded since a base hospital had been established there.

Peacock was one of those admitted into this hospital. He still was only semi conscious and was not fully aware of what had happened or where he was. The doctors seemed to think the burns were somewhat abated by immersion in the cold water in the bay.

The trip to Moji was without incident. Only one troop compartment was occupied and mostly with those destined to return to the states or duty in Japan. The ghastly job of cleaning up after the troops was at its worst. Caution had to be used since left behind were many war time items. Several loaded guns, live grenades and boxes of live ammunition were found along with the usual clutter of clothing and other various and sundry objects. All of which stank from long use and battlefield conditions.

After discharging the troops at Moji and taking on board supplies, the Captain announced that the following day would be the Christmas that the crew missed due to the evacuation. A full blown Christmas meal would be served at noon including turkey and dressing and the mess hall would remain open all afternoon in case any one didn't get enough to eat. Liberty would commence after the meal for all but a skeleton duty crew.

The 3rd division crew decided that they would return to Mamma-san's bar and restaurant to give her the terrible news about Sully and Tony. They weren't sure about contacting Sun-Hi but Mamma-san could take care of that. It would be a very nostalgic visit.

The next day they made the dreaded trip. When they got to the bar they were surprised to see that Sun-Hi was there. When the rickshaws pulled up at the front entrance to the bar, she came running to the door.

"I knew the Columbia sailors would be here when I heard that it docked in Moji" she said with laughter in her voice and a beaming smile on her face. Then she stopped short with a puzzled look.

"Don't tell me that no good Sully has the duty today. When's he coming?" she demanded.

Jonesy got out of the rickshaw. "Let's go inside Sun" he said.

Sun-Hi stood for a moment and then slowly turned and walked into the bar. Mamma-san was standing just inside the door and put her hand to her mouth in anguish when she saw the stricken look on Sun's face.

Sun turned to Jonesy and implored "Please tell me he's okay."

"We don't know Sun. He's classified as Missing in Action. We had to leave him in Hungnam......both him and Tony. He may have been captured.....we don't know. We've gotten no reports from the enemy."

Sun slumped to the floor, sobbing uncontrollably. Jonesy caught her and sat her gently on a futon. Mamma-san ran from the room wailing and beating her hands on her head.

Michi was standing behind the bar looking confused. She asked "Jonesy-san, why isn't Virgil here? Wasn't he with Sully too?"

"Yes Michi, he was with them but we were able to rescue him. He was badly burned and is in a hospital in Pusan. Sit down, I can tell you all of what happened. In fact let's all sit down and I'll go over the whole mission."

CHAPTER FIFTEEN

Sun-Hi, Michi and Mamma-san were all in a bad way. They were crying and Jonesy tried to calm them.

"We don't really know the outcome of that battle on the hillside. I know that the men on the VP were all killed except for Peacock who was badly wounded. My orders were to get as many men safe and evacuated to the ship as I possibly could. The gun fire was intense and the Chinese were setting up to destroy our boat too. I had to move out as badly as I hated to."

"The last glimpse that I had of Sully and Marino was when they were going up the hill to help the squad that got zapped with the mortar. Ya know, Sun, those two are the most resourceful guys that I've ever been shipmates with. I'm not counting them out and neither is the Captain. He's got them listed as MIA but only because he has to report something."

Sun sat up straight and dried her eyes. She said "You're right Jonesy. If I get a map of Korea, will you show me exactly where you left Sully?"

"Sure I can Sun but what do you have in mind?"

"I am Korean. I was born there and still have relatives and many friends there. When Sully and I were together, Hungnam was one of the spots that we pick up shipments and Wonsan was where we had a safe house. It still may be there. If Sully is alive, he will try to make it to Wonsan. Jin Sang's sister lives in Hungnam. She may help me or at least tell me where I can contact Jin Sang if he is out of jail. I have heard that all prisoners were turned loose when the North Army had control of Seoul. I will not stop trying until I know one way or the other about my lover."

Jonsey said "I'll help you all I can Sun but we must hurry. The Columbia leaves for Yokosuka the day after tomorrow."

Back in Hungnam, on the hillside bordering the harbor, Tony and Sully hid in the trees lining the waterfront. It was getting colder and they hunkered down in a makeshift cave on the side of the hill. The Chinese soldiers had left the area, satisfied that all the retreating enemy soldiers had been executed.

Tony said "What are we going to do Sully? Looks like we're the only ones left."

"We sure as hell can't stay here. And it's getting colder. First we've got to get somewhere warm. Next we've got to find some friendly's and that's probably going to be difficult since we're pretty far into North Korea."

"Some of the buildings that our boys blew up are still burning or at least smoldering. Maybe we should head that way." Tony said.

"Good idea. At least we'll be moving. I'm kind of familiar with the town since I used to do some business here. I'm not sure anyone's left that I know or even if they'd be cooperative but at least it's a shot. Let's warm up and I'll try to reconnoiter where we are."

"Sully….I can't believe you. Every time we're in a fix you come up with being kind of familiar with something or some one. I swear."

"I've been around kid. I've been around." Sully said with a grin on his handsome face.

They stood and tried to shake the stiffness out of their muscles. They then carefully made their way to the smoldering ruins of the buildings that were destroyed by the X Corps. They successfully averted encountering any of the Chinese patrols which were still scouting the ruins. These looters were looking for anything that could be salvaged and used. The X Corps boys had pretty well destroyed anything useable and there was no sign of human life so the patrols were soon abandoned, to the relief of the two sailors.

They found that most of the buildings had burned to the ground and some were well on their way but they found one small shack that survived and was relatively warm inside. This would be a good spot to warm up and get some rest. They huddled in a corner and dropped off in a restless sleep.

Meanwhile back on the Marino farm, a U.S. Navy vehicle pulled up to the front of the house. A Navy officer and an enlisted man decked out in their dress blues exited the car and knocked on the front door.

Mr. Marino opened the door and when he saw the men, a stricken look fell across his face. Mrs. Marino appeared behind him with her hand covering her mouth. A glint of tears were already showing in her eyes. They both knew that these men were not bearers of good news.

The officer asked "Are you Mr. and Mrs. Marino?"

"Y…yes we are" answered Mr. Marino.

Both men saluted.

The officer said "My name is Lieutenant John Unger and this is Yeoman First Class Williamson. May we come in?"

"Of course, please come in."

They entered and when the door closed Lieutenant Unger said "The United States Navy regretfully informs you that your son Anthony Marino has been listed as Missing in Action."

"Wh…what does this mean. Please explain." Mrs. Marino implored.

"Of course I'll give you all the details as I know them but why don't you sit down. It will be easier to talk."

They all sat around the dining room table and the Lieutenant went on "Please understand that it is entirely possible that your son has survived this ordeal and could be a Prisoner of War or could make his way to friendly lines. His commanding officer wanted this to be made clear. Now let me explain the circumstances."

He then went on to explain the evacuation and the mission that Tony was on. He did not go into explicit detail of the battle or the extent of the death of the squad of army men. He felt that if another visit was forthcoming more detail could be given if they asked.

He answered some questions from both parents and told them who to contact for any updates if they didn't hear anything further from the Navy.

After the Navy men left Mr. Marino took his grieving wife in his arms, both sobbed and let their grief flow until they were weak.

Mrs. Marino said "Vincenzo I'd like to go to church. We have some praying to do. Father Tom will be there and I think we should tell him, he's known Tony since he was born. God will hear his prayers and the prayers of the parishioners for Tony's safety."

"Yes Maria. Let's go. I need to talk to Father Tom too."

When Tony and Sully woke up it was past midnight.

"We probably should move out of here. Traveling by night would be best. As I remember, there's a ghetto area before we get into town. Let's head for there. We will stick out like sore thumbs among all these Orientals. Maybe we can pass ourselves off as Russian sailors if we run into trouble." Sully said.

"Yeah....Lottsa luck" Tony said. "Do you think we can find something to eat?"

"I don't know. These are very poor people here. We might be able to bribe someone if we find the right kind of a guy. Did you bring any greenbacks?"

"Yeah. In fact the M.A. gave me the rest of my money from the anchor pool and I didn't have time to stash it so I've got a couple hundred."

"We may need it. Greenbacks are very valuable. They can be traded for almost anything. Let's go."

They made their way through the rubble of the destroyed waterfront buildings towards some flickering lights in towards the town. The lights were from camp fires in the ghetto. Electricity was not a commodity here. These were the poorest of the poor and therefore the neediest and hopefully the easiest to help them for a price.

When they reached the outskirts, Sully grabbed Tony's arm and signed him to be silent.

They were closing in on a tin roofed shack and someone was sitting on the ground, leaning his back on the wall, smoking a cigarette. The pungent smoke was definitely from marijuana. As they eased closer they could see that it was a very young boy. Maybe even a pre teen.

Sully winked at Tony and signed for him to stay there. He then crawled closer to the boy and then stood quickly and sternly said in his limited Korean tongue "Hey you. What are you doing?"

The boy jumped up but before he could run away Sully collared him.

"Please sir. Let me go. Don't tell my mother. I only have one joint."

"Just settle down. If you help me I won't tell your mother."

"Okay I'll help you. What do you want?"

"Do you speak any English?"

The boy looked at Sully with suspicion "Speakee scoshi bit. Who are you?"

"I'm a friend. I can give you greenbacks if you help. Can you buy rice and good water. Maybe some chicken or duck?"

"Maybe so. How much greenbacks?"

"Enough for you and enough to buy food. Okay?"

"Okay. You give greenbacks first."

"No. You bring food first. I give enough money for food. You get yours after."

"Maybe you cheat me."

"No cheat."

Sully handed him three singles and said "This for food."

Then he took a ten dollar bill and tore it in half and handed one of the halves to the boy and said "You get the other half when you come back with food and by yourself. If you tell any one about us I will swallow the other half and you get nothing. I have a friend that has more greenbacks and we will give you more if you help us get into town and find a friend of mine. Deal?"

"Deal. I go now. Maybe take me a couple hours to get food. People here very poor. I must go other place."

"Okay. Get moving. We will be hidden and watching for you."

"Don't worry Joe. I not tell. My name Kim. See you later Joe."

Sully crawled back to Tony who was concealed in the brush.

"I sure hope you know what you're doing Sully. That kid could be on his way to the local authorities. He'd probably get a nice reward for turning us in."

"I don't think so. The other half of that ten dollar greenback will be more money than his whole family will get all year." Sully answered.

"Yeah but don't forget this is North Korea and we're at war with them." Tony added.

"It's a little different though. They are still Korean whether its north or south and these poor people have not faired too well under the Communist regime. Many of them have family in the south. I learned a lot about this culture from living with Sun-Hi that last year we were running guns. We might be able to make it back if we can steer clear of the Chinese. That's where we might be in trouble. If only they had stayed out of this thing it would be over by now. MacArthur had planned on a victory by Christmas and would have made it easily."

"Well let's wait for Kim and keep our fingers crossed."

They crawled into the empty shack that Kim was using to hide his enjoyment of the marijuana joint and tried to keep warm.

After a few hours they were jolted out of a slumber when the door slowly opened. They both crouched with their forty five's drawn and ready to fire.

"Don't shoot Joe. It's Kim. I got chow for you" a juvenile voice came from the half opened door.

"Get in here Kim and close that door. Its daylight out there." Sully ordered.

The boy entered with a sack of food which was soon devoured by the hungry sailors. They offered some to Kim which was readily accepted.

It looked like they had lucked into an ally that they might be able to use for their next move which will be very critical.

The two sailors smiled at the way their new found friend dug into the rice and chicken. Yes, this young boy is going to come in handy in finding Jin Sang's sister.

CHAPTER SIXTEEN

Sun-Hi asked the boss' secretary if she could see him for a moment. The secretary left her desk and entered his office and was gone for what seemed like an extraordinary long time.

She finally returned, looking a little disheveled and slightly embarrassed. She said, very coolly, "Mr. Chung will see you in five minutes. He will ring when he is ready to meet with you."

There was an unequivocal jealousy evident in this office towards this beautiful Korean woman. Also contributing was the intolerance of the Japanese people towards Korean people caused by the war in 1910.

She waited patiently. Finally the intercom beeped and she heard Chung's voice but couldn't make out the message. The secretary turned and with a chilly announcement said "You may enter now."

Sun entered Mr. Chung's office and said "Thank you for seeing me sir."

"Certainly, my dear, what can I do for you?" he answered with a smile.

"I was wondering if there was any possibility that I could be transferred back to the office in Pusan? I still have family in Korea and I miss them greatly. My parents are getting very old and need me to be with them."

"Hmm" he contemplated "I was under the understanding that your parents lived in the north. In view of the turnaround in the war wouldn't it be difficult for you to be with them?"

"Oh no" she lied "they moved to the south when it got too difficult to live under communism."

"I see" he hesitated and shuffled some papers on his desk.

"You have become an important part of our system here but certainly not irreplaceable. I will take your request to the CEO and also contact

Pusan to see if they will agree to such a transfer. You must also consider the fact that there is a war going on in Korea and the conditions are not as favorable as here in Japan. Please give it some more thought while I check into this for you.....you're dismissed."

"Thank you sir" she said, as she rose and left his office.

Days passed and the wait was interminable. She became nervous and edgy but did not want to go to Mr. Chung again fearing it would only antagonize him.

She noticed a change in the attitude of her coworkers, even those that treated her with respect before. They now avoided her and when she approached any of them they would turn their backs and walk away.

Finally she was summoned to Mr. Chung's office and when she entered he was very cool.

He said "All right Sun. It seems that you have had a favorable reaction from the Pusan office. Against my recommendation, our CEO has agreed to transfer you to Pusan. You must remain here until I can replace you and you must agree to train her in a manner to create no loss in efficiency here in Moji. The job at Pusan is of a lesser responsibility so there will be a lower salary. Is all of this agreeable?"

"Yes, of course and I am most appreciative of this Mr. Chung. I will do my best to train my replacement."

"Since you also live in my house you may find it convenient to show your appreciation in other ways my dear" he said in an oily, leering tone.

Sun dropped her eyes and blushed. She shakily said "Oh Mr. Chung, I have felt like a daughter to you and Mrs. Chung. It would not seem right for something like that to happen and I'm sure that Mrs. Chung would find out that you even would suggest such an act let alone really happen. I'm sure that would cause much trouble for you at home and also here at the company."

She gave him a knowing look and sat quietly.

"Hmm. Yes. I see" he squirmed in his chair "well you may be right of course. I simply meant that maybe a gift for Mrs. Chung might be a nice gesture. Of course I would not want to compromise our friendship."

"I will be most pleased to thank Mrs. Chung, sir" she smiled sweetly, rose, and left the office.

As she passed the secretary she noticed a look of relief on the girls face. Her demeanor had completely changed since she discovered that a potential competitor to her desirable situation here at work was not in danger.

Apparently the intercom system button had been left on. By accident, of course, she would never intentionally spy on her boss' meetings.

Sully gave Kim the other half of the ten dollar greenback and asked if he would like to earn more.

"Sure Joe. I like make lottsa money. Maybe get enough to move my mother and baby sister to Hungnam town" Kim eagerly responded.

"Okay. This will be a little harder but you will get another ten dollar greenback. I had a friend who has a sister living in Hungnam. His name is Jin-Sang. His sister's name is Min-Ho. I can't remember exactly but I know it's in Hungnam Teukbyeolsi, Yongsan Ward but I can't remember the neighborhood. Maybe in Seocho but you will need to ask around. You can say she is your aunt and your mother is sick and you must tell her. When you find her tell her that an old friend of Jin-Sang's wants to talk to her. If she asks who, tell her Sully-san and take notice of her reaction. If she is calm, ask her if Sully-san can come and see her. If she wants to know where I am staying tell her you don't know. Got all of that?"

"Sure Joe. I'm a smart kid. I know my way around. I do some business in Seocho. Good spot for pot. I go tomorrow morning. First thing. Tonight I change greenback to Won."

After Kim left, Tony said "I hope you know what you're doing Sully. That kid could still turn us in."

"He's our best bet for now Tony. But just in case let's move for tonight. There's another shack closer to the edge of town where we can see the comings and goings. Maybe we should stand a watch while one of us sleeps the other can keep a sharp eye."

"Good idea. Let's move and I'll take the first watch."

The two sailors cautiously made their way to another tin shack. This one was smaller but warmer since it was adjacent to a building that was still smoldering and the hulk gave off a good amount of heat. It actually was halfway comfortable.

Sully had no problem falling off to sleep and Tony was wishing for a cup of hot coffee while he stood watch.....to no avail.

Halfway through the night when Tony felt that he could wait no longer he woke Sully to relieve him on watch.

"What does it look like?" Sully asked.

"Quiet as a mouse" replied Tony.

"Okay get some sleep. I'll wake you up at daylight."

"Sounds good. I'm beat."

Tony hunkered down and quickly fell asleep.

The sun came up but was not visible in the low hanging clouds. There was no wind so it didn't seem quite so cold but there was still a chill in the air. Tony stirred, rolled over and looked at his shipmate. He said "Well I guess your watch was as quiet as mine, huh?"

"Yeah. Not a peep. All we can do now is wait. I heard some gun fire off in the distance a of couple times. Sounded like howitzers or artillery of some kind."

"Yeah, I heard some earlier in the night too. I wonder how it's going."

"I sure hope Wonsan is still in our hands but as fast as those Chinese were moving it may have fallen also."

"Man I never saw so many soldiers as that horde of Chinese coming over the top of that hill. They just kept coming and coming."

"I guess that's just a small example of what our guys saw at Chosan. One G.I. told me they came at them by the thousands. He said you mow one down and three more took his place. I wouldn't trade places with any of those G.I.'s or Marines."

"Well hell Sully. We're not exactly sitting on a beach sunning ourselves now are we?"

Sully chuckled "Yeah I guess we're kind of in a stew right now huh buddy?"

The morning passed slowly. They hunkered down waiting for their young compatriot to hopefully return with good news. They kept an eye out for movement of any kind when they spied a small burst of energy running into the area hell bent for election. It was Kim and he looked all in a panic.

Sully stuck his head out of the ramshackle of a door and whistled loudly.

Kim skidded to a halt and spewed out a torrent of Korean words so fast that they were unintelligible.

"Hold it. Hold it. Speak slower" Sully instructed "What's going on?"

The bug eyed youngster breathlessly spurted out "Chinamen coming. They almost here. You must hide."

"How soon?" asked Tony.

"Very soon" Kim answered.

Sounds of approaching footsteps and voices in a Chinese dialect gave them their answer.

Kim whispered "I have a plan. You guys lay down and get ready if it doesn't work. Help me light this joint."

"You crazy kid. Be careful" Sully said as he lit the cigarette.

Kim inched his way to the door which was hanging halfway open and stuck his head out blowing a heavy fog of white smoke.

Sudden Chinese bellowing cut the quiet calm. The click, clack of rifle bolts accompanied the bark of the squad leader.

"Don't shoot. Don't shoot" yelled Kim, in Korean, as he exited the shack with his hands in the air firmly grasping the marijuana cigarette.

The squad leader ordered in broken Korean "Who are you and what are you doing?"

"My name is Kim and I'm just having a joint. Please don't turn me in. Don't get me in trouble."

The soldiers all relaxed their weapons and enjoyed a good laugh at this scared young boy.

"Are you alone? Is anyone else in that shack?"

"I'm all by myself. I always come here to smoke. No one wants to come here. I come so no one will bother me."

"Okay. We're looking for American stragglers. Have you seen anyone suspicious?"

"No not today. Yesterday I hear voices on the other side of the hill but I'm not sure if they were your soldiers or not."

The squad leader gave orders to his squad and turned to Kim "Okay boy. Enjoy your smoke. We'll check out the other side."

After the squad left, Kim slid back inside the shack.

"Pretty good plan huh Joe?"

"Pretty good Kim, but I think we better get out of here."

"Not yet Joe. We wait until dark and then I take you to house of Min-Ho."

"Well I'll be damned. You are one resourceful kid Kim." Tony said.

"By the way, I suppose you used that greenback to buy pot?"

Kim smiled and said "I buy pot so I can sell it on the street. That way I can make more money. It's called "free enterprise" much better than communism. I think maybe socialism not work so good unless maybe need some capitalism to keep it going."

The two sailors looked at each other in amazement.

"Out of the mouths of babes" said Sully.

CHAPTER SEVENTEEN

"Okay little buddy, tell us what you found in town" asked Sully "Did you see Min-Ho? I'm curious as to her reaction."

"Yes. I talk to lady. She very pretty. When I tell her about Sully-san want to come see her, she say 'Tell som-a-bitch to come. I love to tell him something.'"

Tony looked at Sully, hesitated and then said "Again, Mr. Sullivan, you obviously didn't tell me everything about this lady. Are you sure we're okay with this?"

"We're okay. She might just be bent out of shape a little. At one time we had a few dates. It was before Sun-Hi came along."

"I think I'm beginning to understand" said Tony "well I hope she's over it enough to put us in touch with her brother."

"Don't worry. I'll handle it."

Kim snickered with a knowing look that belied his young age.

"What are you snickering about kid?" Sully asked.

"Nothin' Joe. Nothin' at all. Kim just mind his own business."

The three of them rested for the rest of the afternoon and on past the evening hours. It was well into the night when they started the trek into the town of Hungnam.

Kim kept to the back streets and they stayed in the shadows to keep concealed. They entered into a neatly kept neighborhood. Soon Kim told them to wait in a yard and to hide in the bushes. He left and the sailors nervously waited until he returned.

"Okay Joe, she will open the door when we knock. She will have all the lights out to appear that she is asleep. Let's go."

They approached a small neat house nestled among other similar houses and lightly rapped twice on the door. The door swung open, they entered and the door closed. A candle was lit and in the dim light a lithe young Korean woman was visible. She looked at the disheveled sailors and said "Welcome back lover boy…..you bastard" dripping with sarcasm.

"Now, now Min, is that any way to greet an old friend?"

"You could have explained that you and Sun-Hi were a couple."

"Sun-Hi wasn't in the picture at the time. I had only just met her and we weren't together until later Min. That's the truth."

"Maybe so but I thought we had a start on a good relationship even though we only saw each other when your boat came in those few times." Min said.

"I'm sorry Min. It just wasn't the right time for us. It may have been different if I wasn't in the business I was in with Jin-Sang. We just moved around too much."

"Didn't seem to make a difference with Sun." she interjected.

Sully mumbled something and stepped back. For once in his life he was speechless.

"Oh don't worry, I'll help you get to Jin-Sang" she said "I already made the attempt right after your little friend explained your predicament. He's quite the little salesman. I can't believe he's only twelve. He must be an older midget or something."

"Thank you Min. If only we can get to the safe house in Wonsan we'll be okay."

"You don't want to go there" she answered "It's now a barracks for the North Army. You'd walk right into a hornets nest."

"Oh great! Now what?" Tony asked.

"I made contact with a friend of my brother. He knows how to reach Jin. The message I gave is one which will bring him here. It's a code we set up long ago for when I need him. It may take a day or two before he gets here but he will come."

"Thank you Min. Can we stay here until he comes?"

"Not for long. I have moved on with my life too Sully. The man I'm soon to marry will be here tomorrow night. He is following the ways of our new government and belongs to the Communist Party."

"Wow! What does Jin think about this?"

She answered "Jin doesn't care as long as he treats me good and gives me the few luxuries I now have. Jin has no politics. He does business with everyone. I live in North Korea so I must accept things as they are."

"When do you think Jin will come?"

"It depends on where he is when he gets my message. I have no way of knowing. You must leave here after sunset tomorrow. I will direct him to wherever you go. I'll be discreet with my fiancé, Sang-Yong. I'll explain that Jin just wanted to assure I was okay after the last battle here in Hungnam."

"Thank you Min. I know that you didn't have to do this and you are endangering yourself to help us."

"This will be the last time Sully. There was a time that I felt a love for you and part of it still remains. I even fantasized that I could seduce you into my bed tonight and maybe even convince you to stay and be my lover but such a fantasy could never happen. We would both be doomed."

"You are a beautiful, intelligent woman Min and deserve all the happiness that you can get. Marry that guy and live a good life."

"Thanks Sully. Now you'd better get some sleep."

The night passed quietly and the next morning brought a snow storm which was fortunate since it kept people inside and made it easier to hide the three surprise guests.

It was approaching dusk when an unexpected visitor entered the front door. It was the very surprised fiancé, Sang-Yong who entered from the blustery, snowy outside.

He stopped short after he hurriedly closed the door and scanned the small room in which held four surprised people.

"Min-ho who are these men?" he shouted.

"They came to see my brother, Sang-Yong. But they leave now. Jin-sang will meet them elsewhere."

"That brother of yours brings nothing but trouble. I want you thieves out of this house now or I'll call the authorities" screamed Sang-Yong.

"We're leaving. Don't blame her. She wanted nothing to do with us." Sully said.

"You are American. You should not be here. I think you are spies. It is my duty to report this to my comrades" said Sang-Yong, the Korean communist, as he turned to leave.

Sully and Tony both drew their forty five's at the same time.

"Not so fast. Just stay put and no one will get hurt" Sully calmly ordered.

Min-Ho screamed "Don't hurt him. He will let you go. I promise I will not let him leave if you just don't hurt him."

"It's strictly up to him Min. He won't get hurt as long as he remains here and allows us to get out of here."

The roar of a truck engine suddenly could be heard outside of the small house. It stopped and the engine was turned off.

"Oh thank God, it's Jin-sang" Min said as she rushed to open the door.

As Jin-sang walked in and surveyed the room he saw the two Americans with drawn weapons and he said "Well Sully, I see you've met my future brother-in-law. I knew Min-Ho needed me but I had no idea how badly."

"Hello Jin-Sang. Sure glad to see you're out of jail." Sully said.

"I demand to know what this is all about" said Sang-Yong in a loud authoritative voice.

"Just don't get excited Sang" answered Jin "We'll be out of your hair very soon."

He turned to Sully. "Holster your weapon old buddy. I'm figuring that you want a way out of this town. Right?"

"The quicker, the better, Jin."

"Okay. Both of you, crawl under the bags of rice on my truck. We'll get out of here and somewhere safe. Then we'll talk about the next step and the cost involved." Jin said.

"Sounds good. Kim come outside with me." Sully said

As they left the house Jin turned to Min-Ho and embraced her. He said "Be careful sis. Keep this antisocial boy friend of yours busy for a while. I don't want him blowing the whistle on us too soon."

He then glared at Sang-Yong "I know your politics Sang and I don't give a damn what you believe in but remember that you have a personal life too. My sister can give you a good marriage. If you're smart you won't do anything to screw it up."

Sang-Yong was quiet but his hateful stare spoke volumes.

When they were outside Sully stooped down to be eye level with Kim. He said "I'm going to miss you kid. Here's a twenty. Use it to help your mom and sister. I wish I could do more for you. Can you get back home okay?"

"Sure Joe. I know these streets better than anyone. Maybe some day I come to the States to see you and make free enterprise."

This brought a laugh from both sailors.

"I wouldn't be a bit surprised" Tony added as he grabbed the little guy and gave him a big hug.

"Come on. Load up" yelled Jin as he rushed out the door "I don't know how long my sister can keep that zealot tied down."

Tony and Sully threw some bags of rice aside and crawled in between others. Jin then loaded the extra bags on top of the human cargo and jumped in the cab. He opened a window in the back of the cab so he could talk to his passengers under the rice.

"You guys okay back there?"

"Yeah we're good. I never thought I'd see you making a living hauling rice. Are you going straight now?"

Jin laughed "Don't be silly. The money stuff is in a sealed compartment under the hood made to look like part of the engine. You don't need much room for the white powder that I'm hauling to Seoul. We'll be picking up Chin-Ho in about an hour. It'll be just like old times. He kicked it in gear and moved slowly away."

Back in the house Sang grabbed his coat, mumbling under his breath about foreign dogs and traitors. Min-Ho grabbed him before he could move towards the door.

"Please. Please" she implored "he is my brother. Don't turn him in to the authorities."

"Let go of me woman. He is a traitor and those Americans are our enemies. They are probably CIA. I must do my duty as a party communist."

"Do it for me Sang. Please, I will do anything that you ask if you just wait and give them a chance to get out of the city."

"I know he has a friend that allows him to operate out of his house outside of the city. If he makes it there we will never find those American dogs. In my report I will say that the Americans forced him to drive them. That way he will be set free."

She still hung on to his arm and said "Wait just a short while. Please."

Sang jerked loose from her grip and swung a hard back hand that caught Min high on her cheek. She fell back and landed hard, sprawling on a table. She scrambled up and charged at Sang and he hit her with a closed fist. She raised her bloody head and swore at him but when he drew his arm back for another hard clout she held up.

In a low voice she said "If anything happens to my brother I swear that you will pay dearly." Her words were dripping with hate.

He turned and said in a threatening tone "My status in our party is growing every day and this will help even more. Any other threats like that and you may find yourself out on the street. Don't forget who arranged for you to live in this nice little house and buys your food. You need me."

He turned and quickly left.

Min-Ho sat down, put her head in her hands and sobbed.

Jin-Sang drove down the narrow lane and soon was on more populated streets. The going was slow so as not to raise suspicion. Chinese troops were in evidence and Jin sometimes took the back streets to avoid them.

He continued "Hey that was a pretty sharp kid back there. I may recruit him some day. He must have done you a pretty big favor, paying him so well."

"We wouldn't have made contact with you if it weren't for him." Tony said.

"Well he'll probably get around 50,000 Won for that twenty dollar greenback. If he's as sharp as I think he is, he'll use that to finance himself for a long time."

After several hours of zigzagging through the town, they finally made it to a highway heading south.

"We'll pick up Chin at a farm in about a half hour. That's where I was when I got word that Min needed me. We use this farm as a meeting place when we do business up this way. The farmer and his wife are......... Oh dammit looks like a check point up ahead. Must be new. It wasn't here when I went into town. I'll bet that idiot boy friend of my sisters had something to do with this."

Two other trucks were stopped at the check point. They were being searched thoroughly. Jin was still a hundred yards or so away. He slowed to a crawl.

"Sully you've got to jump off. It's your only chance. Maybe we're far enough away that they'll miss it. Go man. Go now. Try to make your way through the woods south. I'll try to meet you on the other side."

Sully and Tony dug their way out of the rice bags and jumped to the side of the road. As they did Jin gunned the engine and approached the check point. Soldiers were already clamoring over his truck before he even stopped.

One soldier opened the driver's side door, dragged Jin out and threw him to the ground. Jin protested and the soldier slammed his rifle butt into the side of Jin's face. Blood spurted out from a gash next to his eye and he laid there unconscious.

Three other soldiers jumped onto the truck bed and started throwing bags of rice off. They could see the hollowed out space where the two sailors had lain. They jabbered in Chinese to the officer in charge who directed his men to search the area.

Two soldiers pulled the semi-conscious Jin to his feet and the officer started grilling him, screaming in his face.

Jin uttered something unintelligible and the officer backhanded him. Jin's head jerked back and his eyes rolled. He was barely conscious. They let him drop to the ground and one of the soldiers kicked him in the gut.

He laid there, not moving for what seemed to be a long, long time but was probably only a half hour or so. The soldiers sent on the search returned dragging the two prisoners. Both had been beaten and Sully had a flesh wound on his shoulder. Tony's head was bleeding. Maybe from an errant bullet or a rifle butt… it didn't matter. They were captured and they were wounded.

The North Korean officer smiled when he saw the prisoners. He said "So we have captured the American spies. Our comrades will be most appreciative to have them to question. Secure them and load them up for transfer to headquarters."

A soldier asked "Do you want to detain the driver too sir?"

"No. He is of no value. Bring him to me."

Two soldiers pulled Jin to his feet and took him to the officer who pulled out his side arm and faced Jin. He said "Now you pig, I'll show you what reward traitors get. Put him on his knees."

He placed the pistol to the back of Jin's head and pulled the trigger. Jin's head jerked forward from the bullet and he slumped to the ground. They pulled the body to the side of the road and left it there.

Sully and Tony witnessed the execution. It would be etched in their minds for the rest of their lives. Their hands and feet were shackled and they were thrown into an enclosed truck with a locked door.

It was dark with no windows so they had no idea where they were going and they lost all sense of time but when they arrived it was dark and they were stiff and sore. The wounds had clotted and stopped bleeding.

The door opened and they were dragged out and directed to walk into a building. They were thrown separately into small empty rooms. Each had a bare light bulb hanging from the ceiling and a heavy wooden chair in the center of the room.

They lay there for hours not knowing what was happening to each other. Finally Tony heard the lock snap and the door opened. In walked three men. One in an officer's uniform and the other two in shirt sleeves.

Two of them dragged him to his manacled feet and slammed him on to the chair so that his bound arms were stretched behind the chair back.

The officer stood before him and glared at him in silence, dramatically pausing to try to inflict as much discomfort as he could.

Tony raised his head and defiantly returned his stare.

It was very early in the morning. The sun had just risen and Min-Ho had not slept all night. She was sitting on a futon when she heard a knock on the door.

"Who is it?" Min called.

"It is Chin-Ho" came the answer.

She scrambled up and opened the door. As soon as she saw the look on Chin's face she knew it was bad news.

"Tell me" she said.

Chin's voice broke as he said "They killed him."

Min collapsed in his arms.

CHAPTER EIGHTEEN

"What is your mission here and where is your base of operations" said the officer in broken English.

"I am Anthony Marino, Seaman in the United States Navy, service number 571 5814."

"You are not a Prisoner of War. You are not dressed in military uniform. You are a spy and will be treated as such. We will question you and depending on your answers you will be confined or executed as a trial dictates."

"Sir, I'm dressed in foul weather gear. My boat was sunk in Hungnam during the evacuation. I have dog tags."

"YOU LIE, American pig, you have no dog tags. You were searched when you were captured and no dog tags were found."

"Someone must have taken them off when they were beating me in the woods. I think I was out cold for a while" complained Tony.

"QUIET" screamed his interrogator. "You will only answer questions. No talking otherwise. Are you CIA?"

"No. I'm United States Navy."

A sudden blow to the side of his head made his wound start to bleed again. He didn't see the blow coming since his assailant was standing behind him. Blood ran into one eye. It burned and made the room look pink.

"I think we'll give you some time to think about your fate while we talk to your fellow spy. Maybe he will be more cooperative. When we return, we will educate you on the use of heated bamboo spears."

He turned to the two shirt sleeved soldiers and rattled off some Korean orders then left the room.

The soldiers roughly pulled Tony from the chair and pushed him to his knees on the cobbled concrete floor. They then put a noose around his neck and pulled it through a pad eye on the ceiling. They pulled the rope tight so he was now standing with the noose tightly pulling upwards. His arms were bound so he could not loosen it. He could do nothing but stand in this stretched out position. If he tried to sit or kneel or try to move, he would strangle himself.

They left him that way, laughing as they exited.

The two soldiers then joined the interrogating officer in the room where Sully was confined.

The officer already had Sully sitting in the wooden chair in much the same way that Tony was trussed up.

"I hope you are more cooperative than your spy friend, American pig. What is your mission?"

Sully looked up and said "Sean Sullivan, Boatswains Mate 3rd Class, Service number 495 8922."

"You are not Prisoner of War. You are civilian agent. Are you CIA?"

"I told you. I am U.S. Navy."

"YOU LIE" the officer screamed. "You have no uniform. You have no identification. No dog tags."

"My dog tags were ripped off of my neck by your soldiers when they captured us. If you don't have them then they do."

The officer spoke in Korean to the two assailants. He was unaware that Sully understood him.

"Teach this Yankee dog a lesson. Maybe it will loosen his tongue. After you rough him up, put his neck in the noose like the other Yankee pig." He then left.

One of the soldiers grabbed Sully from behind and stood him up, holding him firmly while the other one came at him from the front.

Since Sully was held firmly in a bear hug by the big Korean, his feet were free of the floor. When the approaching guard got in close, Sully lashed out with both feet and kicked the combative guard in the groin. The guard doubled over with a scream. He fell on the floor, grabbing his crotch and rolled over in the fetal position. He was moaning and groaning. Sully had made a direct hit in a very sensitive body area.

The force from the kick propelled Sully and the guard behind him backwards and to the floor. The unexpected kick and thrust caused the guard to land hard on his back. His bear hug grip was released and in an instant Sully was free of this restraining hold.

As Sully tried to scramble to his feet, the restraints hindered him and the guard was able to get to his feet much quicker. He pounced on Sully and started beating him unmercifully with his fists. The other guard was slowly regaining his composure and joined in on the beating. He was teeming with vengeance from that horrible kick that was still excruciatingly painful. So much so, his blows were not as devastating as he would have liked.

Sully pulled himself into the fetal position, trying to protect himself, as much as possible but now they were kicking him. He knew they were going to kill him for the resistance that he gave. Especially the one on which he was able to inflict some damage. The man was consumed with rage and he pulled his pistol out of the holster. He held it to Sully's head spewing hateful obscenities.

Before he could pull the trigger, the door was flung open and the interrogating officer came charging in and screamed "Stop, you idiots. We want him alive. Headquarters has informed me that these two have been requested by members of the Psychology Team for the experimental purposes. They have been beaten enough. Take the other man loose from the noose and transfer both of them to the hospital ward. The Psychologists want them in good health."

Sully had already passed out so he heard none of this. The next thing he was aware of, he was lying in a hospital bed. He looked at the next bed and his ship mate was lying there sleeping.

He took inventory of his body. He was sore and stiff all over but everything seemed to be intact and working. His mouth felt swollen but all his teeth seemed to be there. His lower back was very sore. Probable from a well placed kick to the kidney area.

He glanced down at a tube running out from under the sheet leading to a bag of bloody urine. Probably a catheter.

He thought to himself...*I wonder why they're giving me such good care. I surely thought they were going to beat me to death. Tony looks in pretty good shape too. Something strange is going on.*

He drifted back to sleep.

It had been almost a month since Sun-Hi had requested a transfer to Pusan and finally she was on a ship en route to Pusan Harbor.

She found out from the crew on the Columbia that Peacock was in the military hospital in Pusan and that would be her first stop in trying to find out if Sully was still alive and where she could start to locate him.

As soon as the ship docked she checked into a hotel and called the company office to tell them she had arrived. They asked her to report for work the next morning. The management may have a suggestion on where she could go for a decent place to room and board.

When she reported the next day she felt welcomed by her fellow employees who were mostly Korean and the stigma of working in Moji with mostly Japanese was not evident.

She was shown into the manager's office and was surprised to see an older gentleman instead of the younger man that was manager when she left.

"Welcome Sun-Hi. You have come here with very high recommendations both from Moji and from your previous assignment here in Pusan."

"Thank you sir, I will do my best for the company. Did the previous manager get transferred?"

"He left very suddenly and I came from corporate to temporarily replace him. We will assign a new manager shortly."

"I see" she said "do you know of a room I can rent close by?"

"Of course, see my secretary and she will give you several that you can choose from and she will also introduce you to your supervisor."

"Thank you again sir." She said as she rose and left the room.

She had no problem adapting to her new job and the day passed quickly. That evening she visited one of the suggested homes for a room and was pleased to find one so soon. It was an older couple whose family had grown and left, so space was available. She would move in the next evening after work.

The military hospital was close by the hotel so Sun stopped and asked to visit patient Virgil Peacock. She was given his room number.

When she entered his room, Peacock was sitting in a chair along side of the bed. His hands were bandaged and his face was bare showing some ghastly burns.

He looked up at her as she sharply drew in her breath and raised her hand to her mouth.

Peacock said "Yeah I get that a lot, but it's better than it was six weeks ago."

Sun said "I'm so sorry. I didn't mean to......."

"Don't worry Sun. You didn't hurt my feelings. I know it's a shock at first but the doc's tell me that they can do a lot of repair work. It will take time and they'll be sending me back to Bethesda in the states to do some surgery. It could have been much worse. The cold water, where I landed, curtailed the burns. I'm happy to be here even in this condition. None of the soldiers on the boat made it."

"Please Peacock, tell me about Sully."

"All I can tell you Sun is that the last time I saw Sully and my buddy Tony they were alive. They were under attack and going to help some wounded soldiers. They had come under the same barrage that got the boat and I thought I saw one hit close to Tony. Sully was heading his way to help him. That's the last thing I remember until I woke up in a hospital bed. I'd been out for days. I'm not even sure when or how I got there. They kept me pretty doped up for quite awhile. Even now I get doses of morphine. I was transferred here for some preliminary work. For the real surgery, I'll go back to the States. I think that will be soon."

"I won't rest until I find out for sure if my darling is alive or dead. I lost him and then found him again. I was so worried that he didn't love me anymore and now I know that he does."

"Sun I've just got a good feeling about those guys. The Exec came to see me when the Columbia was in port and he feels the same way. He said their names have not appeared on the KIA or POW reports sent to our government by the Red Cross. They are still classified as MIA. So I think there's hope."

"When Sully and I were together in his gun running days we made regular trips to Hungnam, Wonsan, Hamhung, Kosong and Yangyang so he's very familiar with the area. We even had a safe house in Wonsan. I'm going to try to get some time off at work after I get established here. I must work for a while and make some contacts starting in Hungnam where Sully and Marino were left behind.

"Better be careful Sun. There's a war going on out there."

"I can take care of myself Peacock. I've been doing it all my life and don't forget, I'm from North Korea. I'll come back and see you before I leave."

"If I can find any news I'll get in touch with you at the company."

Sun left for the hotel and the next few days were used to establish herself on her job and her new home. She tried to keep up with the progress of the war and was disappointed to hear that Seoul had fallen back into communist hands. Getting into North Korea was going to take some planning.

If only she had some word on Sully. If he was alive or dead, if he was captured or still free and hiding.

She quietly made a promise to herself "I won't rest until I know. And when I know, if my darling is alive, I will go to the ends of the earth to find him."

CHAPTER NINETEEN

Sun-Hi used all the resources available to her through the company's contacts which were worldwide. And although there was a war raging on between North and South Korea and commerce between the two had all but ceased, past personal contacts were still furtively available.

Using this information was critical to making contact with some of her old acquaintances and the starting point was in Hungnam.

Jin-Sang had a sister named Min-Ho who lived there. There had to be a way to contact her. She had to be pragmatic about this. She didn't want her employer discovering the use of company resources and especially doing it on company time.

She was making headway. Through some legal channels she found that both Jin-Sang and Chin-Ho had been released with many other prisoners when the Communists took control of Seoul at the start of the war. And further she found that both were now fugitives in the eyes of the authorities here in the south.

It only made sense that the two partners in crime were back doing what they did in the old days. Perhaps she could connect with them through some of the old veiled contacts here in Pusan. It may be dangerous since these contacts were mostly felons and smugglers. She would not present a danger to them but there were some who resented any kind of contact that could lead the law to them.

If she was going to do this she might as well go right to the top. The one man that had control of the biggest majority of smuggling in the whole of South Korea was headquartered right here in Pusan. He was known as *The Big One* and he held court in a palatial suite in the back room of a night club. The night club was called *Ecstasy* and was located in the sleazy entertainment district of the city. Going there at night was very distasteful but it was the only time available to her. She would go as early in the evening as possible.

She hailed a cab outside of the company offices and when she instructed the driver to take her to the Ecstasy Club, he slowly turned to look at her and asked "Are you sure you want to go in that part of town? You don't look like the type of girl that hangs around that neighborhood."

"Yes and I am very nervous about it. Can you wait for me while I go in and try to contact someone? I'll pay you for waiting."

"I don't like to wait very long. Strange things can happen while waiting. Even the law goes there in groups, but I will try. Can you pay me for this trip before you go in? I need the money and I may not be able to wait until you come back."

"Yes of course. Please do what you can."

They drove into the brightly lit district with music blaring from open doors even in this cold weather. Servicemen of all description roamed the streets. As they walked by the bars, scantly dressed young women cajoled them to come in. Some even ventured out to the sidewalk and pulled the men in by the coat collar making lewd promises.

The cab pulled up in front of *Ecstasy* and Sun exited the cab. Two very extravagantly dressed women approached her and said "Move on sister, this is our spot. We pay *The Big One* for exclusive rights here."

"Please, I'm not here to take your spot. I just need to talk to *The Big One*, Jong-Cho. I'll be leaving very quickly."

"What did you say? I've never heard him called by that name. You may be in big trouble lady. He is *The Big One* to everyone."

"That name may be what gets me in to see him" said Sun.

She pushed past the two irate girls and entered into the club. After she entered she had to stop and adjust her eyes to the very dim indirect lighting. Slow suggestive music was playing from unseen speakers. She could see a low lit center stage with two scantily clad girls slowly dancing to the music. Surrounding the stage were tables and thickly padded chairs, hardly visible in the smoky bar room with even lower lighting. From what she could see most of the ringside tables were occupied by servicemen and female companions.

She suddenly felt a presence beside her and turned to see a man, somewhat shorter than she, leering at her through very slanted eyes. His teeth showed very white in his wide grin. He had a thin mustache and a small goatee at the point of his chin.

In a low suggestive voice he said "Welcome to Ecstasy you beautiful, sexy creature. May I sit with you and buy you a drink?"

"No thank you. I'm not here to drink. I have business to discuss."

"Well then we can sit and talk. I may have an interesting proposition for you."

"I'm not interested in becoming one of the girls working here or outside of the door."

"Of course, I'm aware that a woman with your refinement and class should be on call for our more genteel clients. I can arrange that also."

"SIR, I AM NOT A WHORE."

"Just simmer down young lady or I'll teach you a lesson you'll remember for a long while" and he grabbed her upper arm and squeezed until it hurt. She tried to pull away and he grabbed her other arm and pulled her to his body.

She screamed "Let me go! I want to see Jong-Cho."

"Who?" said the little sleaze bag.

"*The Big One*" she said.

He relaxed his grip on her arms and she jerked away and staggered back away from him as two larger men approached and one said "What's the problem here."

"This stupid bitch says she wants to see the boss" the assailant said.

"Okay sister what's going on? We don't like trouble here and we don't like girls on their own infringing on our girls."

"She said she wanted to see Jong-Cho. I don't think the boss likes being called that especially from a piece of fluff walking in the door."

The older of the two tall, well built men asked "Who are you and what business would you have with *The Big One?*"

"My name is Sun-Hi and I want to talk to him about locating a former acquaintance named Sullivan."

"The boss does not specialize in locating lost persons. Why don't you hire a P.I.?"

"Please just tell him I want to take just a few minutes of his time. Tell him I formerly worked with Sullivan, Jin-Sang and Chin-Ho. It was three years ago that we were busted by the authorities. That was the last time that we had contact with Jong-Cho as he was known to us then."

"You stay here Miss. I'll see if the boss will even see me. Sometimes he doesn't want to be bothered by anyone."

"Thank you. I understand and I will leave if he won't see me."

The bouncer left while the group waited.

The sleazy little man smiled and trained his most disgusting look on Sun. He said "If the boss won't see you, my offer still stands."

Sun-Hi glared at him and stepped away.

Several minutes later the bouncer returned and in a puzzled voice said "Well I'm very surprised but the boss said to show you in. So come with me."

She followed him through the club, passing by tables of ogling servicemen, some of which expressed various invitations and offers to join their table. She smiled at some of the boyish remarks knowing full well that most of them were young and inexperienced. But also with the knowledge that even as young as they were many of them had recently left the hell of battle. For this reason she could forgive their sometimes crude remarks and laugh it off as having a good time.

When they reached the door leading to the back of the club, the bouncer knocked and her demeanor changed. This was serious business. The door opened and a lovely woman elegantly dressed and coifed bade her to enter.

The bouncer turned and left her standing in the open doorway. She walked in to a palatial, elegant room.

The woman closed the door and beckoned her towards a beautiful mahogany desk behind which sat a huge man dressed in a western style suit of the finest Italian fabric that she had ever seen.

She drew in her breath at the sight of him. She had forgotten how big he was. The Korean people tend to be of bigger stature than other Orientals but this was the biggest man she could remember ever seeing.

Although huge, his features were not distorted. He could almost be considered a handsome man and could be very debonair and charming with the ladies. But it was also rumored that he was heartless if crossed or lied to. He was known to beat his many women admirers at the slightest provocation.

His strength was also legendary. To eliminate a competitor who was showing signs of growth he set up a meeting in a remote location and when the man showed belligerence *The Big One* wrapped his huge arms around the unfortunate man and squeezed him in a bear hug that broke every bone in his torso including ribs, clavicle, spine and both arms. The air rushed out of his lungs and he died an agonizing death flopping on the ground like a fish out of water.

The dead man's body guards quickly ran away quaking in fear.

Sun knew she had to approach this man with the utmost tact.

The lovely hostess showed her to an overstuffed chair opposite the desk. She sat with all the grace and poise that she could muster. She wanted to show confidence but not arrogance.

"Ah yes" he said "now I remember. When first I met you, you were a very pretty young girl. You did not disappoint. You have grown into an elegant and beautiful woman."

She appropriately blushed and said "Thank you Jong-Cho."

Butterflies fluttered in her stomach while she waited his reaction to his given name.

He hesitated, gave her a hard look, then softened and slowly grinned. "Not many have the courage or have earned the right to address me as so.

"I do so out of respect and in memory of times in the past when we were all in a different situation." She offered.

"Yes, I do remember. It was unfortunate that you and your companions were caught up in that sting. Someone set you up. I was grateful that I was not fingered as the source of the merchandise. I agreed to see you because of that but I will not promise anything further."

"My sole purpose in being here is to get any information I can to locate Sean Sullivan."

"It was my understanding that Sullivan was taken to the States by the CIA and probably jailed. Since it didn't interest me I checked no further. I also found out that you three, Jin-Sang, Chin-Ho and you, were taken in custody by the police. Chung-Hee had been killed, you escaped and the other two were jailed only to be set free by the Chinese a few years later. I heard that you disappeared after that. Am I right so far?" He said.

"That is very accurate and that is why I came to see you. If anyone can tell where to start it would be you."

"Hmm. I can bring you up to date but I don't think you'll like it."

"I'll take any information that I can get."

He drank from a cup on his desk and said "I have no information on Sullivan. After Jin-Sang and Chin-Ho were set free they set up an operation and we have done business. In fact they were in the process of delivering a shipment to me when the North Korean Army intercepted them. Jin-Sang was killed. Chin-Ho escaped but lost the truck with the merchandise. I don't know the details except that Chin is trying to recover the truck. The merchandise is well hidden and may have not been discovered. I have only heard all this by a third party. I have not talked to Chin and with the war not going well for the south it is unlikely that I will."

"Jin-Sang had a sister in Hungnam. Do you know anything about her?"

"Rumor has it that she is the paramour of a communist official and he may have been the one that caused the problem with the shipment. If so, I'm not sure what the relationship is now. What makes you think she knows anything about Sullivan?"

"The CIA turned Sully over to the U.S. Navy. They made a deal and Sully reenlisted. I saw him in Moji and we are lovers again. His ship was in Hungnam during the evacuation and Sully was left behind. He is listed as MIA. I must find out if he is alive or captured. He has not been reported as a POW or KIA by the Red Cross. If he's alive Min-Ho might know something. Can you help me get to Hungnam?"

"Hold on lady. I said I would tell you what I know and that's all."

"Please Jong-Cho, I must find him. Maybe I can get some information on your shipment. Don't forget I'm from the north."

He was deep in thought and waited a long time before he said "Hmm... ...I wonder......maybe. Wait outside. I will send for you."

CHAPTER TWENTY

The two sailors had been confined in the hospital for about a week. They both were feeling much better after the beatings they had received and were to the point of wondering if they were going to be transferred to a POW camp or maybe a jail cell.

When a doctor or nurse attended them it was always under the watchful eyes of a guard or sometimes even a pair of guards. Their questions were never responded to, whether Tony asked in English or Sully asked in Korean. They tried posing the remarks to both the medical and to military persons. No information, not even medical questions, was responded to.

"Well this gets more interesting every day" Tony said very thoughtfully, as a doctor and nurse team left. "I'd call that visit as close to a complete physical as you could get, especially under these circumstances."

"Yeah and we got the same kind of blank look from both of them when we asked questions." Sully said.

"I did notice a slight reaction from the doctor when I asked when we would be discharged. He must understand English."

"Hmm" Sully stared off while contemplating. "Maybe something is brewing. I've noticed that the guards are more attentive too."

The locked steel door opened and two uniformed officers entered. One was a tall North Korean with unusual chiseled features and in what appeared to be a dress uniform. The other was in a drab Chinese battle dress uniform and much shorter in stature than the Korean.

They approached the beds and stopped between them. The Korean was smiling and in perfect English he said "Gentlemen, I see our medical team has treated you well.........or at least from all appearances it seems so."

The two American sailors sat up and looked at each other with astonishment. Neither spoke.

The Korean chuckled and said "Yes, I guess you are surprised that someone is finally speaking to you. Please forgive our procedures here. We thought it better that no one speak to you rather than give you inaccurate information. I am Doctor Rho."

"Can you tell us when we will be released and where we are going?" Sully asked.

"The attending doctor has just given us a report that you both are in good health and will be transferred tomorrow."

"Are we going to a POW camp?" Tony asked.

"Not exactly. The facility, where you will be confined, is one that we reserve for special prisoners such as yourselves. You will receive indoctrination and perhaps partake in our new program, that is, if you demonstrate the characteristics we are looking for."

"Indoctrination huh…..don't you mean brainwashing?" lashed out Sully.

"Please" interjected the Chinese officer in an oily tone "I am Doctor Chan, we ask that you cooperate and no harm will come to you. You will come out of this much better than some of your fellow American prisoners."

Tony bristled "Listen you…."

"QUIET TONY" Sully said in a firm tone.

Both officers smiled weakly.

"You can indoctrinate all you want but we will give nothing but name, rank and serial number. And we expect to be treated as Prisoners of War as outlined by the Geneva Convention." Sully said.

"We are sure that you cannot complain as to your treatment so far gentlemen since you are both spies and working directly with the American CIA…… You will be transferred tomorrow."

They turned to leave and then stopped and faced the sailor's beds again. Doctor Rho said "Today you will meet a fellow comrade doctor who will direct the treatment you will be receiving. He has just arrived from Moscow and we understand he is quite capable in the specialty of indoctrination. It will behoove you to cooperate with this doctor. In fact your survival will depend on it."

They both turned and left the room.

Two armed guards entered as they left and stationed themselves on either side of the door.

Sully looked over at Tony and said "Looks like we've been picked for some experiments. The Nazi's tried some of this in the war. I'll bet these gooks have expanded on the science of brainwashing."

"QUIET!! No talking" yelled a guard.

"Yeah, yeah" said Tony.

Just then the door opened and a slight, young male orderly entered with a tray of pills. He said something in Korean that was unintelligible to the Americans.

He walked to Tony's bed and stationed himself between Tony and the guards. He handed Tony a cup of water and a small capsule. He very quietly said, in a muted voice, almost too quiet for Tony to hear *"don't swallow the pill"*.

Tony took the pill and while looking at Sully he slightly shook his head as he put the pill up to his mouth.

Sully gave an acknowledged look in response.

The orderly walked to Sully's bed and as he gave him the water and capsule again stationing himself between Sully and the guards. He said in the same low tone *"Bravo one is coming. Don't blow his cover".*

"NO TALKING" yelled the guard and he made a threatening move towards the orderly.

"Don't scream at me. I'm merely giving medical instructions. I don't want him to choke and spit up the capsule, you uneducated, crude dolts. After all they are still patients." said the orderly firmly.

He turned and gracefully left the room muttering to himself and glaring at the guards as he passed them. He slammed the door closed as he left.

The soldiers laughed and made some crude remarks as to the sexual orientation of the slightly built orderly. One of them talking in a falsetto and the other roared with crude laughter.

The sailors used this distraction and each made a coughing sound and raised their hands to their mouths. They discretely spit out the pills and crushed them, spreading the remaining debris on the floor under the bed.

After the North Korean Doctor Rho, in his ornate dress uniform, and the Chinese Doctor Chan, in plain battle dress had left the room, they entered an office and sat at a table. A tray holding hot tea and cakes awaited them. The Korean poured for both of them.

"Yes" said the Korean "I think we have chosen wisely. They are both young, healthy men who obviously have a patriotic background. They are listed as MIA by the Americans so there is no danger of them being traced to our experimental clinic. This new drug from Russia is designed to alter their personalities as we had hoped with the other drugs we have tried. It is unfortunate, but we must terminate that experiment. The four remaining patients will be disposed of as was done with the others. If this plan is successful, we can steer these new ones back to their own lines and they will be fine operatives for us. The exciting part is that they will not be aware of any wrong doing. When they come under our direction they will have no memory of what they have done. Even when we set them up as assassins they will have no memory of their own actions and therefore no guilty conscience."

"It is a brilliant plan Doctor Rho, and of course, even more so, because they will have no memory of ever being here in our clinic, they will go back to their normal lives as civilians after their discharge from the Navy and none the wiser that they are under our beck and call. " said the Doctor Chan.

"I'm not happy about the Russian interference with our plan. The doctor from Moscow has arrived and wants to oversee the inoculations. But we have no choice in the matter what with all the military assistance from them. I have ordered the preliminary oral drugs to be started now. After they are moved and have sufficient drugs in their system we can start the personality altering inoculations and of course the verbal indoctrination."

"What is your estimate of time to complete this experiment Doctor?" said the Chinese officer.

"From past failed experiments, I estimate at least one month. Maybe more. Past failures were partly because we rushed the experiment. We must be patient. This will be a new procedure but I still have hopes for the one American officer still in the clinic. He is responding better since we cut the dosage on the old drugs. We may just use him as planned with this new group. Perhaps try some of the new drug as a test. He is a Harvard graduate with a Masters degree. I have hopes to put him in some political office in Washington D.C. and be under our guidance. His uncle is in the Senate. Perhaps he could follow in his footsteps."

The orderly came in just before lights out with another pill and as he gave them out he whispered *"act groggy tomorrow."*

The night passed without incident and the next day the orderly came in with their dungarees and foul weather jackets and another pill. He winked as he gave them the pills and quietly said *"Bravo One comes now. My name is Tae"*

As he left, the door remained open and a Russian officer entered. The boys did a double take. It was Bravo One, at least what they knew him by in the past. As he entered he gave an almost non perceptible shake of his head, meant only to be noticed by the two Americans.

In a Russian accent he said "I am Major Nikolai Baklova, Chief Medical Officer, First Detachment, of the Soviet Socialist Republic. I will be administering treatment after you are transferred to our clinic at the Peoples Hospital just outside of Wonsan. Please to follow me."

He turned and started towards the door. The sailors, as instructed, slowly crawled out of their beds, staggered a bit and followed the guards, acting groggy and disoriented. They left the building and were loaded into the back of a military ambulance. They sat on benches which were on each side of the truck bed and appeared to nod off. The two guards accompanied them and one of them commented that the prisoners seemed out of it since the new medication was administered.

"Wait until they get the strong stuff in an I.V. They'll really be out of it then. Remember the last two American dogs?"

They both laughed heartily.

"The young one went completely berserk. I had to help subdue him. It felt good giving that one a good beating."

"I think the doctors are hoping for some better results this time. Major Baklova has brought a new medication. It will be humorous to watch." They enjoyed another good laugh not aware that Sully understood every word that they uttered.

The driver and Major Baklova sat in front.

They rode for several hours and entered a long driveway that led to a large hospital building. They drove past the large building and finally pulled up to a smaller but very secure looking building with high heavily screened windows and a single front entrance with armed guards.

They exited the ambulance and were led into the building by the guards. The Major had already entered the building and was standing at the main desk studying a stack of papers along with several Korean medical men as well as the orderly that had brought the capsules to them in the hospital.

He glanced up when they entered and said "You will be shown to your rooms after you've been given a meal in the dining area. I will begin treatment tomorrow. Reading material can be found next to your bunk.

I suggest you make use of it. These are American newspapers, The Daily Worker printed in your city of New York and Peoples Daily World printed in San Francisco."

"Medication will be administered by my assistant. He will bring it to your room after you eat. The more cooperation that you give, the easier your treatment will be." He dismissed them by turning away.

They were given a Spartan meal, rice and bits of fish, in a very basically furnished dining area with the ever present guards hovering over them. When finished they were ushered into a sparsely furnished room with two bunks and a toilet which was nothing more than a hole in the floor behind a partition. No other plumbing was evident. It left no doubt that they were prisoners and not patients any more.

The heavy door was locked from the outside but at least the guards were now out of the room. However, at least one of them was in the hall at all times. He could be seen through the small heavily screened opening in the door when he occasionally checked on the prisoners.

Communication between Tony and Sully had been difficult but at least now it was possible. They decided to devise a way of using hand signals when verbal communication was prohibited.

"I'm really curious about Bravo One. He's got to be on an assignment of some kind" whispered Sully "maybe we'll find out something tonight when the orderly comes in with our meds."

"Yeah that's another mystery. Who is this guy?" said Tony. "Could he be CIA?"

"Well we know he's on our side or else I think we'd both be in la la land. This whole operation has got me confused. What kind of hospital is this?" Sully said.

"Hey Sully did you see these newspapers? Do you think they're really from the States? I heard there was some Senator gonna check into who's Commies and whose not back home."

"At least we're alive" they said in unison.

CHAPTER TWENTY ONE

That evening Tae, the young Korean orderly, entered the room with their medication. He wheeled a cart in with all the medical supplies for preparing the sailors for I.V. injections. He also had a tray of pills. He talked to them in a low modulated voice.

"You can swallow the pills I'm going to give to you, they're just A.P.C.'s but keep acting like you're only half conscious when the doctors come in tomorrow. I'm afraid they'll discover the remains of the real ones when you spit them out. I'm going to insert an I.V. tube in your arms but don't worry, the bags I hook up tomorrow will just be saline. My name is Tae-Hyun. I work with the Major."

While he worked on them he quietly continued "The Major will try to get in to brief you on what's going on this evening or maybe late tonight. Needless to say he didn't expect to see two men here from a former operation but he's glad it's you two. He can use you guys to help shut down this barbaric operation. Maybe he'll brief you on what we've seen so far in the POW camps. This will be the last enemy asylum we will infiltrate. The ones we've seen up until now are ones we can't do anything about except make a report to officials about the violations of The Geneva Convention and also article 6 of the Charter of the International Military Tribunal. But this one needs to be eradicated. Okay, I've got to go now. Remember act groggy."

He turned, pushed his cart to the door and called out through the screened opening "Open up. I'm finished in here."

The door clanked open shortly and the orderly left pulling the door shut after him.

The lights went out soon after he left and the only illumination was from a dim night light over the door.

"Might as well try to get some sleep" Sully said and rolled over.

"Yeah, who knows what tomorrow might bring" answered Tony.

Before they could fall asleep the lights came on, the door opened and the Major Baklova came in. The Korean guard was with him.

The major spoke to the guard in Korean "You may leave us now. I want to test to see how sedated these men are and I don't want any outside stimulus. Close the door, after you leave, and keep watch down the hall. See that it is kept quiet with no traffic while I'm performing my tests."

"Yes sir. I will make sure it is quiet sir" he answered.

He turned and left closing the door behind him.

The major put his hands up in a motion to hold up and keep quiet. He waited for a full minute before he softly said "Well this was a hell of a surprise. How in the hell did you two get yourselves in this predicament?"

Sully chuckled "It's a long story sir, but we're sure glad to see you. It started out when we were stranded in Hungnam during the evacuation. I won't go into details now but we were captured and beat up pretty badly. But for some reason, they stopped and we ended up here. Can you enlighten us?"

"The Koreans, Chinese and now Russians have been dabbling in psychological warfare for some time now. We knew they were operating a clinic and actually had been somewhat successful in some mind warping experiments. Many times it ended up with some good men going berserk and dying in a mentally deranged state. From some of the feed back that we got, the experiments were inhuman. The CIA was given orders to shut it down. Two of us were assigned. I was able to neutralize the real Major Baklova and his aide en route here to assist in this latest program. He was sent to create two assassins as well as to try to culminate the most successful experiment.....so far. They are programming an air force officer that has political connections. They've concocted some sort of plan to use the officer in a position of power by means of killing off officials and automatically moving him up. It's a long process but they feel worth the effort. They apparently feel that you two would make good assassins. They've been somewhat successful in doing this elsewhere in the world. Anyway boys it looks like we are banded together for some action and we're going to get it done quickly. If allowed to continue, it could be devastating to our government."

"We'll do what ever we have to do to get out of this hell hole and put them out of business, sir. Just give us the word" Sully said.

"We'll cool it for now. My assistant will keep the fake meds going but you guys gotta do some play acting."

"Hey, what about that little Korean Tae-Hyun? Does he work for you? He sure isn't your typical CIA agent" Tony asked curiously.

"Don't let that guy fool you. He could lay you out cold in two seconds flat. I've promised him that before we leave here he can do a number on those two smart ass guards. He's a ninth degree black belt and he's just itching to turn it loose. I'm glad he's on our side."

"Wow. I never would have guessed" said Tony "he said you've been infiltrating some POW camps. Are they as bad as we've heard?"

"They're worse than anything you've probably heard. In the prison camp at Taejon they took 60 prisoners 14 at a time, wired their hands behind their backs, sat them in hastily dug ditches, dug by themselves. And then shot them with American M-1 rifles at close range with armor piercing ammo, one at a time. These were the lucky ones."

"I saw dead soldiers that had been given the bamboo spear treatment. This is where heated bamboo spears are inserted into their bodies time after time until they die."

"The death marches were the worst. They take them from point of capture to a collecting point. Here they wait from 2 weeks to 5 months. They remove their heavy clothing and boots which leaves them exposed to the freezing cold. Then they march them to a permanent camp. On a march from Seoul to Pyongyong, about 250 miles, 376 men started out. Only 296 made it. One poor devil's feet were frozen and rotting. A Chinese guard amputated all but two of his toes with garden shears without benefit of anesthesia. Many others had frozen feet and hands. This is a deliberate Communist Policy to weaken prisoners and make them more vulnerable to incessant political probing and forced communist indoctrination."

"Okay. I've got to go. Tomorrow I'll be in with the two *mad doctors*. They'll have a laundry list of questions. Just act very sedate and even doze off a time or two. Answer the questions in a very confused state. Whatever you do don't get riled up. Remember you're just acting. Tae-Hyun will inject something in the I.V. line and when he does it will put you to sleep. Just flow with it. It won't hurt you and it will keep you out of trouble. I won't let them do any damage. Good luck. I'll be getting back to you."

He got up. Banged on the door and said. "Okay open up."

The major left the room.

"Sully, I don't go for all this business. We could just break out of here. I'm feeling pretty good now. What about it?"

"Belay that sailor. Let's go along with Bravo One, or whatever his cover is now. I think our best shot is to stick with what he says, at least for now. Let's get some shut eye and see what happens tomorrow."

"Okay, okay but I'm getting nervous. What did we get ourselves into here Sully? I keep thinking, maybe I should have joined the Air Force. My cousin Rosie was a pilot."

It was only a few days after her meeting with Jong-Cho that Sun-Hi found herself on a nondescript fishing boat heading north along the east coast of Korea. She was dressed in the typical crude, fish smelling clothing of a female fishing boat crew member. Her face had been scrubbed of any semblance of makeup and even stained to give her the look of a peasant with an unkempt face. If stopped and boarded by authorities they had to all look like poor fishermen.

The rest of the crew was also made to look like typical Korean fishermen with a freshly caught batch of fish to be unloaded at the market in Wonsan. The real cargo was some contraband that she didn't even want to know about. Some things were left better unsaid was the message she got from Jang-Chow.

He also told her that she was on her own after she got to Wonsan but her best bet was to try for a contact with Chin-Ho and he gave her instructions how this may be accomplished.

The fishing boat entered the harbor under cover of darkness and joined a fleet of other fishing boats gathered at the north end of the harbor. They rafted off of another boat.

The leader of the group said "Okay Missy, you come with me. I will do as *The Big One* instructed and put you in touch with a contact. After that my responsibility is done and my debt to *The Big One* is paid."

"I can take it from there" Sun said "just get me to the dock" as she picked up her ruck sack.

They climbed over the rafted fishing boats and finally got to the dock area. They were met by a seedy looking character who accepted a package from the fishing boat captain and the captain accepted a sack full of greenbacks. A short conversation ensued, of which was hardly audible to Sun. She caught a few words, one of which was '*The Big One*' and another was 'big favor'. She understood the gist of it.

The seedy character took a closer look at Sun, ogled a bit, and suddenly got very interested. He said "Yes I will be happy to assist the lady. I'm sure she won't mind staying at my humble abode while I locate Chin-Ho. It may take some time."

He turned to face her and with carnal desire in his eyes he cooed "You may even find comfort while I'm helping you and choose to stay longer to show appreciation for my help, sweet little lady."

Sun tensed up, got a no nonsense look on her face and very demurely said "You are very kind sir. And I also know you will be very cooperative since I am under the direct protection of *The Big One* and of course I promised to give him a complete report of how I'm treated on this journey. I'm sure you will find Chin quickly........as instructed. Now.......Shall we go?"

The seedy one blanched, looked around sheepishly and shakily said "Oh yes missy. We go now and I will make contact quickly."

They left the dock and climbed into an awaiting rickety car. They drove through the back streets of Wonsan, many of which Sun was familiar with because of her early years here. Soon they stopped at a typical house in a poor residential neighborhood. She had no history here but felt safe and waited until her driver spoke.

"I will leave you here at my house while I scout around and try to make contact with Chin-Ho. I know he is in the vicinity because he is still trying to recover a truck confiscated by the army. He's in the same business that I am, with *The Big One* as our benefactor. You will be safe here. Don't worry about my wife. She is sometimes excitable and does not understand all my comings and goings."

They went into the house. It was very unkempt and not clean. A woman with a small, dirty child in her arms arose from a sleeping mat and very irately blurted out a torrent of obscenities. She screamed "Who is this woman you bring into my house? Have you no regard for me, at all, to bring your whores here?"

"No, no. Be quiet you hag. She is not my woman. This is business. She has been sent by *The Big One* for us to give assistance. I must locate Chin-Ho and send her to him. I must do so or answer to *The Big One*. You cannot interfere with this. Failure would bring dire consequences and a severe beating for you."

The woman calmed down and withdrew to the next room muttering something obscene.

"She'll be okay. Since the baby came she has been very unhappy. I've promised to move her to the country soon. When she comes back from the benjo she'll be calmer."

"Sounds to me like you've given her reason to be unhappy. I intend to be here only as long as necessary. Please hurry." Sun said.

"Aw don't worry. She was on the street when I took her in. She knows she has no options."

"You pig. Get going. I want out of here as soon as possible."

"Don't get your panties in an uproar sweet lady. I'll find Chin. I will leave now and make some deliveries to my associates on the street. I'm sure one of them will have some information as to where I can get a message to Chin. I'll be back by daylight."

After he left, Sun opened her ruck sack and found a change of clothes. She was happy to get out of the fish smelling peasant clothes that she wore for the boat trip.

As she was dressing the woman came back into the room and stared at her.

Sun looked up and softly said "I won't intrude on you any more than I must. As soon as your husband finds a contact, I'll be out of here."

"He is not really my husband. Only in name. I would not stay with him if I didn't have the child. He is not even the father but he does not know this. I don't hate you. It's him that makes my life miserable."

"Why don't you leave the miserable cur?"

"Where would I go? Things are very different here in the north now. My family is either dead or in prison. I'm not beautiful like you so I must take what I can get."

"You poor woman. Here…..let me give you some money."

"No, no. He would only find it and take it from me after he beat me."

"Can I do anything?"

"No. Please sit and hold the baby. I will make tea."

They talked into the night and then both dozed off. When they awoke it was light and they soon heard the door open. The husband entered.

He gruffly said "I need breakfast, woman. MOVE!!"

The wife jumped up and scurried into the kitchen.

He turned to Sun. His tone changed and he said "One of my dealers saw Chin yesterday. He is in town. My man will make contact with Chin and tell him I must see him."

"Will Chin listen to him?"

"I also mentioned that this was direct from *The Big One* so he will listen. If he finds him today, we will hear from him soon."

The drug dealer ate his breakfast and went to bed. The woman followed him and Sun was alone. She sat and contemplated her fate. Was this a fruitless quest? What will she do if Sully is dead or a prisoner? Whatever the outcome, she must know. She won't rest until she knows if her lover is alive and if he is, she will find him.

CHAPTER TWENTY TWO

It was quite early when Tae-Hyun, the young Korean orderly, entered the room with his cart of medications. The two prisoners awoke from a drugged sleep and felt groggy and disoriented.

Sully said "What the hell did you give us? I feel horrible."

Their Korean ally smiled and said "I intentionally gave you both a shot of a drug to keep you sedated. Today is the first day of the oral part of the experiment and there will be questions and the start of the mind warping suggestive propaganda. At this time you should be entering the stage of submissive behavior. They will try to trick you with questions to ascertain if you have reached the point in the procedure that you should be. The Major and I want you to be disoriented and very unaware of your situation. In other words we want you to be spaced out, like you're on another planet or something. We weren't sure that you could carry this off without some assistance from drugs. As the days go by their plan is to bring you back from this drugged up state slowly after they have implanted a new electronic personality in your brain. You would then be, for all intents and purposes, outwardly the same person that you were before the treatment started. But inwardly, without your own knowledge, you will be under their hypnotic control. You would be robotic with a device implanted in your brain that can be turned off and on like a light switch."

"My God!! Can they do that? It seems impossible" questioned an unbelieving Tony.

"They've already come close. There's an Air Force pilot that's been here for months and he's now pretty much under their control. We've seen him and they gave us a demonstration to show the Major how far they've come" said Tae-Hyun.

"Are there any others like us? Asked Sully "I heard the guards talking about some other Americans. They don't know that I understand Korean."

"Yes, there are others here but we haven't found them as yet. We think they are failures in past experiments. There's a lot we don't know about this place yet. And apparently they don't tell the Russians everything. The Major is doing some nosing around and was up early today before the rest of them checking out the other wing. I haven't had a chance to find out if he was successful in locating any more patients."

"Wow this is some pretty serious stuff. I hope you and the Major have a plan on getting us out of here. I don't go for this psychological, mind warping junk. It pretty well shakes me up that they could do something to control my mind and I wouldn't even realize it" said Sully.

"Yeah, you're right. Okay, I'm going to give you guys another little boost of opiate to get you spaced out more. It's very important that they feel comfortable with your present condition. Both the Korean Doctor Rho, the Chinese Doctor Chan, as well as the Major and I will be in the treatment room with you. I'll be back here in about an hour with some help to get you moved to *The White Room*. Just remember to be very serene and just plain dopey. If you feel like it, you can even doze off from time to time. Just lay still while I shave a couple of spots on your heads."

"I'm feeling dopey already" Tony slurred.

Tae-Hyun left and the sailors dozed off.

The night before when the CIA operative, Pete, posing as Russian Major Baklova, left the two sailors, he returned to the small office that the Korean General had given him for his base operations. He also had been given a folder of reports which explained the history of past experiments. He wanted to study them to determine the outcome of the other Americans used up to this time. No disposition was given but in his own mind he feared the inevitable. They were probably disposed of after the study was made. It may have been the humane thing to do after driving them to the brink of insanity which was indicated by some of the reports.

He looked up as someone entered the room.

"Good evening Major" said the Korean Doctor Rho "I see you are burning the midnight oil."

"Yes General. I want to be prepared for tomorrow's session with the Americans. I feel we can make some headway here."

He answered "I am very optimistic about these new ones, what with your new serum available and the recent success with the American Air Force officer."

"Will I be able to interview this patient? I met him but was not given the opportunity to interview him. Also, how about the other ones in the east wing. I understand there are four more in process?"

"Of course. I can set up a session with the officer later tomorrow. But I'm afraid the other four will be transferred to a more secure facility and would serve you no purpose."

"Hmm. Very well then, I will look forward to a session with the American officer."

"Goodnight Major. Don't work too late. We have a full day for tomorrow."

"Goodnight General. I will retire to my room as well. Will our Chinese comrade be joining us for the session with the two Americans?"

"Oh yes. He has had success with this type of experiment in China. He can give valuable input."

The Major retired to his room and remained until all was quiet. He slipped out into the empty hall and made his way towards the east wing.

When he got to the closed door he peered through the glass window in the door and saw a soldier sitting at a desk just inside. He was reading and seemed very comfortable with his feet up on the desk.

The Major tried the door and found it was locked. He rattled the handle and the soldier was startled and looked up wide eyed. He arose, walked to the door and with muffled voice said "Yes sir. May I help you?"

"Open the door" Pete said in a commanding tone.

"I am under orders to allow no one to enter sir."

"You fool" in a raised voice "I am the one who gave the orders. Do you realize who I am? Open the door. I'm checking on security here and it seems you are pretty lax at your station with unauthorized reading material and inattentiveness. I was standing here observing you for five minutes and you didn't respond. UNLOCK THIS DOOR NOW."

The soldier nervously unlocked the door and stood back as the Major entered.

"When was the last time you made your rounds?"

"Well…Ah..ah…I checked on the patients when I came on duty and they are all comatose as they have been for several days."

"What were their vitals?"

"I don't take vitals sir."

"How do you know their status?"

"There is no status to report sir. These men will be transferred tomorrow."

"Transferred? Transferred where?"

"Well...well...I guess to the same place the rest were sent."

"I want to see them."

"Yes sir. Come with me."

He followed the soldier into a large ward where six beds were lined up on one side of the room. Four of the beds had men lying in them. The Major observed each one. They were all unconscious and one seemed to be breathing very shallow. Two of them gave an occasional spasm with their heads jerking from side to side. When he approached the fourth one, the man's eyes fluttered open. He looked at the Major and with a pained look on his face he started crying.

"The Major said in English "What's the matter son?"

The soldier blurted out "Please. No more. No more."

He sobbed and closed his eyes and drifted off in a troubled state of half consciousness sobbing like a child.

The Major turned to the soldier and said "I don't want these men moved out of here. I will speak to the General the first thing in the morning."

"I only do as I am told sir. I have no authority to do anything."

"You will hear from the General."

He gruffly turned on his heel and left. When he got back to his room he sat on the edge of his bed, put his head in his hands and muttered "Those bastards."

The next morning he went to the main office and asked to see the General and was shown in immediately.

"Good morning Doctor Rho. I'd like to speak to you about the four Americans in the east wing."

"Yes, I heard that you paid them a visit quite late last night. It was fortunate that you observed them before they were transferred this morning."

"You mean they are gone?"

"Oh yes. Quite early, in fact."

"Where will they be sent?"

"Oh come now Major. They served our purpose and now will be disposed of very humanely. Your concern should be the success of future experiments and not the learning curve that we discovered on the past ones. Shall we have tea before we start with today's patients?"

As the Major stood speechless, the Chinese Doctor Chin entered and said "Am I late for tea?"

"No, of course not. The Major and I were just going to indulge. Please join us."

"If you gentlemen would excuse me, I have arranged an inspection of the prisoner's wing in the main hospital. I would like to compare it to the Russian facilities where we housed German prisoners in the last war" said the Major.

"By all means, Major. I think you will find it more to your liking. We have some interesting procedures there."

The Korean Doctor Rho turned and poured his tea.

CHAPTER TWENTY THREE

Sun tried to busy herself during the day. The man and his wife were sleeping and she heard the baby crying. She looked in the bedroom and saw the baby lying in a filthy baby basket. She quietly stole in and picked up the child. The poor thing was hungry and very dirty.

She cuddled the baby and he quieted down and sucked on his thumb. She went into the kitchen, looked in the cupboard and found a crust of bread and in the ice box was a half bottle of milk. She mixed bits of bread with the milk and spoon fed the baby. This seemed to satisfy the child and it soon drifted off to sleep. She took him back to his bed and the woman roused and followed her back to the front room.

The woman said "I can give you some rice and tea. That's all we have until my husband wakes up and goes for food."

Sun answered "That will be fine. I hope to be gone by tonight or tomorrow.

The rest of the day passed slowly and when the man of the house awoke he left to get some groceries. He returned later with chicken and more rice which the woman fixed into an evening meal. They ate in silence.

It was late into the night, the man had left to tend to his dealers and Sun was dozing. A rap was heard at the door and the woman ran to answer it. It was Chin-Ho.

He entered and said "Well Sun-Hi, it's been a long time since our skirmish in Seoul. I'm surprised to see you back in the north. I thought you were lucky enough to get out of here and live in Pusan."

"I have been very fortunate since then Chin. I even found Sully and we have become a couple again. But he has disappeared and I'm trying to locate him. Can you help me?"

"I heard the rumor that you and Sully were together again. So it's true. But I'm afraid I don't have good news for you Sun. From what Min-Ho tells me, Sully, Tony and Jin-Sang were captured by a NK patrol. Jin-Sang was killed and the other two were taken as prisoners."

"I have checked with the Navy and neither has been reported as POW's. They are listed as MIA" added Sun.

"I know Sun. I also heard that but these people here in the north don't always follow the rules of the Geneva Convention. God only knows their fate."

"Do you think Min-Ho will tell me more?"

"The last I heard, you weren't Min-Ho's favorite person Sun, but you could try. She is supported by a Commie guy who I think was responsible for those guys getting caught. Maybe he knows something."

"How can she be with the man that had her brother killed?' Sun said.

"Things are not good here in the north Sun, even worse than they were when you escaped. She doesn't have much choice."

"Yes. I've heard the same story from this woman" lamented Sun.

"I will help you Sun, for old time's sake. Do you want to go see Min-Ho?"

"Oh yes. Yes. Can we do that?"

"We're in luck. I'm able to get the truck back through my brother-in-law who is working for the Commies, but I've got to get it out of town tonight. I'll get it as soon as I leave here and pick you up in about two hours. Be ready. Hopefully the shipment is still intact and I can deliver it tonight before day break. Then it's off to Hungnam where I pick up more merchandise. I can get you to see Min-Ho during the day when her paramour is off doing his Commie business. You can decide then if you want to stick with me or make your own plans. Is all of that okay?"

"Can I come with you now? It may save some time and I'm not very comfortable here."

"Sure but we have to move fast."

"Hey Chin. Don't forget who you're talking to. I might be a little older but I still remember the old days when we had the boat. We came through some pretty tight squeezes then too."

Chin smiled and said "Let's go Sun. This might be fun again."

She hugged the woman before she left and stuffed a few bills in her apron pocket. "Don't let him find it. Hide it and buy some food for the baby."

She left with Chin and piled into a car driven by one of his cohorts. They got to a fenced in area and got out of the car. Chin whistled and heard a return whistle. Soon a skinny little guy came out of the shack on the side of a parking area filled with trucks of every description.

The skinny guy was very uneasy and said "Hurry, hurry. Get the truck and get out of here. We've only got a little time before boss man comes back."

He opened the gate and tossed Chin a set of keys.

"Hurry. Must hurry" he said nervously.

"Okay. Okay. I'm just as anxious as you are."

Chin and Sun piled into the truck. The little guy had warmed it up so the engine kicked right over. Chin put it in gear and pulled out through the gate and onto the road.

He said "I'll stop as soon as we're clear and check for the shipment. It's well hidden in a compartment under the engine."

He drove for a short time and pulled into a garage. He hopped out, crawled under the truck and was back in about ten minutes.

He said "*The Big One* is going to be very happy with me. Everything looks intact. Let's make a delivery and go to Hungnam."

They drove the rest of the night after Chin dropped off the narcotics to his man for distribution on the street.

It was day break when they entered the outskirts of Hungnam and Sun had been napping.

"So do you recognize any of this area Sun?"

"Yes, some of it seems familiar but it's been a long time. If I remember Min-Ho lives pretty close by."

"That's right. It's only about a half hour away. We can't get there too early. We don't want to run into Sang-Yong. He's a gung ho Commie and got a real boost when he turned in our guys. We're dead meat if he sees us."

"What about Min-Ho? Can we trust her?"

"I'm pretty sure we can. I don't know how much help she'll give us but I don't think she'll turn us in.......at least as long as we don't get her in trouble."

"Can we stop somewhere so I can go to the bathroom?"

"Yes. I will make a pick up of the stuff from *The Big One* in about ten minutes. It's a safe house so we can get a bite to eat there and take a break. I'll load the stuff in the engine compartment and then take you to Min-Ho. I'll drop you off and go for my pickup of rice. Hauling bags of rice is my cover for the other stuff. It will be up to you to handle the meeting with Min. I'll give you about three hours and then return. You can decide then on your next step."

"I'm getting nervous now. What if Min hates the sight of me?"

"It could be so. You know the saying about a woman scorned."

"Well I have no choice. She's my only hope of finding Sully or at least finding out what happened to him."

They soon got to the safe house. They had driven through an area of military vehicles and NK soldiers. They even saw a detachment of Chinese soldiers in their pajama type uniforms.

After resting and eating they felt revitalized and Sun's confidence returned. She was taking needed steps to find her lover and this gave her strength.

They drove by Min's house and all looked quiet. No car was parked in front which hopefully meant that Sang-Yong had left for the day. One more drive by and they decided to stop down the street on their next pass.

Chin got out and walked to the house, leaving Sun in the truck just in case he ran into trouble. He arrived at the house and rapped on the door which opened immediately.

Min urgently said "Quickly. Come in before the neighbors see you."

Chin ducked inside and said "Hello Min. How did you know it was me?"

"You drove by enough times to make anyone suspicious. How many trucks do you think come down this street? I knew it was you. Now what do you want?"

"I have someone in the truck that wants to talk to you Min."

"Who would want to talk to me? And why? I must be careful who I'm seen with Chin. You know my situation here."

"Now just relax and sit down for a minute. This person needs information about Sully and feels that you may be able to help."

Min-Ho's face got a sad look. "That will only dredge up bad memories about my dead brother and that terrible night. Who is this person?"

"It's Sun-Hi."

It got very quiet.

Finally Min said "I'm not surprised that she would be concerned about him but I am surprised that she would have the courage to come here."

"She was very hesitant Min, but her love for Sully overcame any thought for her own well being."

"I will talk to her but there is not much that I can say. Bring her in but please be careful about being seen."

Chin left the house and hurried to the truck to bring Sun back to the house. He took her to the door and left.

When she entered Sun stopped just inside the door and faced a standing Min-Ho. Both stared at each other and neither spoke at first.

Finally Min said "Well Sun you have retained your beauty. You always could dazzle the men without saying a word."

"Thank you Min. I'm sorry if you were hurt. Neither Sully nor I would do anything to affect our friendship with you. Can you forgive us?"

"All that is past history, Sun. So much has changed and not all for the better. I live pretty well here now but not without drawbacks. If you are not a Communist then you must at least agree with the Communist beliefs. I live with a man who is advancing higher in the local regime which gives me some luxuries that others would love to have. This creates some jealousies with people who used to be my friends. But now without my brother, who was my only family left because of these awful wars during the last ten years, I must fend for myself. I put up with the occasional cruelties of Sang-Yong because it is my means of survival."

"You are a brave woman Min. I don't envy your situation but I can sympathize with you. I will not jeopardize you. Can you give me any information about Sully and Marino?"

"The only hope I can give you is that they were taken alive when my brother was killed. Sang told me that he tried to have them all taken as prisoners but an Army officer executed Jin before he could intercede. I don't know if that is true. A farmer that lives nearby the spot where they blocked the road said that the two Americans were beaten and taken away in a truck. I can't tell you anymore."

"Is there anyone that would have this information?"

"I guess the Party Headquarters would have someone who knows where they were imprisoned or possibly worse."

Sun looked mournfully at Min. Her eyes filled with tears and she stammered "I....I must know. I cannot rest until I find out if he is still alive."

"I've told you all that I know Sun."

"Could Sang-Yong find out more?" Sun asked.

"He may be able to but there is no way he would cooperate with you and I cannot take any chance in asking. He would not hesitate in putting me on the street or worse."

"Is Party Headquarters located in the old municipal building?"

"Yes but what are you thinking?"

"You didn't know me then, but my family lived here when I was young and when I was in school my father worked as a janitor there. He used to take me to work at night and I would pretend to be a city official sitting at the big desks. I have a plan. Can you give me names and positions of the main officials there?"

"Yes I can but you are taking a big chance."

"Give me the names of the men that Sang must report to and what is Sang's family name?"

"Sang's last name is Rah. His immediate superior is Park Yong-Sook Nahm. He is a defector from the south. The top man in Wonsan is Lee Suk-Chul Shinn. Those are the only ones that I have met."

"Where did Park Yong-Sook come from?" Sun asked.

"The story goes that he was a police officer in Seoul and got in big trouble. He ran away to the north and became a Communist."

"That's interesting. His name is familiar. I noticed women in uniform when we drove here. What are they?"

"That is just standard dress for Party Workers. If you belong to the Party you can wear one while you perform any menial duty."

"Do you have one of these uniforms?"

"Of course. Since I live with Sang, it is required of me."

"Would you consider letting me use it?"

"Oh my God! I couldn't do that. What if Sang found out?"

"I will return it. I will be very careful. If I was caught I would say that I stole it."

Min was wringing her hands and pacing the floor trying to make up her mind.

Just then Chin showed up. He said "Okay Sun we've got to hit it. I'm all loaded and I want to move this stuff."

Sun turned to Min and said "Please Min."

"All right. All right. I've got two of them. Take it and leave. Don't come back. I don't want to see you again."

She ran from the room and came back with clothing wrapped up in a ball. She was crying as she roughly pushed the bundle at Sun and said "Now go. I will deny that I ever saw you."

CHAPTER TWENTY FOUR

Sun and Chin ran down the street where Chin had parked the truck. They jumped in and he quickly got it underway.

"Okay, unless you want to come with me on my run you will be on your own Sun."

"I have a plan Chin. Just drop me off at your safe house where I can change clothes and you can be on your way. Thank you for everything. I've got to see this thing through."

He looked at Sun with disapproval and said "I think you are either nuts or a very determined girl,"

She smiled and said "You'd be surprised at how determined I am and maybe a little nuts too. I've struggled all my life and managed to beat the odds. I'm not giving up now."

They pulled in at the farm house and Chin said "Good luck and I hope you find Sully. Ask the farmer to take you into town with his truck load of produce. He goes in once a week and I think today is the day."

"Good bye Chin and be careful."

Sun changed into the uniform she had gotten from Min-Ho. Min was a bit smaller than her so the skirt was shorter than she liked but for her purposes it might be even better to have a short skirt and fit a little snug.

She packed the rest of her belongings in her ruck sack except for a few necessities which she kept in her purse. She rode to the edge of the Central Market where the farmer delivered his produce. She walked to the center of town and checked into a small inexpensive hotel.

If she had not been dressed in the uniform, she may have been refused and even then she was questioned to ascertain if she was a prostitute or not.

By explaining that she was going to do clerical work for Park Yong-Sook Nahm and only needed temporary lodging she was readily accepted.

She went to the room and freshened up and decided to try her luck at Party Headquarters.

Her first stop was at an office supply store where she bought a small leather portfolio, a steno pad, two pencils and a clip board with a small amount of paper.

She confidently walked up the stairs of the Party Headquarters offices. A uniformed guard sat at the entrance desk and stopped her.

"Can I be of assistance" he cooed.

This will be easy thought Sun.

She gave him her biggest dazzling smile. "I am here to see Captain Nahm. I'm to assist him on a project, but I'm ashamed to say that I have never met him."

"Of course. Please sign in. You are new here. I've never seen you before and I'm sure I would remember."

"I just arrived in town from Party Headquarters in Wonsan and I'm still struggling to find my way around. Can anyone guide me? I would be very thankful" she breathed a sigh.

The guard clearly melted. "Please wait while I get my assistant to relieve me and I would be most pleased to take you on a tour."

He rose and scurried off and quickly found a relief. He said to the soldier "Take over the desk. I think I've got a live one. Boy that Captain Nahm can really pick 'em."

When he returned he said "My assistant will take over so I'll be free to show you around. What may I call you?"

"My name is Sun-Hi and what is yours Sergeant?"

"My name is Lee and I haven't made sergeant yet. But very soon, I am sure. Please come with me."

They started the tour and Sun made special note of the offices of Sang-Yong Rah, Park Yong-Sook Nahm and where the empty offices were as well as noting how many women were in the steno pool.

"Will we see the offices of Comrade Suk-Chul Shinn?"

"You really are an ambitious lady aren't you" said Lee. "No. Comrade Shinn is on the third floor and only special passes go there."

"Oh of course. How silly of me. It is the same in Wonsan."

"I've shown you the building. Would you like me to take you to Captain Nahm's office?"

"I have seen where it is and I have some preparations to make before I see him. I'm so lax, I should have done it last night but I guess some fun time got in the way." She giggled.

"Maybe you could use one of the empty offices. There are a few. Will you be long?"

"Probably a few hours and then I can meet with him."

"Come, I'll take you. Would you like me to show you the town tonight after work? Perhaps have a bite to eat. Maybe a drink?"

"Let me see how much work the Captain gives me. I will see you on the way out. If not tonight, perhaps tomorrow."

"It will be my great pleasure" He said and bowed.

He showed her into an office and left, leaving the door open.

She busied herself, opening her portfolio, shuffling papers and waiting until the hall was clear.

She gathered her papers and started to rise to leave when an official looking man stopped at the door and said "Good morning. I didn't know that this office was in use. Are you new here?"

"Yes, my name is Sun-Hi Kyu-Bak. I'm new in the steno pool but don't have an assigned desk as yet. I was told to be attentive to Comrade Rah and Comrade Nahm but I have not had the opportunity to report to them. My escort told me to wait here until arrangements have been made but perhaps he forgot. Could you direct me to Comrade Rah?"

"I am Comrade Rah. And I saw the guard escorting you. I can't understand why he didn't leave you at my office."

"Oh please don't blame him. I think he was trying to impress me. He wanted to take me to see Comrade Nahm first but Comrade Nahm was busy."

"Yes….sounds like he was trying to feather his own nest. I will take over now. Please come with me."

They walked down the hall to Sang Yong's office. He closed the door and asked her to sit across from him.

He asked "Who assigned you to this office?"

"I came from Wonsan sir. I was in the pool there but the other girls felt that I was no longer needed. A group of them went to my boss and asked that I be transferred" she answered and then looked at him with a sheepish glance.

"Hmm. I see."

Tears welled up in her eyes "I worked very hard sir. I don't know why they didn't like me. Everyone else seemed to like my work."

"I think I understand young lady. Perhaps you should use the empty office for now. I will take you to meet Comrade Nahm and we will decide the next step. In the meantime I have some correspondence to get out and a stack of files to be put back. You can do that while I advise comrade Captain Nahm of your arrival."

"Oh thank you sir" she gushed "I'll get busy on that right away."

After he left she busied herself putting the files back in the cabinets and took the correspondence to the empty office to get it ready for mailing.

While she was working in her temporary office, Sang-Yong Rah entered with another gentleman in a Captains uniform. She stood and drew in a startled breath when she saw his face. It was the same Captain that she had an encounter with in Seoul.

When he saw her he slowly grinned and said "Yes it is the same Sun-Hi that I knew while I was with the Seoul Police Department. How are you Sun? It seems that time has made changes for both of us."

She quickly composed herself and with a confident voice said "Why Comrade Captain, I had no idea that you had decided to join us here in the north. I was very happy to return here to my home after my encounter with the authorities in the south."

"Yes I remember your escape very well. In fact the result was a determining factor in my enlightenment to join the Communist Party. When Seoul was retaken by our Chinese comrades shortly after we met, I made an easy transition."

Sang-Yong looked pleased that his boss seemed happy and said "I was not doubtful that you would welcome Comrade Sun-Hi but I had no idea that there was a previous relationship. Of course she will primarily be your secretary. I would not want to tie her up."

"Nonsense Comrade Sang-Yong, we can share. I think giving her the empty office is a good move. Let's keep it that way."

"Oh thank both of you" again she gushed "I hope this is alright with the other girls."

"Don't worry about them" Captain Nahm said sternly "they will do as they are told."

As the men turned to leave, Captain Nahm said "When you've finished with Comrade Rah's letters, Sun, come to my office for some dictation."

"Yes sir. I'll be along soon."

After they left, Sun sat and breathed a sigh of relief.

Now that I'm in, I've got to make some friends in the steno pool. That's where I'll get the information that I need. Stenos know everything, even more than the bosses. She thought to herself.

She finished up her work for Sang-Yong and walked into the bullpen where the stenographers were stationed. She picked out an older woman who looked to be in charge of the pool and stopped at her desk.

"Good morning Comrade. My name is Comrade Sun-Hi and I just arrived today. You've probably been notified about my transfer here but I'm very confused. I hope you can help me. I don't want to get started on the wrong foot."

"Well first of all I have no notice of a transfer. Where did you come from?"

"Party Headquarters at Wonsan. It was quite sudden."

"It's not unusual that we don't get notification before the fact. It may follow. Who are you to report to?"

"Comrade Rah and Comrade Captain Nahm is what they told me and they have already given me assignments even before I reported to the pool. I hope it won't be a problem."

"Oh, now I understand. Yes Comrade Captain Nahm. He sometimes circumvents protocol. I'm not surprised. Do you know him?"

"Yes, I met him when he was with the Police Force in Seoul. He had somewhat of a reputation there."

"Well he brought his antics with him here in Hungnam. You'd best be careful with that man. I wouldn't let him get you behind a closed door if you know what I mean."

"I'm very aware, but I'm also concerned because they gave me an office. Shouldn't I be out here with the other girls?"

"Hmm…These office politics are frowned upon by Comrade Shinn. I will take care of it my dear. Just do as they say until you hear from me."

"Oh thank you Comrade Madam. You are very kind" she said dripping with sweetness.

She left the bull pen and went to the next floor to the office of Captain Nahm. She knocked on his door and heard him say "Enter".

She entered and leaving the door open she said "I'm here for dictation sir."

"Please sit" he said "I notice that you left the door open, my dear. Perhaps when you become more familiar you will prefer it to be closed. You will be well advised to know that I can make things very comfortable for you here. I have even more authority than I did in Seoul."

"Please, sir, let me get situated here. I don't want to be forced to leave as I was in Wonsan."

"I understand. I am a patient man. Now I have several letters to dictate."

"I am ready. Please proceed."

After an hour of dictation she left and was going back to her office to type the letters when she encountered Comrade Madam who said to her "I have taken care of the private office situation Comrade Sun. Bring your belongings to the bull pen and I will assign you a work station with a typewriter. You will continue to work for Comrades Rah and Nahm but you will be under my direction. I'm sure we will work well together."

"I'm very relieved Comrade Madam and very thankful to have made a friend. I will be very loyal to you and the Party."

"You may come in very handy, my dear."

CHAPTER TWENTY FIVE

Tony and Sully were in a dreamless sleep when they were roughly jolted awake by two Chinese orderlies. Tony was disoriented and momentarily confused as to where he was. The room was spinning as the orderly sat him up in his bed but he felt strangely relaxed and compliant to the rough treatment he was getting.

An outburst of Korean that he couldn't understand came from the doorway. When he looked through the haze he could see that it was their young Korean friend, Tae-Hyun, who obviously didn't like the rough treatment they were getting. Tony glanced over at Sully who was half sitting up and had a blank look on his face.

One of the Chinese orderlies answered the reprimand sharply but immediately changed his demeanor and handled Tony with more care. They placed him in a wheel chair and then they left him to roust out Sully and also put him in a wheel chair.

Next came a trip down the hall to an elevator and up one floor. They then entered a large room with a bank of electronic devices along two walls. The room was painted white and seemed antiseptically clean. A pungent odor was evident, like a combination of electronics and strong soap.

The confusion was still there and it was difficult to sort things out. Tony decided to just flow with it and see what happens. He looked at Sully who just grinned and slightly shrugged his shoulders. He was spaced out too.

Both were stationed under a head set and the orderlies busied themselves attaching wires with sticky pads to shaved spots on their heads. The other end of the wires terminated in two large electronic devices, one for each of them, that had a round greenish screen that reminded Tony of an oscilloscope.

The Korean Doctor Rho and Chinese Doctor Chan came in dressed in medical scrubs. They were in a somewhat heated conference with Major Baklova.

The Korean orderly, Tae-Hyun, stood to the rear of them and soon broke away and sauntered over. He whispered "Just relax. They will begin soon. Don't be frightened, this is a preliminary session. No permanent therapy will take place. The electronic leads attached to your heads are to establish a base for future therapy, but we don't plan on reaching that point. The Major will discuss a plan with you.......sh...sh... here they come."

"Well I see that our American friends have reached a very comfortable state of mind. How about it, Marino, are you comfortable?"

Tony stared at him and nodded his head.

"Good, good....and how about you Sullivan, are you okay?"

"I'm....O..kay" Sully slurred.

"Very well then. My Chinese colleague will perform some tests on each of you. No response from you is required at first. There will be a series of tones getting louder and shriller at times. It may cause some discomfort but will not last long. The doctors and orderlies put ear plugs in their ears and the Chinese doctor disappeared behind them. They could hear him adjusting a device and soon a tone sounded. This was followed by succeeding tones each getting louder until the noise caused pain in their ears.

When Tony raised his hands to cover his ears an orderly pulled them down and tied them to the arm rest. The Korean doctor made a note on his pad. Soon after, the same thing happened to Sully.

Thankfully it was soon over. The ear plugs came out of the observer's ears and a conference between the doctors took place in front of the electronic screens.

"We will now apply electronic stimulus and let your hearing return to normal before the oral tests begin."

These tests took the best part of the rest of the morning with much hustling and bustling of the doctors and orderlies. The Russian Major Baklova was an observer and not a participant so far.

Soon they rested.

The Korean doctor gathered the group and said "This will be enough for this morning. I want to break for lunch and examine some of the data."

He turned to Tae-Hyun and said "Bring them some light refreshment. Some rice and water will suffice. No more medication for now. I want them somewhat alert for the oral tests."

They all left except for the two Chinese orderlies who stayed to watch over them.

While the doctors ate a plentiful lunch, they discussed the notes and printed graphs from the morning tests.

The Korean Doctor Rho was not happy with some of the results and with obvious concern he said "The noise levels are not a concern but the electronic stimulus should be more pronounced. Have they been getting the proper dosage? Prior results on the other subjects were different than these."

The Major said "It is obvious to me that some problems existed with your other subjects otherwise you wouldn't have had to exterminate them. Why would you want the test results to be the same?"

The Korean squirmed in his chair and was noticeably embarrassed by his Russian comrade.

The room grew quiet and finally the Chinese doctor said "I agree with our Korean colleague but perhaps understandable since we have adjusted the medication. Let us continue with the experiment and perhaps make another adjustment. I have other medication from my Chinese lab that we can try."

"And I also have had experience with this procedure" said Major Ballova "it would have been helpful if the elimination of the four patients was not so rushed. I would have perhaps gained some knowledge on what was done in error."

"We made no error" Doctor Rho adamantly proclaimed "we are still experimenting."

"That is exactly why I'm here! To help you correct the procedures you've used up to this point. I still have not been given the courtesy of examining the Air Force Officer. Why?"

"You may examine him later today. There had been a slight set back early this morning but all is in order now."

The rest of the lunch was eaten in silence. There was a definite uncomfortable feeling among the three comrades.

Tony and Sully had eaten their sparse lunches and had been allowed to use the bathroom since they were no longer tied down.

"You okay?" Sully whispered.

"Yeah. Not as dizzy. How 'bout you?"

"Okay but gettin' tired of this crap"

"Me too. Let's just act woozy and out of it. Maybe they'll quit for the day."

"NO TALKING IN THERE" a command came from the outer room.

The boys went back to their chairs and nodded off.

Finally the doctors came back in and the Chinese doctor shook them awake.

He said "I will give you a word and you respond with the first thing that comes to your mind. I will ask you first Marino."

Tony looked at him with a blank stare.

"Mother" said the doctor.

Tony slurred something unintelligible.

The doctor gave a questioning look to the other doctors.

He again said "Mother".

Tony just stared and his eyes drooped.

The doctor tried several other words and got little or no response.

He arose and said "This is useless." He looked at Sully who was softly snoring.

"I suggest that we change to the medication that I brought from my lab in China. It has less of a drug effect and more stimuli. A twenty four hour dosage will tell us if it will be more effective than the meds that they are now on."

"I agree that some other procedure be adopted" said the Major "these experiments up to now are worthless."

The Korean Doctor Rho bristled with indignation "How can you say they have been worthless? The experiment with the American pilot has gone very well."

"You've kept him pretty well hidden. I must make a report to the Kremlin very soon. They are getting impatient. When can I talk to him?"

"Very soon" he said sharply and turned to the orderly Tae-Hyun. "Take these men back to their room and see our Chinese Comrade for their medication." He turned on his heel and stalked out.

After they were settled back in their room, the friendly Korean orderly said "Make sure you don't swallow the pills I give you later. Try to clear your heads because the Major may want to make a move soon. When he does it will be fast."

It was several hours later the orderly came in with his tray of pills. He had a very serious look on his face.

"Looks like this is it, guys. The Major went to interview the American pilot and found him hanging from the overhead by his belt. He committed suicide. He is really pissed. He's not sure that this wasn't contrived because when he took the body down, the marks on the throat didn't really match up with the way the belt was around the neck."

"That poor bastard. Well maybe he's just as well off. No telling what his mental condition would be after what he went through." Sully lamented.

"Okay listen, Doctor Chan gave me some capsules that I'm supposed to give to you every two hours for the rest of the day up until midnight and then again at 0400 hours and 0800 hours. Each time I come in I'll flush them down the toilet. If anyone comes in other than me, pretend like you're asleep. If they give you meds, don't swallow them."

"Do you know what the Major plans to do?" asked Tony.

"All I know is he's ready and his assignment was to infiltrate, gain intelligence and put them out of business. He's checking out the prisoner wing of the hospital here on the grounds. It's not good."

"If he operates anything like he did at Inchon, he'll be moving quickly and thoroughly" said Sully "we'll be ready when he needs us."

"Good. See you in two hours."

CHAPTER TWENTY SIX

"I hope Major Baklova moves quickly" complained Tony "I'm tired of all this play acting."

"I don't think we'll have to wait much longer" answered Sully "you could just sense his disgust when we were in the treatment room. There was one time when I thought he was gonna take a swing at that Korean Doctor Rho. I wonder who made him a General anyway. Prob'ly a political thing. He sure isn't a Line Officer."

They waited in silence for several hours and were getting impatient and ready to jump into action. The adrenalin was starting to flow and they had been out of circulation all too long.

The door clanked open and Tae-Hyun entered in a flourish.

"The Major has decided to hold off any action but he's really chompin' at the bit. It seems that some higher ups in the Party are getting impatient with the operation down here in Wonsan and supposedly a contingent of political authorities are being sent here to investigate. The two doctors are all aflutter. They've wasted a lot of lives with nothing to show for it."

"Oh man…C'mon….me and Sully are ready to knock some heads. What's the hold up? Can't we just do the job before they come?"

"The Major said to wait. Maybe we can eliminate the replacements as well as the ones that are here now. Might be some prime Commies in this bunch."

"What do you want us to do?" asked Sully.

"Just play it cool for a while. They want me to continue with the Chinese medication and then they plan on injecting some serum before the investigation team shows up late tomorrow. I think they want to put on a 'dog and pony' show the day after tomorrow. It's rushing their plans a little but I think the two mad doctors are struggling to keep their positions. These Commies don't mess around and once the Russians get into it, human lives are immaterial. Even their own comrades."

"Hey Tae-Hyun, we don't want more of that stuff that zonked us out, like you gave us before. We want to be aware of what's going on so we can react if this thing is getting close" Sully said.

"Yeah, we can put on the act a while longer" Tony said.

"Don't worry, I'm only giving you APC's and I'll make some kind of a switch on the serum if it even gets to that point" Tae said.

He called the guard to open the door and left the room.

Sully turned to Tony and said "Stay alert pal. Tomorrow afternoon should be real interesting.

Back in the Party Headquarters at Hungnam a meeting was taking place among the hierarchy of the Communist Party leaders from Russia, China and North Korea.

The Russian, obviously in charge, made an announcement to the throng of ten men with various degrees of high responsibility in the Party.

"After hearing the report of operatives that have secretively infiltrated the operation in Wonsan, it is obvious that we may have some failures in the experiment. It has been somewhat successful, in the past, in the Mother country. It is time to make some changes either in medical people or certainly in operation procedures. I feel that certain personnel at Party Headquarters in Wonsan may be too close to the situation to come to a successful conclusion. It is therefore my decision to send an advisory unit to the Wonsan Laboratory to ascertain our next steps."

The high ranking Chinese representative declared "We have sent a very reliable doctor to assist in these experiments. In our contact with him it seems that the Korean General has control of the situation and does not take kindly to any interference with his actions."

A North Korean official bristled "This was not a cut and dried activity. It is still experimental and any success by the Russian Government is still not entirely determined. We asked for input from both of you and all we are getting is distasteful arrogance."

"ENOUGH" exclaimed the Russian "we will investigate before any decision is made. I understand there is a former police captain that defected from the south here in Hungnam. He is experienced in investigative police work and is in charge of Security here. He seems to be the type of man to ferret out any misuse or ineptness prevalent in Wonsan without favoritism to any individual. My superiors in the Kremlin have given this experiment a high priority. My orders are to proceed post haste."

The men sitting around the table all nodded or spoke in agreement to proceed right away.

"Good. I will contact Captain Nahm, brief him on the assignment and give him the authority to head up a team. I, of course, will be on the team as a civilian observer. I have brought with me a Psychiatrist, who is very experienced in this type of procedure. I will include him on the team even though we have a capable Russian doctor already on site. The team should leave for Wonsan tomorrow to arrive before dusk. This meeting is adjourned"

Sun-Hi was busy typing at her desk when she felt a presence behind her. She looked up and said "Good afternoon Comrade Madame. I was engrossed in my typing and didn't hear you approach."

"Quite all right Sun. I have been told to summon you to Captain Nahm's office. You will be meeting with him and several other officials. I have also been told what this meeting will entail and I want you to know I resisted sending you but I was overruled."

"Oh my, this sounds like something I might not like" Sun said.

"Well it means going back to Wonsan but not to Party Headquarters. It's to an experimental laboratory at Peoples Hospital."

"But I am not a medical person. Why me?"

"It seems Captain Nahm has requested you to be on a team to investigate an experiment. An office person is needed to audit office records and transcribe the findings of the investigation. I recommended a more experienced girl but was told to mind my own business. I did not want to lose you. I…I like to be near to you."

"Oh…oh…ah…How many are going?"

"I'm not sure, at least two Russians and the Captain. I have heard it involves some experimental procedures on prisoners."

"Are the prisoners criminals or POW's?"

"My understanding is that they are Americans and involve psychiatric findings. You better go now. They are waiting."

Sun left in relief and quickly walked to the Captains office. She thought *This may be my opportunity to talk to American POW's who may have heard where Sully has been sent. It's a remote chance but at least it's a chance.*

She knocked on Captain Nahm's door and got a quick response to enter. She observed two Russian civilians and the Captain sitting around his desk. They all rose and the older Russian leered, turned to the Captain and said "Oh yes, I see."

"Please sit Comrade Sun" said Captain Nahm.

She sat in the one empty chair and said "Thank you."

"I want to introduce you to our Russian comrades from the Kremlin. This is Comrade Ivan Yushakova and Comrade Igor Robachov.

Both Russians nodded, smiled and uttered a Russian phrase not understandable to Sun.

They sat and the apparent leader nodded to Captain Nahm to begin.

"Sun-Hi, we have been given the honor of accompanying our Russian Comrades on a special assignment in Wonsan. I know you are familiar with the city and are very adept at transcribing notes. It has been ordered that you accompany us. We will be leaving early tomorrow morning therefore when we are finished here, you are to go to your hotel and pack for a possible extended stay. Living quarters have been arranged in the Peoples Hospital in Wonsan."

He continued " I would like to make it plain that this is a secret mission and you are to tell no one of the findings nor are you to notify anyone at Wonsan Party Headquarters about the mission, either before we arrive or after we have completed it. Do you understand?"

"Yes sir. I understand. This is quite sudden but I will be ready to go in the morning. Should I come here?"

"Yes. There will be a vehicle to take us to the hospital."

Sun left and picked up her personal belongings at her desk. By then it was getting late into the day. When she passed Sang Yong Rah's office he motioned her in.

He said "You are very fortunate to be assigned to this mission Sun. I have worked for years to achieve my status. You have an opportunity to advance yourself in the Party quickly."

"I am aware of this chance to help the Party but do you know anything further about it?"

"All I know is that it is an experiment with high priority. It involves American prisoners. I have heard that some captured here in Hungnam are confined there."

"Thank you Sang-Yong. I will do a good job for our comrades."

She walked away, trembling, and left for her hotel afraid to believe that this may be the first concrete lead to find her lover.

When she arrived she packed all her belongings. If Sully was there or if someone could tell her where she could find him, she would not be back. In her heart she knew that he was still alive.

CHAPTER TWENTY SEVEN

The team of investigators traveled in a six passenger, Russian made vehicle. It was very utilitarian, not many creature comforts and had a very stiff suspension. The three hour drive to Wonsan over war torn roads was very uncomfortable. Sun-Hi was stiff and sore from the constant bouncing in the military vehicle.

When they arrived it was late in the afternoon. They were met by a Russian civilian whose attention was focused on Comrade Ivan Yushakova. He was not introduced to them. The two conversed quickly in Russian. It was obvious that Comrade Yushakova was of importance.

"There will be orderlies to unload your luggage and show you to your quarters" said Comrade Yushakova "I will notify you of our itinerary as soon as I meet with my aide."

Sun-Hi was shown to a room in the nurses quarters. She settled in and decided to explore and perhaps ask questions. The hospital was predominately for military men. She noticed both Korean and Chinese male patients. It was a typical military hospital except for one area that was heavily guarded. When she reached the heavily barred doors she was stopped by guards and asked her business.

She replied "I am here with the inspection team from Hungnam and just familiarizing myself with the facility."

The guard at the desk said "Welcome Comrade, but this area is for prisoners and only those with special passes are allowed entrance."

"I see. Thank you. I will try to obtain this special pass."

As she turned to leave, the doors swung open and a high ranking Russian officer came bursting through the entrance and almost knocked her over. He looked distraught but he pulled up to a halt and said "Excuse me Comrade. I am late for a meeting and did not expect anyone on this side of the door."

"You are forgiven Comrade Major. I should not be standing in a vulnerable spot."

He saluted, turned on his heel and left.

She turned to the desk and asked "He looks like an important man. May I ask who?"

"That is Major Nikolai Baklova from the Kremlin. He is also visiting. But his work is in the laboratory on the grounds. They deal with mental patients there."

"Ah yes, then I will probably see him tomorrow since our inspection involves that kind of thing. How many patients are there?"

"It is difficult to say Madame Comrade. We are not allowed access. But once they are admitted they usually are not seen leaving except by hearse."

She shuttered and walked back to her quarters. She didn't want to cause any suspicion or raise any alarm.

As she was entering her room Captain Nahm stopped and spoke to her.

"Good evening my dear. Are you comfortable in your quarters?"

"Yes they are more than adequate, thank you for asking."

She turned to enter her room.

"Please wait a moment Sun-Hi. I suppose you know it was me that made the decision to bring you on this trip. I could have brought anyone. Male or female, I chose you."

"I am aware that you chose me Captain and I will do an efficient job for you."

"I have no doubt of that. I have been told that you are a very good worker. I can see to it that you are moved along very quickly in the Party if you play your cards right."

"Please, Captain, I'd prefer not to be in the same predicament that I was faced with in Seoul."

"Of course not, my dear. I will wait until you feel the time is right. I am a patient man but I do have a limit. I'm sure that when you see the benefits of working towards a common goal with me as your benefactor, your intelligence will weigh heavily in the matter."

He paused and leered momentarily before he said "I am patient my dear. Please do not hesitate to ask if you need anything. Anything."

He turned and left.

She entered her room and closed the door. Her room mates glanced up and saw that she was shaken.

The youngest one asked "Are you okay? You look in distress."

"Yes, I'm alright. Just tired from the trip, I guess."

"Can I get you a glass of water?" The young nurse asked.

"That would be kind of you" answered Sun.

Sun sat on the edge of her bed.

The nurse came and handed her the water.

"Thank you" said Sun.

"You're very welcome. My name is Mae-Hin. What is yours?"

"I am called Sun-Hi."

"Are you here for administrative purposes?"

"Yes. I am with the inspection team from Hungnam."

The girl dropped her eyes and said "Oh".

Sun waited a minute and then said "Is something wrong?"

"No, no. Please, I am new to ways of the Party. Please don't say anything to anyone. I am in enough trouble speaking out against the psychiatric experiments."

"I would not say anything. Tell me about the experiments. I have heard that no one leaves alive from there."

"I can't say any more. Please don't ask."

"Have you been there?"

"Yes. Unfortunately psychiatry was my specialty in school. I was sent to work there but I've asked to be transferred. They do not do things as I was taught in school."

"How many patients are there now?"

"Most of them are gone. It's terrible. Even if they are Americans and they are our enemies, they are still human beings."

Sun was devastated.

"Are there any Americans at all there?"

"I think only two are left and they are scheduled for treatment tomorrow. The Russian Major has brought some serum from Russia which will be used in tomorrows experiment."

"I think I met the Russian coming from the prisoners ward."

"He is the only Russian here so you probably did. Why was he in the prisoner's ward? That is not his specialty."

"I don't know but he seemed very preoccupied and abrupt."

"I've heard about that ward from my coworkers. Perhaps he was surprised at some of the conditions of the men."

"Mai, could you take me to the experimental lab tonight?"

"Why would you want to go tonight? Aren't you scheduled to go tomorrow? My supervisor said that the team from Hungnam would be present for tomorrow's procedure."

"I'm not sure if I'm to go or if I'll be in an office doing transcription. I would like a first hand look so I can translate properly."

"Well, I suppose we could go for a short visit. The only ones there now would be guards. My shift starts in about an hour. I could go a little early but you must leave when I start my duties" answered Mai.

"Yes, yes. I will do that. I would just like to peek in at the two Americans. Can I see them?"

"The door to the cell is locked but you can get a quick glimpse through the security window. The guards are very strict with them."

"Thank you Mai. It will be helpful in my job."

"I just hope we don't get in any trouble. Oh, I so much want out of this place."

Sun changed to a new Party uniform to appear more official and primped to appear more feminine. It wouldn't hurt if she encountered trouble.

The girls left the hospital to walk to the laboratory.

Sully and Tony were relaxing in their cell when they heard the key in the door and looked up as it opened.

The Major stalked in and the accompanying guard closed and locked it from the outside.

He, as before, held up is hand for silence until he heard the guard walk away from the door.

The look on his face was grim. His voice was almost a guttural growl.

"I just left the prisoner wing at the main hospital. I have seen deplorable conditions in the POW camps but what I saw today was inhuman. Prisoners are allowed to die without any attempt at relief. After arriving there I asked to see the prisoners. They were kept in chambers that reminded me of barn stalls, nothing more than little boxes. I opened one door and there laid two men, both naked, too weak to even turn over. The flies were in their mouths and in their eyes. They were too weak to brush them away."

"I went to a Chinese doctor and asked *Can't you do something for these men?* He said *later, later.* I then went to the next stall. There was only one man in this one. He was almost dead. Maggots were coming out of his nose, eyes and ears. I almost felt that I should put him out of his misery. The next stall held a naked dead man. I saw first hand what heated bamboo spears could do to a man. It was horrible."

"But the next sight was the most vicious atrocity that I could imagine. It is called the *Monkey Gland* operation and the procedure originated in Russia. An incision is made under the prisoners arm and a chicken liver is inserted into the slit. It is then sewed up and allowed to heal. It soon festers and becomes infected. Of course no treatment is made and the man subsequently suffers an agonizing death."

"I'm afraid if I stay longer I'll snap and wreak havoc taking as many out as I can before they get me. But then my report on these atrocities would never be made and the perpetrators would go scot free. I have collected the names of the ruthless commanders of the POW camps. We must proceed slowly. I have just about all I need but I want to see this group from Hungnam. After tomorrow we'll make our move. Most of the bastards here will pay the piper before we go. Here's the plan."

As the Major was laying out the next day, he heard someone outside of the door and looked up to see a female face in the window. Sully and Tony also looked and Sully jumped to his feet and bellowed "It can't be….. it can't be." He started towards the door and when he got to the window there was no one there.

The Major abruptly stood and sternly said "SULLY, what the hell's wrong with you. Settle down before you alert the guards."

"It was Sun-Hi. I only got a glimpse but I know it was her" Sully exclaimed.

"I don't know who Sun-Hi is sailor" said the Major "But I'm pretty sure that's the same woman I saw at the hospital and if that's the case she dressed in a Commie uniform."

"Tony, you saw her. Wasn't it Sun?" asked Sully.

"I only got a quick look Sully. It definitely was an Oriental woman and I guess it could have been Sun but I only met her in Moji. I can't be sure."

"Major, if that was Sun, she's not a Commie. Back when I was running guns I rescued her from North Korea right in this same area. She was with me for almost two years. We were going to go back to the States to live but we got Shanghaied by some of your CIA guys."

"Oh yeah, I remember why we chose you to run the boat at Inchon. But that doesn't mean it's her or maybe she decided to go back and work with the Commies."

"Please Pete, can you check it out?"

"I can't take chances Sully. This operation is too important. If it is your friend and she is an enemy she may become collateral damage."

"Pete, I know this woman. I repeat, if it's Sun, she's not a Commie."

"Okay, okay. I owe you that much. I'll check her out. But I warn you, if she's present tomorrow and you give any indication that you know her or if she somehow screws up this assignment, it's curtains for both of you."

"Aye, aye sir" agreed Sully.

"Okay I'm out of here. You know what to do tomorrow. And call me Major tomorrow."

He called the guard and left the room.

CHAPTER TWENTY EIGHT

Sun-Hi and Mai-Hin walked the short distance to the building that housed the labs and the Psychiatric Experimental Group. They entered through the front and approached the guard at the desk.

"Good evening Mai-Hin" he said "Aren't you early for your shift?"

"Good evening" she answered "yes I am. I was given the instruction to show Comrade Sun-Hi the facility. She is with the inspection team from Hungnam."

"Hmm. Yes. Well you know the restricted areas. Please stay in the halls and corridors. I will give her an I.D. Pass but please make it a short tour. The Russian Major is with the two experimental patients. Please bypass that room."

"Thank you" said Sun as she gave him a lingering look "I will be brief."

He smiled and squirmed in his seat while he was making out the pass.

They walked into the main part of the building, passing by closed laboratory doors. Sun could see very well equipped labs through the closed windows. It was obviously well funded.

"Where are the patients rooms?" she asked.

"Down this hall, but we shouldn't go there" said Mai.

"Don't be silly Mai. I will be with them tomorrow. What could it hurt if I just peeked in quickly?"

"Well….okay….But let's be quick."

They quickly walked down the hall.

"This is the only room occupied" said Mai.

Sun looked in through the small window in the door and was startled at what she saw. The Russian Major had turned and looked directly at her and one of the patients leaped up and started towards the door.

It's him. It's Sully. She was wide eyed in disbelief but was pulled away by Mai.

"We must leave quickly. The guard is coming and really coming fast" said Mai in a frenzied voice.

They turned and walked back from where they came.

"Hold it" ordered the guard "who are you and what are you doing here?"

"It is Mai, comrade, and we took a wrong turn. I am giving an orientation to a visitor. We are leaving now."

"Oh it is you Mai. It seems you are always doing something wrong. You know you should not bring visitors here. Does she have a pass?"

"Yes. I have a pass and don't blame Mai. I requested to see where the prisoners were housed. I am part of the inspection team from Hungnam."

"I see. Well I must make a report."

"What's the problem here" an authoritative voice boomed.

"Good evening Comrade Major. These women are not authorized to be in this area" answered the guard.

"I see. Who are you and what is your business here?" said the Major to the women.

Mai answered "I was giving Comrade Sun-Hi a tour of the facility. She is with the Inspection Team. I am Mai-Hin, a psychiatric nurse."

"All right young lady, report to your station. Comrade Sun-Hi you will come with me to return to the hospital where you belong and are to stay until you are given your orders."

He turned to the guard "I will handle this. Go back to your station."

"Yes sir. Thank you sir."

The Major strode towards the front entrance with Sun-Hi in tow. When he reached the front desk he handed the guard Sun's pass and said "I am returning Comrade Madam back to her quarters in the hospital. I will give a report to her superiors on her visit here."

The guard acknowledged and the two left the building.

When they were outside he asked "What is your full name Sun-Hi?"

"My family name is Kyu-Bak."

"And what is your job with the Inspection team?"

"I am a stenographer. I will record the report given by Captain Nahm."

"Don't you mean COMRADE Captain Nahm?"

"Oh yes of course."

"One of the Americans thought that he might know you. Have you had contact with Americans?"

"It was many years ago Comrade Major. I work for the Party now."

"How long have you worked in Hungnam?"

"I have only been there a short time. I was in Wonsan before."

"I am very familiar with Party Headquarters in Wonsan" he lied "I don't remember seeing you there."

"Oh….oh….I was on a sick leave for a long while. Maybe that's why."

"Yes. Well here we are at your quarters. I assume I will see you tomorrow. Please do not leave your quarters tonight."

"Yes sir."

He left and went to the entry desk and inquired of the guard "Has the car that I ordered been delivered?"

"Yes Comrade Major. Do you need a driver to take you into town?"

"No. I am familiar with this area. I will drive myself. I expect to be gone until past midnight. Is that the car out front?"

"Yes sir."

The Major left the hospital, got in the car, and drove away.

After he left Captain Nahm approached the desk and asked "Was that Major Baklova that drove away?"

"Yes sir. He requested a car to drive into Wonsan."

"Did he say where he was going and why?"

"No sir but he had a brief case with him so I assume he may have business at Party Headquarters."

"Hmm…..yes I see. Thank you."

The Major made the half hour trip into town and took a circuitous route using back streets. He finally pulled up in front of an inconspicuous dwelling nestled among thick trees and then drove up a winding driveway stopping where the car could not be seen from the road.

He got out and entered the house through a side door hidden by foliage. He was met inside by a very small Asian woman who spoke to him in Chinese.

He followed her into a room containing two men and a bank of radio equipment.

One man greeted him with "You sure make a good looking Russian Pete. Are you still on our side?"

"Very funny, pal. Let's hurry, I've got to get back. I've got a feeling one of the visiting Russians has some suspicions about me."

"Why do you say that?"

"Well when they arrived and asked to meet me, I gave them a quick hello and the Psychiatrist said that he's read about my experiments and thought I was an older man according to the description in a report. I just pooh-poohed it and said reporters never get anything right. And then I got out of there."

"Well the job's about done anyway. Show us what you've got."

"It's worse than we ever thought and I've got all the details here in my brief case. But before we start, can you radio Pusan and check on a suspect? Her name is Sun-Hi Kyu-Bak. She was caught up in a sting that we made back in '48 in Inchon. It involved a guy named Sean Sullivan. Find out what happened to her. Get her history and mostly what's her politics at present."

"Got something going on Pete? I never knew you to get sweet on someone over here."

"No no not at all, Stan. She could be very helpful if she turns out to be one of the good guys. Check her out and do it quickly. I need it before I leave."

"Okay, okay, I'll get right on it and have Harry check it out while we go over your report."

The next several hours found them deeply engrossed in the paperwork and pictures in the Major's brief case.

When they finally quit the CIA agent said "Those inhuman bastards. It's bad enough to kill people during war time. We both have experienced that but to inflict murder, torture, starvation, experiments both physical and mental and degradation like this is almost unbelievable. I'll get this back to headquarters ASAP so our government can take action."

"Okay, it's in your hands now. Part of my assignment was to put the laboratory out of business and the best way to do that is rid this earth of the animals performing the experiments. I won't get 'em all but the worst ones will take the fall. Did Harry get anything on the girl?"

"I sure did Pete and I think you'll be happy."

"What's the scoop?"

"She dropped off the map for a while and then resurfaced, going straight and working for an Import outfit. I won't go into all the details but to answer your main question, we made contact with a smuggler king pin that we sometimes use for clandestine purposes. He said he set her up for transport to Hungnam to help her hunt for her lover who was captured by the NK. And guess what, it's this guy Sullivan. I think she's okay Pete. And it also sounds like she's quite a looker."

"She's a pretty girl alright and I think very courageous. This is good. She can work very well in the final plan. Okay now the final piece of business. What are my orders when I finish this?"

"I've got a suitcase for you and one for Tae-Hyun. It's got what you need for your next identity and instructions on a tape. Destroy it when you are finished memorizing it. You guys will split up. Tae is going back to Pusan for shipping out. Do you need any more guns or ammo?"

"A couple more pistols with silencers and a box of ammo should do it with what we have. Okay I'm on my way. Get that report to headquarters."

He made the drive back to the hospital and when he arrived he left word for Sun-Hi to report to his office the first thing in the morning.

Tae-Hyun was waiting for him in his office and he gave him his suit case and said "I won't be seeing you after tomorrow Tae. You're going back to Pusan. It was good working with you. Maybe we'll do it again some day."

"It's good working with you Pete. Let's wrap this up tomorrow and be on our way."

"We've got a little unexpected help Tae."

He told him about Sun-Hi and how she could work into the plan of destruction.

"When you go into the sailors room in the morning tell Sully that all is okay with Sun and we'll have them back together in no time. But what ever he does he cannot show any recognition of her. It could be fatal for both of them. Now let's get some sleep. Tomorrow's going to be a long day."

CHAPTER TWENTY NINE

When Sun-Hi arose the next day, she was given two messages. The first was to report to Major Baklova, in his office upon arising. And next to report for stenographer duty's, after her morning meal, in the conference room. Her days schedule will be given to her at that time.

She walked to the Major's office in a very nervous state. She was sure her cover was blown by the questions that he asked. She was prepared to protect herself. She had a dagger with a six inch blade, in a holster, strapped to her thigh. It could well be her last act but she'd go down trying.

She knocked on the closed door of Major Baklova.

"Come in" came the response from inside.

She entered. He was sitting at his desk and he said "Please sit down Sun" in a pleasant voice.

She was suddenly confused. This was not the greeting that she expected nor did she expect that he would be alone.

"I had a message to see you first thing today Comrade Major" she said in a voice as confident as she could muster.

He answered in English "You can drop the Comrade stuff Sun-Hi. I know who you are and what you're doing here."

She stared at him and steeled herself as to what was coming next. Was he trying to trap her with his relaxed demeanor? Would his attitude suddenly change to one of aggression when she let down her guard? Her hand crept to the pocket in her uniform that allowed her access to the dagger.

She slowly answered with "I'm not sure what you mean."

"I know that you're here to help Sully and you've only been in North Korea for just a short time. I know about the clandestine operation that got you here. I'm not Russian Sun. I'm American."

"Oh my God" she exclaimed "oh my God."

He smiled and said "I was sent here by the CIA to shut down this horrible hell hole. I was lucky to get to Marino and Sullivan before any damage was done to their mental stability. We're ready to wind it up later today. You can be of great service. Will you help?"

"Of course….Of course…..Can I see Sully?"

"In due time, in fact you'll probably see him very soon but you cannot in any way show that you know who he is or even show sympathy or concern over his welfare. I've told him the same thing. You'd both be dead and the whole operation would go down the tube. Do you understand?"

"Yes. I understand but it will be hard. I love him so much."

"You can show your love by following the plan we have laid out."

"I will cooperate. What should I do?"

"Good. Here's the drill. You will continue your duties as if there has been no contact with me. Since you are working for Captain Nahm, I want you to be able to isolate him later this afternoon for elimination. I'll give you the word when."

"That will be no problem. He's been trying to get me alone for some time now."

"My partner is Tae-Hyun. He's the only one you can trust. He has his assignments. Marino and Sullivan will be ready even though it will appear that they are under the affects of a drug."

"Will you be the one to dispatch Nahm?" asked Sun.

"It will be one of us, probably you. You'll need to use that dagger strapped to your thigh. Can you do it?"

"Yes I can. But…the dagger… how did you know?"

"I've been around this type of thing for many years, Sun. It's an old trick usually used by femme fatales. And I must say you are an attractive one. Besides that I saw your hand sliding towards you right thigh when you thought your cover was blown.

She smiled and said "If you would have truly been a Russian, I may not have had a chance to use it."

"When the occasion comes, make it fast. Don't hesitate just react. Don't give your opponent time to see it coming. He will be stronger and has more fire power. Now go get your breakfast and report to the conference room. I will be there also."

She arose and left the room. She felt much more relaxed than when she had entered even though she knew the rest of the day could prove fatal if she didn't make the right move at the right time.

It was mid morning when Tae-Hyun entered the prisoner's cell. The guard that unlocked the door made some obscene remarks to Tae, all being geared to his sexual orientation.

Tae was seething inside but knew it would soon be over for this crude monster so he just smiled and said "Is your friend here today also?"

"Yes he is here today too, my sweet little fellow. He looks forward to seeing you as much as I do."

"Oh that's good. Will you both be here late this afternoon?"

"We will make it a point to both stay as long as you want us to little fella."

After the door closed Tony said "Oh my God Tae, I could hardly keep from busting a gut. Are those guys going to be surprised when they realize that you are a black belt."

"Their surprise will be short lived. I've been waiting for weeks to vent my frustration" said Tae in a low menacing tone.

"Has the Major talked to Sun yet?" asked Sully.

"Yes he has and she's on board with the plan. Don't forget this all hinges on you guys showing no recognition of her in any way. The Major thinks the Russians are suspicious of him. He may need to step up the plan a notch or so. Keep alert. Here are your silenced pistols. You'll know when to use them if we have to move more quickly."

"I can't wait to wipe that smile off of the Chinaman's face" said Tony.

"I've hidden your dungarees in the White Room. Get them on as soon as you can after the fireworks are over. Keep the noise down as much as possible. The staff car will be waiting out back. You guys, Sun and me will be in it. She'll drive and have on her Communist Party uniform until we clear the area. I'll be up front with her. You guys will be in back. If we're stopped, you guys will be prisoners for transfer. We've got some fake manacles for you, but also keep your piece close in case we run into trouble."

"What about the Major?"

"Don't worry about Pete. He's already been given a new assignment and will be well on his way. Major Baklova will have dropped off of the face of the earth never to be seen again."

"Wow! That guy's something else." Sully said.

"He's probably the best that the CIA has. It's a pleasure to work with a guy that has it all together like he has." Tai said.

"And we've done it twice in the last year" Tony said.

"Okay guys" said Tae "I'll be coming back to pick you up with my friends the *happy guards* after lunch. Act your usual dopey way. After I give you the IV upstairs you can be semi alert. The Major will ask you questions about 'cooperating with the Party' and 'how happy you are to be here' and all that stuff. Give positive answers, as sick as you may be to give them, but remember it will all be over by late today.

The meeting in the conference room lasted all morning. It turned into an inquiry by the Inspection Team.

Present were the North Korean Doctor Rho who introduced himself as the Head Psychiatric Physician for Mental Studies, also his Chinese associate, Doctor Chan, the expert on Mental Studies in Beijing, the Russian Major Nikolai Baklova, who noticeably distanced himself from the pair, and of course the team from Hungnam. The Russian civilian observer, Ivan Yushakova, the Russian Psychiatrist Igor Robachov, the North Korean Security Expert, Captain Park Yong-Sook Nahm and the stenographer Sun-Hi Kyu-Bak.

The first questions came from Comrade Robachov and were directed at both the North Korean and Chinese doctors. They were technical in nature and required detailed answers. Both men were very uncomfortable with the directness and at times it became heated.

Next, Captain Nahm questioned them on procedures of security and of disposition of failed experiments. Predominately, can any of this be recorded or traced.

Comrade Yushakova had several questions for clarification of prior inquiries. And then he turned to Major Baklova and asked very pointed questions as to his qualifications, background and pertinent information on his duties here in Korea.

Comrade Robachov was very attentive and scribbled notes all the while.

The Major bore up under this interrogation very well.

When Comrade Ivan hesitated the Major jumped in and said "Comrade, I see that the noon hour has passed and I know that a grand lunch has been prepared for us. May I suggest that we adjourn, have lunch and return for my briefing on the demonstration of the serum that I brought from our Moscow lab." He hesitated and looked for objections.

"About an hour after the briefing we will resume in the White Room where our two patients will have been injected with the serum by my assistant and will be ready for questioning."

They all rose to leave and the Major stopped Yushakova and whispered "Comrade, I would like you and Comrade Igor to stop by my office after my briefing and before the demonstration. I feel that we must clear up this matter and I would like to do it in your strict confidence."

"Yes, of course Comrade. I'm sure that you may clear up a few points. We will be there."

The lunch was sumptuous. All were satisfied and happy by its end. Pete's plan was to make them full, relaxed and slow to react.

They returned to the meeting sporadically and it started later than scheduled. Finally all were in attendance and all a bit sluggish.

The Major said "I see that everyone enjoyed lunch. I will be brief and perhaps a rest in your rooms would be in order before the demonstration."

He rushed through his presentation and dismissed the group.

"Can you come to my office Comrade Ivan? I will be brief."

"Yes. We will accompany you, Comrade."

"Very well. Pease come with me."

They left the lab and crossed over to the hospital to the Majors office. He sat at his desk and showed the two Russian civilians to the chairs directly opposite him.

"Now Comrade Igor, I get the impression that you have questions about my credibility."

"My questions stem from the fact that you don't entirely match up with the description I was given and for that matter your medical capabilities" said Comrade Robachov.

"I too have some reservations Comrade Baklova. I am waiting for a reply from the Kremlin. I'm sure you understand our concern" interjected Comrade Yushkova.

The major stood and said "I certainly do."

He opened the center drawer of his desk, quickly removed a pistol with a silencer, without saying a word and before either Russian could react, he raised the gun.

Pfttt….Pfttt

He put a bullet in each of their heads. He then walked around the desk.

Pfttt…….Pfttt

He placed another head shot in each, felt for a pulse and finding none, he dragged the two bodies behind the desk out of view.

He removed his suitcase from the closet and exited the room, locking the door behind him. He quickly left the building and placed the suitcase in the trunk of a Russian made car parked in the lot.

He then went back into the hospital and made his way to the prisoner's wing. The guards recognized him, saluted and opened the iron doors for him to enter without question.

At the nurses desk he asked to see the doctor in charge. They directed him to a main office. When he knocked, a voice answered in Chinese, to enter. He opened the door and entered.

He said "Good afternoon Doctor. Do you remember me?"

"Ah yes. You are the Russian sent to us by the Kremlin."

"Well that's what I appear to be. But really my name is Pete Greenwood and I'm a CIA agent. Remember when I asked you to help one of my fellow Americans who was suffering and you said *later, later*?"

The Chinese doctor stood and with bulging eyes tried to speak but with mouth hanging open and lips quivering, all he could do was drool. He stared at the pistol in Pete's hand which was pointing at him.

"No…No….Please. I…I.

Pete continued "Well that poor devil is probably out of his misery now and I won't even respect the profession and call you *doctor*.

Die and burn in hell, you miserable bastard"

Pfttt….Pfttt

Pete put two shots between the Chinaman's eyes with a silenced pistol.

Again he laid the body behind the desk out of sight, left the room and closed the door.

He left the hospital and made his way to the lab.

On his way to the White Room he encountered the North Korean and Chinese Psychiatric doctors, Rho and Chan. They too were on their way for the demonstration.

"Good afternoon gentlemen. I hope you are rested" said the Major.

"We are fine, thank you" a very cool reply came from the North Korean.

"My Russian comrades, Ivan and Igor may be slightly late. I think the lunch and a touch of vodka may have made them in need of a nap. We can proceed without them. They are somewhat familiar with the demonstration I will give" said the Major.

"Hmm. I am anxious to see the results of your serum after only one injection" offered the Chinese doctor.

"Oh I'm sure you will be very surprised at the outcome of the session today. Yes in fact I can be positive that you will have an unexpected surprise."

CHAPTER THIRTY

The cell door opened and Tae entered with the two guards. Each guard pushed an empty wheel chair. The two prisoners lay there, sluggish and apathetic, just as they were instructed. It was difficult because internally the adrenalin was flowing.

The guards rousted each one of them out of their beds and directed them into the wheel chairs. They moved slowly and carefully since each had a pistol and silencer strapped to the inside of their thighs. They had been issued loose fitting pajama bottoms and a jumper which easily concealed the weapons. Tae smiled to himself when he saw how well they were carrying out their roles.

They were wheeled to the elevator, up one floor and into the White Room. On this trip they remained in the wheel chairs and placed beside an IV stand.

Tae hooked up the IV's to their arms, turned to the guards and said "We've got to let this serum drip for about an hour before its effective. You can leave if you care to."

"No. Our orders are to stay for the whole session. And besides we like being with you, sweet little fella."

Both guards burst out in a raucous round of laughter.

Tae grimaced and thought to himself... *just a little longer...just a little longer.*

Tae busied himself, checking the IVs, making sure the liquid was flowing correctly even though it was only a weak saline solution.

He turned to the guards and said "Well if you two will be here to watch them I must attend to something in my quarters. He glanced at one of them with a lingering look on the way out and left.

After Tae was gone the guard that he had glanced at said "I think he wants me to follow him. Take over here. I won't be long. It will be an hour or more before the doctors get here" He left the room.

Tae was in his quarters when the guard suddenly burst in on him.

"Well here I am Tae. Did you want to see me about something?"

Tae answered softly "Yes I did. Come on over here. Lay down your automatic weapon and take off your holster."

The soldier leered at him. "I'd be happy to. Are you going to show me a good time?"

"Come closer and find out."

When the soldier approached, Tae suddenly lashed out with a Karate chop at the base of the soldier's neck. He dropped like a rock on his knees but still very conscious of his surroundings. He started to rise up when Tae hit the base of his nose with the heel of his hand and drove his septum up between his eyes. The man screamed but he was still fully conscious. Blood gushed from his nose. Tae grabbed his arm and snapped it like a twig. The man fell and rolled over groaning.

"You wanted some sexual pleasure for yourself?" Tae sneered as he stood him up.

"Okay, try this" and he drove his knee deep into the man's groin smashing his testicles. The man doubled over in agony and again fell to the floor retching and groaning in painful sobs.

"I wish I had time to make you suffer more but I'll put you out of your misery you filthy piece of cow dung."

Tae grabbed his head and twisted it breaking his neck and severing his spinal cord. He dropped the lifeless body to the floor.

"Your fellow soldier will get much of the same" he said as he left the room.

When he returned to the White Room he again checked the medication bags and turned to the leering guard. "Your friend will be delayed" he said "it may be a while, he is resting."

The guard chuckled.

The door opened. The Major and the two Psychiatric doctors entered and approached the prisoners.

"How much time have we on the serum Tae?" asked the Major.

"We probably need at least another 15 or 20 minutes sir" answered Tae.

"Very well, that will allow me time to explain my procedure to the doctors."

"Major, I have some equipment in the store room that I'll need for the later session. May I take the guard to help me and get it out of the way before we start?" asked Tae.

"Of course, he is not really needed here. Try to be back before I start the session" answered the Major with a slight grin.

"It shouldn't take long. It's a pretty simple procedure" said Tae and he turned to the guard and said "Come along with me and you won't need your automatic weapon. You can leave it here."

The guard stood his weapon in the corner and hurriedly joined Tae as they left the room. He was smiling broadly while walking down the hall.

When they got to the store room, they entered and once inside Tae closed and locked the door.

The smirking guard ogled Tae and approached him with an extended arm to embrace him.

Tae quickly grabbed the extended hand and with a sudden twist and turn he flipped the guard head over heels. The surprised guard landed hard on his back and the air whooshed out of his lungs and a low moan came from his gaping mouth. He tried to get up but Tae was over him in a flash and while pulling up on his arm he roughly placed his foot on the man's throat and held him down.

"Do you have anything to say smart ass?" asked Tae as he applied more pressure.

The man choked out "n..no...p....please."

Tae placed the right arm of the man over his bended knee and gave a sudden downward thrust, bending the arm backwards at the elbow. After a sickening crunch which tore the biceps muscle away from the forearm and roughly dislocated the elbow, the man screamed in agony.

Tae dropped the arm which lay lifeless beside the man's body. He then grabbed the left arm at the wrist and bent the hand backwards until he could feel the tendons tear. The man moaned a deep guttural sound and tears flowed down his cheeks.

Tae pulled the arm upward and slowly dug his heel into the man's throat.

The man kicked his legs and struggled but the slight Korean was stronger than he looked. As the pressure increased the choking and gagging got worse. His eyes were bulging out and Tae purposely let him suffer until finally he lunged and drove his heel in to crush the entire throat back into the spine. The prone body became limp and Tae released his hold.

Satisfaction was accomplished.

Tae returned to the White Room and all participants except for the two Russians were present.

Tai said "I told the guards that their assistance was no longer needed but to return when the session was over to take the prisoners back to their room."

"That's fine" said the Major "I'm sure the Captain and I can handle any situation that might arise, Tae. Thank you for the information."

The Captain swelled with pride and said "There will no problems here that I can't handle."

"Very well then, we can wait a little longer for our comrades from the Mother country to show up but I have the feeling they may have other thoughts."

Tae and the Major busied themselves with the patients. It was obvious that Sully became more alert and nervous when Sun-Hi entered the room.

Pete whispered "Easy son, easy. It will soon be over."

The doctors and the Captain had moved aside and were conversing in confidence. Sun-Hi was being especially attentive to Captain Nahm and it was evident that he enjoyed it.

Sun had made it a point to engage in personal conversation with Nahm, on the walk from the hospital.

Comrade Major Baklova formally announced in Korean that he could wait no longer and must start his demonstration of the affects that his serum has on properly prepared patients.

The two doctors approached the drugged men.

As Captain Nahm started to join them, Sun gently took his arm and whispered "Comrade, I will do my best to make notes but I'm sure I'm going to need help and further explanation when I transcribe them, as well as having other needs. Would it be possible for you and I to go some where in private, when the session is done and work things out?"

Captain Nahm could hardly contain himself "Of course my dear. I will be most happy to give you the help that you need. Follow my lead when I give the word."

They joined the group to watch the experiment.

The Major stood in front of the two patients, looking at one and then the other.

"Good afternoon gentlemen" he said in English.

They both replied "Good afternoon Comrade."

The Major smiled and said "Are you both feeling well?"

"Very well" answered Tony.

"Tip top" answered Sully.

"Marino, can you tell me what you are doing here?"

Tony sat up straight and said "I'm here to learn about social justice and the power of the people."

"And how about you Sullivan?"

"To join the Bolshevik's in the struggle to overthrow the imperialistic Capitalists" said Sully in a loud firm voice.

The Major blinked and hesitated.

He then resumed the questioning along the same vein for the next hour asking pointedly how they would handle situations when back on American soil. The answers were all as rehearsed.

Finally the major said "Would any of you gentlemen like to try a question or two?"

The two doctors mumbled something among themselves while Captain Nahm spoke up and said "I think we have a good idea of what you can do Major. I think we should call it a day and perhaps resume tomorrow. I would like to document all that we have for my report, if my assistant and I can be excused."

"Yes by all means Captain. Could the good doctors please remain? I have some technical data to discuss."

"We will stay Major. Let's sit in the lab office if that will be suitable."

"Very much so gentlemen. Tae please attend to the prisoners" answered the Major.

They walked to the office. The Major took a seat at the desk facing out and the two doctors sat in chairs in front of the desk facing in.

Captain Nahm and Sun-Hi left and walked to the hospital where Nahm led the way to his quarters.

When they arrived he closed and locked the door.

"Please put your stenographic materials on the desk Sun. You won't need them for a while. I knew you would come to your senses my dear. It was just a matter of time and this will be much more enjoyable for both of us."

He approached her with lust in his eyes.

"Please Captain, may I use the bathroom first and get myself ready?"

"Of course my dear and I too will be ready when you come out."

She went in the bathroom and locked the door. She then reached through the pocket of her uniform pants and withdrew the dagger. She slipped it up her sleeve so it lay on the inside of her forearm easily within her grasp when she needed it. She splashed water on her face and fluffed her hair.

When she emerged, Nahm had changed into a kimono and stood by the bed with a pleasured look on his face.

She approached him and he took her in his arms. She encircled his waist with her arms and withdrew the dagger from her sleeve.

He lifted her chin and bent his head to kiss her. As his mouth touched her lips she spat and while holding his body with her left hand she plunged the dagger deep into his belly with the right hand.

He jerked his head back with a puzzled look on his face. He couldn't believe what was happening but couldn't seem to react. Sun twisted the blade back and forth causing agonizing pain. He screamed, trying to push this demon woman away but she overpowered him and held him close. He couldn't move back because he was up against the bed.

She extracted the dagger in a rapid motion and quickly plunged it in a little higher on his abdomen and this time the dagger caught the aorta. Blood gushed forth and then filled his stomach cavity.

Sun pushed him back and he fell across the bed. He clutched his stomach and watched the blood now flowing freely out of both wounds. He looked at Sun who was standing over him with a bloody dagger in her hand and then he gagged and coughed up a huge glob of blood. He was choking on his own blood and he was bleeding out quickly.

He suddenly became dizzy and the room got hazy just before it all went black. He would be dead within minutes.

Sun was trembling. She could only stare at the body lying on the blood soaked bed. As much as she hated this man, killing him with her own hands was terrifying. She felt sick to her stomach and gagged.

She quickly turned away and went into the bathroom. She tried to clean the blood from her hands and what had splashed on her uniform.

After cleaning as well as she could she went to her quarters, thankful that no one saw her with blood spattered clothes. She changed to a new outfit and packed her rucksack.

Before returning to the White Room she put her rucksack in the staff car trunk that would be their escape transportation.

CHAPTER THIRTY ONE

After the doctors and the Major left for the lab office, Tae removed the IV needles from the arms of the two Americans. He cleaned the entry wound with alcohol and taped a cotton ball to the spot of entry.

He glanced around and seeing no one in ear shot he whispered "Are you guys Okay?"

"You bet we are and ready to get out of this hell hole" said Tony.

"It won't be long now. As soon as Sun-Hi gets back and verifies that the Captain is compromised we can take care of the two 'mad doctors' and we'll be good to go."

"You mean Sun is going to take care of the Captain? Hey isn't that a little scary?" asked Tony.

"Sun is a very capable girl Tony" interjected Sully "I saw her handle some pretty tough guys in the old days.

"Pete said that she has a dagger with a six inch bladed strapped to her leg and she looks like she knows how to use it" offered Tae.

"Sounds like a throwback to the smuggling days" said Sully "she used that trick then but she only threatened to use it a few times. I think once she sliced a guys hand when he tried to grab her. God I hope she doesn't get buck fever. That could be bad with that little bastard she's with."

As he said that, the door opened and Sun walked in. She looked a little pale as she halted a few steps inside the room and saw her lover. A broad smile erupted across her face and she slowly approached Sully.

His smile equaled hers and he stood and extended his arms. She melted into him and with damp eyes kissed him fully on the lips. He enveloped her in his arms and returned her kiss with love and tenderness.

"Hey be careful you two we still have the two doctors to dispose of. They're right in that office with Pete and within shouting distance" warned Tae.

"Let's get this over with" said Tony.

"Okay. You two get your weapons out and make sure the silencers are on the muzzles properly. We don't want any noise to raise the rest of the soldiers" ordered Tae.

The four of them rounded the corner and approached the open door of the office. They halted and listened to the conversation barely audible from that distance.

The Major was speaking. He continued "……..and so doctors, or whatever you choose to call yourselves, I've been around for many years and have seen many despicable scenes, but never have I experienced the mental brutality that I've seen here."

Both men sat up straight in their chairs and bristled with indignation.

The Chinaman, Doctor Chan, emphatically said "I've heard of the Russian experiments and they are the epitome of brutality so who are you to find fault with our experiments here."

"Yes, you are correct, there is little if any difference in the inhuman practices of all three of the Communist countries. But you see gentlemen I am not Russian. I am an American CIA agent assigned to uncover the many atrocities committed here and in your POW camps. My orders are to report them to the War Crimes Committee. My assignment, further, is to shut down this ghoulish laboratory and dispose of its perpetrators."

Both doctors leaped to their feet. They glared at this enemy of the Party. Now was a time for confrontation. The two men were engulfed in hatred and stripped of any vestige of civilized restraint.

The Korean, Doctor Rho, screamed "Comrade Ivan was right. Where is the real Major Baklova?"

"He's probably in Hell and recently joined by Comrades Ivan and Igor" said Pete in a menacing tone.

Suddenly the Doctor Chan whipped out a pistol and hurriedly squeezed off a shot at Pete. His shot missed Pete's left ear by inches.

Pete rolled out of his chair and came up with his own gun. In the close quarters behind the desk it was cumbersome, what with the elongated barrel from the silencer extension, to handle the weapon.

But before he could aim his weapon…..Pfttt….Pfttt. Shots came from both Tony's and Sully's silenced pistols. Both hit home. Doctor Chan slammed up against the desk and fell to the floor, blood seeping from a pair of wounds.

His pistol flew from his grasp and slid toward Doctor Rho who was crouched down hiding from Pete on the other side of the desk. Rho saw his opportunity and picked up the pistol. He quickly raised up, took aim at Pete and fired two quick rounds. But in his haste, the bullets never had a chance to hit home and they went wild. Pete snarled, showed his frustrated hatred for this animal and put a round between Doctor Rho's eyes.

"You okay Pete?" yelled Sully.

"Yeah but those shots from Chan's gun is going to alert the rest of the troops. We've got to move out" Pete yelled.

"Okay boss. What do we do?" asked Tony.

"You and Sully grab the clothes we got for you and get in the wheel chairs. Tae and Sun will push you. I'll lead the way waving my gun after I take off the silencer. Get down the hall and into the car as quick as you can. I'll misdirect the soldiers.....oh oh...Here they come."

Pete ran ahead of the wheel chairs, waving his gun and yelling at the soldiers "Quickly. Quickly...after them...they killed the doctors. The Russians are spies and Captain Nahm is after them. They went into the hospital."

The squad of soldiers reversed and ran down the hall. Another group of soldiers came bursting in.

"Follow the other squad. They may need help. The Russians have automatic weapons. We will get the prisoners back to their cell" ordered Pete, still in the Russian Major's uniform, giving loud, authoritative, commands.

The soldiers were in a sate of turmoil. They spun around and ran towards the hospital only because they were ordered to. They had no idea what or who they were looking for. Confusion is what Pete had hoped for.

Pete said "Tae, you get to the car with the others. It's all stocked for the getaway. You know where to head. Good luck. I'm going to set the timers on the charges and then I'm on my way. Major Baklova is no more. He will disappear from the face of the earth. My job here is done. I hope you can get these guys to the U.N. battle line. I hear they are moving north. Seoul may be ours again."

Pete turned to the two Americans "I was able to salvage the dog tags from some of the poor devils that got butchered here and turned them in with my report. Yours was among them. Here, I separated them from the bunch. Put 'em back on. Hopefully they'll help if you run into some friendly's. You're both good men, a credit to our country. Now get going."

Tony, Sully, Sun-Hi and Tae-Hyun ran for the car. Sun unlocked the trunk and they threw in some extra gear and clothes. It was piled on top of the two automatic weapons that Tae confiscated from the two Guards that he dispatched earlier.

Tae also grabbed the NK uniform that he would wear until they cleared any road blocks. Sun hopped into the driver's seat and kicked over the engine. They took off, out of the hospital grounds and headed south.

Shortly thereafter a Russian made car with a lone civilian left the grounds and sped north.

They were less than a mile away when a fireball rose in the sky and quickly after, three distinct explosions were heard.

"Mission accomplished" said a smiling Tae-Hyun.

Sun drove on as the two Americans changed to Navy dungarees and Tae changed to the NK uniform. Sun was still in her Communist Party uniform.

Tai said "On the floor are some manacles that you can wrap around your wrists if we are stopped. Our cover is that we are delivering two POW's to a POW Camp in Changsong. That's one of the bad ones, on which Pete made his report. If we are questioned I will explain that you two are destined for some brutal treatment because of your escape from a forced march from Seoul. Hopefully they won't check into us any further. I have some fake written orders but they're not perfect. Pete had to make it up pretty quick back at the hospital."

They continued on and soon were on an open road and cruising along very well.

Sun said "I think I see headlights way behind us and they look like they are coming fast."

Sun kicked up the speed on the cheap Chinese car but an old four cylinder junk heap on war torn roads could only do so much and not any more. It was slow going.

Soon they could hear the engines throbbing and headlights glaring in pursuit. The lead truck of the convoy blasted its horn again and again.

"Pull over Sun, pull over. I think they want to pass. I don't think they're tailing us. There's too many of them. I think it's a troop convoy."

Sun throttled down and pulled to the side of the road. The convoy sped by kicking up so much dust it almost blinded them. There were at least ten trucks, all loaded with troops.

"It's my guess that they are headed for battle. The front may be closer than we think" said Tae hopefully.

"Wait 'till the dust clears and then let's hit it again" he added.

After the convoy had long disappeared Sun pulled back on the road and drove on for several hours. They had about another two hours of darkness and then prudence dictated that they find a place to hole up for the day.

Sun said "I saw a sign that marked a road to Kosong. That means we've made about 75 miles. Between here and Kansong is an old dirt road that leads to an old coal mine. We used to go there and camp when we were kids. It's pretty isolated. With any kind of luck I might find it."

"Let's keep our eyes peeled. That's exactly what we need" said Tae.

The sun was just breaking over the horizon when Sun said "I see it" and she made a hard right onto a rutted dirt road. The car creaked and moaned as it bounced along.

"Slow down. You're shaking my teeth loose" yelled Tony.

Sun laughed "Sorry" she said "I came upon it suddenly."

She slowed to a crawl.

They soon came to a spot where she could pull over and get some cover among the trees. She stopped and they all bailed out and stretched their limbs.

"Okay let's get a bite to eat" said Tae "I was able to stash some grub in the trunk. It's not much but it'll do. There are three or four canteens of water too. After we eat let's get some sleep. I'll take the first watch. Tony, I'll wake you up in about four hours and then Sully can relieve you in another four. That should get us close to travel time again. Sun, you get some rest since you're doing all the driving."

"I'm okay" she said as she looked at Sully.

Sully returned her look, walked over and embraced her and said "You're an amazing woman my darling Sun. How you managed to find me like you did is a miracle."

"I had a lot of help. There never was a doubt that you were still alive and somehow we'd be together again" said a misty eyed Sun.

CHAPTER THIRTY TWO

Darkness came quickly as the sun was setting behind the barren hills. The motoring travelers were all weary in spite of resting throughout the day. No one got much sleep and all were stiff and sore from lying on the bare ground except for Sun who slept in the car.

Tae was the unspoken leader and he announced "We should probably wait a while before we start out but I'm anxious to hit the road. The later it gets, the less likely we'll run into a checkpoint."

They quickly ate the few last bits of provisions in the trunk.

"Tony, grab the two weapons that I confiscated from the guards. I'll keep one up front. If we're stopped, I would be expected to be armed. The other one can be in back with you guys but put it on the floor and out of sight. Can you cover it up with some clothing?" said Tae.

"Good idea Tae. We can at least offer some resistance if we are rousted out. Let's get moving" said Sully.

They were soon on their way even though the sun had not quite set. The further south they got the more activity they encountered. Mostly it was military trucks carrying troops south and what appeared to be wounded men heading north. They passed through a very congested area that looked like a field hospital and possibly an out post. So far they had not heard any gun fire so the front must be a ways off.

They got through without any notice and were on a stretch of open road when another troop convoy came barreling up behind them. Sun slowed and pulled over to let them pass. The very last vehicle was a staff car similar to theirs but larger and heavier. As it passed it slowed and the officers in the back seat eyeballed them.

It stopped and made a U-turn when it was about a quarter mile away. Just as it was approaching them the roar of attacking planes blasted the evening silence.

Everyone looked up at the Navy AD Avengers coming out of the sunset firing 5 inch rockets at the troop carriers ahead of them. As they passed over the trucks they dropped 500 lb. bombs.

Even at this distance from the trucks the noise was ear splitting. Bomb blasts were rapid and the sky lit up with exploding gas tanks. The Avengers were getting some direct hits.

Next a squadron of Corsairs came, strafing the troops trying to escape the burning vehicles. A trailing Corsair spotted the two staff cars and swung around to strafe the NK leaders in the cars.

Sully yelled "Get out! Get out! They think we're a car load of NK officers. Head for cover under the trees."

They bailed out of the car and scrambled into the woods just as the Corsair opened fire on the two cars. The car holding the N K officers was riddled with gunfire and it careened off the road wrapping itself around a tree.

The driver slumped over the wheel, bleeding profusely from fatal wounds. The officer beside him was wounded and tried to get out but the door was jammed and he was moaning in pain. He slumped back weak from blood lose and exertion. He was bleeding out. The two officers in back were able to get out although both had minor wounds and injuries from the crash.

They ran across the road towards the other staff car which was also heavily damaged by gunfire. They knew that this car held the spies that were reported as escapees, to all Company Commanders before they left. The order stated that locating and killing these spies and traitors was a top priority. They knew that their convoy had been decimated by the U.S. Navy airplanes and killing these spies could put them back in good graces with the Party.

The Americans were hunkered down in the woods and could see the officers running towards the car with drawn weapons. When the NK officers saw that the car was empty they scanned the surrounding trees and spotted the escapees hiding in the brush.

As they raised their weapons they barked an order. "Show yourselves American dogs. Give up and we won't kill you."

Tae and Tony stood and opened up with their automatic weapons. It was no contest. The two NK officers slumped to the ground before they could even fire a round with their pistols.

The Americans slowly came out of the woods and looked for other soldiers but none were evident. The Navy planes were strafing the wooded area adjacent to the trucks, most of which were in ruins. They made one final pass and then headed back to the carrier from where they had come.

"Wow" said Tony "Those guys sure know what they are doing. I'm glad we stopped when we did or we'd be toast."

Tae had been inspecting the car which was riddled with bullet holes.

"This baby is shot and I know the other one that's wrapped around that tree is no good either. We've got no transportation."

"I wonder how many soldiers made it through the attack" said Sully "maybe we could confiscate a truck."

"By the sounds of it there isn't much left down there" Tae answered.

Just then they heard the rumble of a truck coming their way. They waited until the truck drove up. It appeared to be some of the surviving soldiers.

Tae stepped into the road still wearing his NK officer's uniform and waved them to a stop.

He spoke to the driver "My staff car and driver were killed along with the commander. Is there any transportation at the battle site?"

"Yes sir" responded the driver." There are a few trucks picking up wounded. You can probably get a ride with them. My truck is over loaded as it is. Could you walk back to the site? I will radio them and tell them you are coming and need transportation."

"Yes, of course. Alert them that I'm coming and proceed on your way. I will acquire transportation from the men" answered Tae.

The truck pulled away and Tae went back to his companions.

"We may be in luck. They think I was one of the officers in the staff car. I'm sure the other soldiers will also. I'm going to walk down to the bombed out trucks and tell them that I need a truck to pick up my fellow officers that are with me from the destroyed staff cars. They probably saw the one we were in parked along the road. Wish me luck and be ready when I come back. Make sure I'm alone and no soldiers rode along with me."

Tae left and the others pulled back into the woods. It was now well into the night and with no moon it made for a really dark night.

They impatiently waited until they finally saw headlights coming up the road.

"Stay back" said Sully "it may not be Tae."

The truck slowed as it approached and finally stopped and Tae stuck his head out of the open window and said "Anyone need a lift?"

"Hot dog" shouted Tony "come on gang, let's get outta here."

They tumbled out of their hiding places and climbed in the covered bed of the truck.

"I was able to confiscate a map. Sun, are you familiar with this part of the country?" asked Tae. "We may not be able to get through the bombed out area. It's pretty plugged up with wrecks."

"Just a little bit, but let me ride up front with you and read the map. I thought I saw a cross road back about two or three miles. Maybe we can detour."

"Sounds good. Let's go."

Tony and Sully rode in the covered rear but were able to converse through an access window in the back wall of the cab.

"Can you drive this thing Tae?" asked Tony "it rides like a tank."

"Don't worry about my driving, Tony. Just keep an eye on our rear in case they catch on to us."

Sun said "I think I see a road ahead. Slow down...slow down. Yes... yes...turn left here."

Tae turned and the truck jostled back and forth in the ruts.

"Geez, this isn't a road, it's a cow path" he said.

"Might be all the better. They're less likely to find us here" she said.

"Yeah I guess you're right. I'll take it slow."

Sun studied the map.

"I don't see this road on the map so I'm not sure where it takes us. There's a main road in the general direction that we're heading or at least from what I can tell."

"We'll keep going until daylight and then try to find out where we are. I can see some high ground ahead against the night sky. It might be the hills south of Kumhwa. We've got to be getting closer to our guys, sooner or later."

They bounced along for the rest of the night and the hills were getting closer. Soon the sun was fighting it's way into a blue sky. Tae pulled the truck off the road when he got to a wide spot.

When they got out they all stretched achy muscles.

Sully said "Hey be quiet and listen. I think I can hear artillery over in those hills."

"Yeah, I hear it. It sounds away off but that means we're going in the right direction."

"Okay, let's rest up. Tony you take the first watch. I'm beat" said Tae.

"Will do. Go ahead and get some sleep. I'm not tired at all" answered Tony.

As the other three were bedding down Tony exclaimed "Hey, I thought I saw some movement over in those trees. Give me an eye Sully. It could be troops. I don't think it was an animal. Grab your piece just in case."

They all scanned the area in front of the truck.

Suddenly Tae screamed "BAZOOKA...BAZOOKA...HIT THE DECK."

They all dove to the ground and rolled into the brush as the missal from a bazooka streamed towards them.

KABAM came an explosion as the truck engine erupted in smoke and flame.

Soldiers poured out of the woods yelling and charging right at them.

Sully screamed "That's our guys. Those are UN uniforms."

He stood, threw his weapon down and raised his hands over his head.

"DON'T SHOOT.... DON'T SHOOT.... AMERICAN.

Tony rose up and threw his weapon down too. "Hey guys, we're U.S. Navy. Don't shoot."

A shot rang out and narrowly missed Tony's head.

"Hey...come on....we're Americans."

A staccato of shots blasted the quiet and a hail of bullets clanged into the truck body behind them. The sailors dove for cover and both screamed "HOLD IT! HOLD IT! AMERICANS!"

The squad leader barked an order in a strange language. No more shots came their way so it was probably a cease fire order.

Tae and Sun now stood when the boys rose up again and rifles quickly cocked when the NK uniform on Tae was spotted. Some of the rifles had fixed bayonets and they were now close enough to be used. One soldier took a menacing step towards Tae with the bayonet in position for the kill.

They all raised their hands high above their heads and again Sully said "Americans. We're escaped POW's. We need help."

The squad leader said in broken English "You have I.D.?"

"Just our dog tags. We're Navy."

"You lie. What Navy do so far from ocean? Why you have enemy soldier with you and Communist woman?"

"We were captured by the NK" explained Sully "We are all American citizens. The man is Korean/American and works for the CIA. The woman is a dual citizen and is my fiancé. We are going to be married when we reach a Navy base where I can apply for permission."

The look on Sun-Hi's face changed from one of deadly fear to a soft contented look of heartfelt tenderness. She turned towards Sully with moist eyes and a beaming smile. She wanted to rush into his arms but prudence dictated that she stand her ground.

"Hey Sully, I think these guys are Turks. Let me try something."

"Okay with me. I'm not making any headway."

Tony said "My friend is 'Big Turk'. He's an officer in the Turkish Army. We transported him and his men on our ship the USS Columbia. Can I show you his name?"

"What you mean 'Big Turk'?" sneered the squad leader.

"I have a paper in my pocket. Can I show you?"

"Reach in pocket very slowly. I look."

Tony slowly reached in his dungaree pocket and retrieved a very dog eared scrap of paper with the name of the Turkish officer that he met in a bar in Yokohama. It was a remote chance but the only option at this critical time. He stepped forward and handed the scrap of paper to the Turk.

He noticed that the rest of Turkish soldiers were fingering their bayonets and becoming very edgy. He glanced nervously around and stepped back with a silent prayer on his lips.

What a strange turn of events. What if we were wiped out by our own United Nations soldiers after going through all we've gone through up until now.

The Turk Squad Leader studied the writing on the note for what seemed to be an eternity.

He looked up at Tony and said "Where you get this? Steal from a dead Turk?"

"No, no, he gave it to me when we drank together in a bar in Yokohama" said Tony quickly.

The Turk read the scribbles again and turned to a soldier. He talked at length with the man, finally handed him the paper and sent him away. The man hurriedly disappeared into the brush.

The Turk turned to the four prisoners.....which they had again become.......and said "Move out here in the open. Remove your side arms slowly and give them to my men. You can sit on the ground back to back. You may lower your arms but keep your hands where I can see them. It will be several hours before I will receive instruction on what to do with you."

The four of them sat as instructed with Sully and Sun sitting next to each other.

She gently nudged Sully with her elbow and with a smirk on her lips and a slight lilt to her tone she said "Well Mr. Sullivan, I don't remember you asking for my hand in marriage or was that disclosure just a ruse for benefit of our captors?"

Sully got a broad grin on his handsome face, turned to Sun and said "I didn't want to ask for fear of getting turned down."

"Why don't you try me sailor?"

"Will you marry me Sun-Hi?"

"Yes, yes a thousand times yes."

"I love you, Sun."

He leaned over and gently kissed her awaiting lips.

The Turk guard grinned and politely stepped away with moist eyes. He was remembering the wife he left in Turkey.

CHAPTER THIRTY THREE

The day wore on and sitting on the ground in a cramped position was beginning to wear on the four prisoners. It was getting warm and they were thirsty.

"Do you think you could spare us some water?" asked Sully.

The squad leader turned and looked at them. He barked an order to one of the soldiers guarding them. The soldier made some remark and removed his canteen. He handed it to Sully who unscrewed the lid and gave it to Sun-Hi before he drank. She took a swig, passed it around to the other three and then gave it back to the soldier.

"Thank you" she said.

"You velcome" he responded politely.

Off in the distance the rumble of an engine could be heard. All the soldiers snapped up their weapons. A verbal command from the squad leader regrouped them into defensive positions.

They all relaxed as an American made Jeep emerged from the trees and quickly approached them. In the Jeep rode the soldier that was sent away with Tony's note and a very large Turk officer along with the driver.

The Jeep skidded to a stop close to the squad leader and the huge officer unwound himself from the back seat. He stood and stretched giving out a big, loud groan.

The squad leader snapped to attention and saluted. The officer returned the salute and asked him a question.

The squad leader answered. He then turned, facing the four Americans. He pointed at them and said something further in the Turkish tongue that was not understandable.

Still pointing, he then gruffly spoke to the Americans in English saying "Stand up so the Captain can look at you."

They stood.

The officer carefully approached them, eyeballing each one. Finally he got to Tony, broke out in a huge laugh, and loudly proclaimed "TONY! My little friend. It is me. Hakan."

He then scooped up Tony and enveloped him in his huge arms in a gigantic bear hug.

Tony let out a big "Ugh" as the air rushed from his lungs while he tried to laugh and talk at the same time but couldn't get it out.

"I could not believe it when they told me a prisoner gave them my address in Ankara. You must have quite a story to tell. How can a sailor be this far away from the sea?" expounded the officer.

"It's a long story Hakan. Do you remember my shipmate Sully?"

"Of course, the Coxs'n."

And he tossed Tony aside and grabbed Sully in a similar bear hug, laughing all the while.

"Now tell me who is with you. Is this man an NK deserter?"

"No sir. He is an American CIA agent who saved our lives. His name is Tae-Hyun and his orders are to report to his headquarters in Pusan." answered Tony.

"I see. How about this pretty woman? She is dressed in a Communist Party Uniform. Defector?"

"She is also American/Korean with dual citizenship. She and my shipmate are going to be married. She traveled from Pusan to try to find Sully when we were captured. She also helped in our escape."

"Hmmm. She must be very resourceful to accomplish that."

Sully piped up "She's probably one of the most resourceful women you'll ever meet. I couldn't believe my eyes when I saw her at the Commie hospital."

"This is becoming very confusing to me. And I'm sure you can explain it, but this is not the time or place to do so. We are an advance scout force and there are many enemy soldiers very close to us. With all due respect we must, first of all, accomplish our mission and then we can escort you back to the American authorities behind the front line."

He turned and gave an order in Turkish to the squad leader who quickly gathered his force and moved out.

Hakan, the Turk, turned to Tony and said "I will ride up front with the driver. Can the four of you fit in the back? If not we will have to leave someone and return for you."

"We'll manage" answered Tony as they piled in with Sun and Tae sitting on the laps of Sully and Tony.

It was an uncomfortable ride but doable.

About an hour later they arrived at an encampment of more Turk soldiers and half track troop carriers. One soldier was sitting at a radio with ear phones on his head.

Hakan talked to the radio operator and the operator immediately began transmitting. He turned to the four Americans.

"I'm going to ask that you find a comfortable place to sit while I work on a report. We have almost completed gathering the intel that we were assigned to obtain. I have two patrols out and when they return we will prepare to return to the front line headquarters."

"Don't worry about us Hakan. We could use a little rest. We've been traveling all night" answered Sully.

The morning passed slowly and the four of them dozed.

It was early afternoon when the two patrols returned and after they talked at length to their commander they sat and waited while he conferred with his noncoms.

He soon approached the Americans and said "Okay. We've done all we can do. It's time to go back. You can ride in the half tracks and we'll be home by dark."

The soldiers broke down the equipment and the tents and loaded them a on the half tracks. The four Americans rode in the bed of a truck with a squad of Turk soldiers.

Tony said "I'd sure hate to have these guys mad at me."

The ride was long, bumpy and dusty.

They arrived at a bivouac of mostly U. S. Army soldiers. The trucks stopped and Hakan, the Turkish commander walked back to the truck containing the four Americans.

He said "Okay my friends this is where we part company. I will turn you over to the detachment commander here and he will direct you on the next step. His name is Captain Nelsen. Please come with me."

The four jumped down from the truck bed and walked with the Turk.

Judging from the stares and puzzled looks from the G. I.'s while they walked through the bivouac, they must have presented quite a sight.

They entered a large tent with open sides containing a huge table, covered with maps, and with a group of Army officers gathered around it deep in thought and conversation.

As they entered, all heads turned their way.

Captain Nelsen spoke to his men "That will do it for now men. We'll meet first thing in the morning after I've had a chance to go over the report from the Turkish patrol."

The officers and noncoms left and Captain Nelsen turned to the newly arrived group.

"Well Hakan, I didn't expect you to bring survivors back along with your report. But then you've given me surprises in the past so I should have expected something."

Hakan laughed "I always try to please Captain. May I introduce you to my companions and then come back, after I feed my troops, to go over the report?"

"Of course, now who are these folks?"

"The two sailors are Boatswains Mate 3rd Class Sean Sullivan and Seaman Anthony Marino. They were crew members of the USS Columbia and were left on shore during the evacuation of Hungnam when their small craft was sunk by the enemy. They were captured and sent to an experimental hospital for mental programming. They escaped with the help of the CIA."

He continued "The Korean is a U.S. citizen and is employed by the CIA. He was on assignment with another CIA operative to infiltrate the hospital as well as POW camps. They were successful and a report has been made."

"The Captain said "Welcome gentlemen and a job well done. I already got some preliminary information on all this when Hakan radioed me. From what I understand the mission will hopefully help some of our boys that are imprisoned and have undergone brutality."

He shook hands with all three.

"Now my curiosity has gotten the best of me. Young lady, can you enlighten me on how you managed to do what I've been told you've done?"

Sun smiled "I don't know all of what you've been told sir but when I heard that Sean Sullivan had been left behind in Hungnam, I made up my mind to find him or his body. I wheedled my way and by hook or crook ended up in the same hospital that he was in. Through some stroke of luck the CIA had operatives there that were sent to eradicate that house of horrors. With their help we escaped and were eventually found by the Turkish patrol."

"Well I'm sure there is a lot more to that story and I'd like to hear the details but that's for another day. I'm going to turn you over to my aide. He will get you some chow and a place to sack out for tonight. I'm hoping to arrange something to get you further south by tomorrow. Good luck to all of you."

A sergeant was waiting just outside and he said "Follow me folks."

They had their first hot meal in several days and were shown to tents for the night.

CHAPTER THIRTY FOUR

The three men awoke to a sunny spring morning, rested and hungry. They dressed and left their tent to locate Sun-Hi and eat some chow. They were anxious to hear what the captain had arranged for them, so they could get back to their duties.

When they got to Sun's tent, they found her already up and about.

She said "I was hoping you guys would show up soon. I'm starving."

"Yeah and some hot coffee sounds good too" said Tony.

They made their way to the mess tent and sure enough the morning meal was being served. They fell in line with the soldiers and soon were filling their bellies.

As they were eating, the Captain's aide approached them.

He said "After you've had your breakfast, stop by the command tent and talk to the Captain. I think he has some news for you."

"That sounds good. We'll head over there as soon as we're done" answered Sully.

"Man oh man, I'll sure be glad to get back to normal shipboard life" interjected Tony.

"Yeah, me too" piped up Sully.

Sun-Hi became very quiet while she finished eating.

When they all had their fill they headed to the command tent. They waited off to the side while the Captain was meeting with his men who were gathered around the map table. When the meeting broke up, the group left. The Captain and his Sergeant remained and they entered the tent.

Sully saluted and said "Reporting as directed sir." He had now reassumed the role of leadership.

The Captain returned the salute and said "Okay I think I've got things sorted out. There's a MASH unit about 10 miles south of here. There's a Colonel in charge who can arrange for a helicopter flight, probably to Pusan via Seoul. He'll have more detail for you when you arrive. I can get you to the MASH unit by half track."

"We're ready to go anytime sir. The sooner the better" Sully answered.

"The truck and driver are standing by" said the Captain. "Give me an hour or so to assign a patrol to escort you. There are still some straggler NK troops in the hills between here and there. They'd love to ambush an unarmed single vehicle."

"Thank you, sir. We'll wait at the motor pool until it gets organized."

"Again I want to commend you on a great service to our country. And I want to alert you, Miss Kyu-Bak, when you arrive in Seoul, there may be some questions for you by the Seoul Police Department. Good luck and God Speed" said the Captain as he returned Sully's salute.

Sully looked at a stricken Sun-Hi and asked the Captain "Any thoughts on what they want sir?"

"No I don't" he replied "only that they want to question her."

Less than an hour later, the small convoy headed south with the four travelers. They arrived without incident at the field hospital which was buzzing with activity. Helicopters were coming and going with wounded soldiers aboard.

After they unloaded, the Sergeant traveling with them escorted them to the command center in a small Quonset hut.

They entered the building and found themselves in a reception office with a Corporal manning the desk.

The Sergeant said "These are the four people from the Kumhwa bivouac area to see the Colonel, Corporal."

"Yeah Sarge, he's expecting them. Let me give him a heads up."

He arose, entered the Colonel's office and closed the door.

They waited a short time and soon the Corporal emerged and announced "Okay Sarge, you can head back to your outfit. We've got 'em now."

"Good enough. Good luck to you guys and to you too, Miss"

He left.

The Corporal said "follow me folks." He turned and opened the office door.

When they entered they observed an older, gray haired Army officer dressed in fatigues and sitting at a large desk.

Both Tony and Sully saluted and Sully said "Reporting as ordered sir."

The Colonel quickly returned the salute and said "We don't stand on much ceremony here sailor. My main job is Chief Surgeon. You men can stand at ease. There's a chair Miss, if you'd like to sit."

"Thank you sir, but I can stand" she answered.

"Very well then, I understand that I'm to arrange a helicopter to fly you folks to Seoul. At that point you'll be transferred to another copter so mine can return here and get back to duty transporting wounded soldiers."

"Yes sir, I think our final destination is Pusan" said Sully.

"That's correct. Are you Sullivan?" asked the Colonel.

Yes sir" replied Sully.

"Okay Sullivan, you and Marino will report to the Navy BUPERS in Pusan for reassignment to the USS Columbia."

"Yes sir. That's our ship."

He looked at Tae and asked "I guess you're the CIA operative Tae-Hyun....right?"

"Yes sir" answered Tae.

"They tell me that you know where and who to contact so I won't even go there. You're on your own when you get to Pusan."

"Thank you sir" answered Tae.

"And now you, young lady" he turned to Sun-Hi "the Korean authorities in Seoul have asked us to have you available for questions and possible detainment. They will meet the copter when you land."

Sully looked stricken. He turned to Sun who stood with her mouth agape.

"Sir, she's an American citizen" said Sully.

"I know that son, but she's also a Korean, originally from the north. I'm only following orders" said the Colonel.

"Sir is there any way I can communicate with my office in Pusan?" asked Tae.

"We don't have that capability here but I'm sure you can reach them when you get to Seoul" answered the Colonel.

Tae turned to Sully "Let me see what I can do when we get to Seoul Sully. There may be a way."

"I won't let them detain her. I'll stay with her if I have to" growled Sully.

"Don't do anything foolish Sullivan" said the Colonel "it may not be as bad as it sounds. Now the copter is ready. Good luck and God speed. Get a move on."

They left the office and boarded an awaiting helicopter which took off as soon as they were strapped in.

The flight to Seoul was uneventful and they landed at a helicopter pad right at the Army Camp.

They disembarked and were met by an army Lieutenant who yelled above the rotor noise to follow him. Two Jeeps were waiting to transport them to Command Headquarters.

When they arrived they were shown in to the Adjutant's office. Seated with him was a Seoul Police Department Officer.

The Adjutant said "The Base Commander has asked me to intervene for him in this matter. This shouldn't take long. We have a helicopter standing by to take you to Pusan."

"Yes sir" said Sully, eyeballing the Police Officer "is there going to be a delay for Miss Kyu-Bak?"

"We'll address that in due time sailor."

Tae interrupted "I'd like to communicate with my Pusan Base of Operations, if that's possible sir."

"I don't think that will be necessary" answered the Adjutant. "And since it seems to be a problem, this is Lieutenant Jung of the Seoul Police who has a statement from his headquarters."

He turned to Lieutenant Jung and nodded.

Jung stood and said "You are Sun-Hi Kyu-Bak. Correct?"

She answered "Yes, I am."

"In our files is a several year old report of the escape of a Sun-Hi Kyu-Bak who was under arrest for smuggling and subsequently never tried. The capture of these smugglers was under the aid and direction of the American CIA. One of the smugglers, being American, was detained by them with the three Koreans turned over to the Seoul Police. It has recently come to our attention, by the CIA, that Miss Kyu-Bak is also an American citizen. Therefore they have requested that she be turned over to them. We will relinquish you to a CIA authority who I understand is in your party."

A loud sigh came from Sully and Tony. Sun-Hi beamed and Tae smiled broadly. Sully grabbed Sun and hugged her.

"Okay…okay, that's enough celebrating. Settle down, he's not through" said a stern Adjutant.

The Police Officer continued "We do this on the condition that you do not return to Seoul. If so, your record will be expunged."

"Thank you, sir. I will abide by your decision" said Sun in a very relieved tone of voice.

"The chopper is waiting. I suggest that you move on out of here as soon as you can and get aboard" ordered the Adjutant.

They moved quickly and were soon winging their way to Pusan.

Upon arrival Sully and Tony reported to the Navy BUPERS Office and were told to report to ships stores and be issued proper clothing. They were assigned a temporary barracks where they could await transportation on an MSTS Transport to Yokohama. There they would meet the USS Columbia which was en route from their home port of San Francisco.

Sun-Hi and Tae-Hyun were driven to the CIA office where Sun picked up her U. S. Passport and was told she was free to go. She visited her place of employment and explained that she would be leaving Korea. She received the compensation due her and was able to buy clothing. She then checked into a hotel.

The CIA had arranged that she take the same MSTS Transport, with Sully and Tony, to Yokohama.

When they all arrived at Yokohama, the sailors reported to the Navy Base to await the Columbia which was due to arrive in about a week. Sun again went to a hotel.

It took a special request and intervention from some higher navy brass but Sully was able to arrange a wedding ceremony for him and Sun.

They were married at the Base Chapel by the Base Chaplin. Tony was best man.

Since she was now a dependent of a serviceman, Sun was able to travel by an MSTS Transport to San Francisco where she could live while Sully was at sea. For now she remained in Yokohama until Sully shipped out.

Finally the Columbia tied up in Yokohama with a load of soldiers for deployment to Korea. Tony and Sully climbed the gangway, saluted colors, turned and saluted the Officer of the Deck and asked "Permission to come aboard sir?"

The O.D. said "Permission granted, sailors. Welcome aboard."

"We're happy to be back sir."

"The XO asked that you report directly to him when you arrive, Sullivan" added the O.D.

"Yes sir. We'll go right up."

When they got to the Commander's cabin, he shook their hands and said "Let's go see the old man."

The Captain welcomed them and commended them on a job well done.

Sully said "Thank you sir, but I only wish I could have brought my whole crew back. Peacock bought the farm when our boat blew sky high back there in Hungnam."

"I've got good news for you boys. Peacock's alive. He was badly burned and is now at Bethesda getting extensive work done on his face and arms by plastic surgeons. He's going to come out of this with some scarring but intact."

Tony brightened up and enthusiastically said "That's wonderful news, sir. Oh my God. I can't wait to talk to him."

"You might be able to do that son. I'm granting a 30 day leave for each of you as soon as we reach San Francisco. Also effective immediately, Sullivan you have been promoted to BM 2nd class and Marino you are now BM 3rd class. You've also received commendations in your permanent records."

"Now go down and see your shipmates. They want to hear all about it and welcome you back." He then stood and smiled.

"And then get ready to get underway. We're going home."

EPILOGUE

Anthony Marino served out his enlistment, staying aboard the USS Columbia. He was able to travel to many ports in the Pacific and Indian Oceans. When he received his discharge in the spring of 1954 he fulfilled his promise to his Dad and went to college. While at Kent State University he met the love of his life, Rosemarie. Eventually they married and raised a family. Tony went on to have a successful career in manufacturing. One of his suppliers was a Korean immigrant who furnished him with electronic parts. His name was Kim. Tony and Rosemarie enjoyed a long, happy marriage with their children, grandchildren and great grandchildren.

Sean Sullivan stayed in the Navy until retirement. Upon reenlisting he requested shore duty in San Francisco to be with his wife Sun-Hi. He was stationed at MSTS Headquarters on the Search and Security Squad. He was eventually transferred to San Diego Naval Training Center where he was a Drill Instructor and retired as a Chief Boatswains Mate. He now runs a charter fishing boat out of San Diego. He and Sun-Hi had no children.

Virgil Peacock spent a year at Bethesda Naval Hospital going through successful plastic surgery. He became interested in the medical field and studied medicine becoming a surgeon specializing in burn cases. He never married. He dedicated his life to medicine.

The four high school boys in the detention room all remained friends through the years and occasionally were able to see each other.

Jay remained in California and after his discharge he married a California girl that he met at the U.S.O. He became a bailiff in the Fresno courthouse and retired early. He passed away from complications of cancer.

Tom was stationed in Texas and took his discharge there. He enrolled at Texas Tech and became an Electronics Engineer. He and his wife settled in the northwest where he worked for an aircraft manufacturer.

Ray joined the Air Force when the Korean War broke out. He was sent to Germany where he tried out for the baseball team at the airfield where he was stationed and ended up winning the European Championship. Upon discharge he worked for Alitalia Airlines. Ray acquired sugar diabetes and died of kidney failure.

The two CIA operatives Pete and Tae retired from the CIA and opened a Private Detective Agency in San Francisco. They work closely with the Federal government.

The author, Ken Filing is a retired entrepreneur who sold his company in 2007. He and his wife Teddy divide their time living in Ohio and Florida. He joined the Navy at age 17 in 1949, one year before the Korean War started and remained in the Navy until 1954, one year after the end of that war. His ship, USS General J. C. Breckinridge, saw action during the invasion of Inchon and the evacuation of Hungnam. He has always loved the sea and currently owns a 42 foot Grand Banks Trawler docked in Lake Erie. His broadest experience was sailing a 30 foot sailboat, the Rosie II, more than 20 years. He once sailed the Rosie II from Cleveland, Ohio to Jupiter, Florida, a 42 day trip. Teddy joined him on the 37th day to help finish the voyage. Ken now spends his time golfing, fishing, boating, writing and enjoying his loving wife, his three children, his four grandchildren and one great grandchild.